Enemies of the mind
The Watchers Series: Book 2

Eilidh Miller

Copyright © 2020 Eilidh Miller

All rights reserved.

Eilidh Miller has asserted her rights under the Copyright Designs and Patents Act 1988 to be identified as the author of this work. This book is sold subject to the condition that it shall not, by way of trade or otherwise, be lent, resold, hired out, or otherwise circulated without the publisher's prior consent in any form of binding or cover other than that in which it is published and without a similar condition, being imposed on the subsequent purchaser.

This is a work of fiction and any resemblance of the fictional characters to real persons is purely coincidental and non-intentional.

This work was not written with the use of any AI and no authorisation is granted or implied to allow its use in training any AI models.

Cover Photography by TJ Drysdale

Cover Design by Matthew Weatherston

Griffith Cameron Publishing

ISBN - 978-1-7345367-6-8

Chapter 1

Euan depressed the clutch, shifted the car into the next gear, and then eased off it. The sound of the engine gaining power as the black Aston Martin DB11 streaked down the road made him smile. He loved that sound.

Grace had taught him how to drive once they'd settled in Scotland, then å with him to select the car he wanted. They'd been in Scotland for almost a year now, and Euan had settled into this life more comfortably. He'd discovered a fondness for the rapid drumming and heavy riffs of rock music, and Grace had already taken Euan to his first concert experience; it had been incredible. It was what he was listening to now as the car sped down the motorway, the music pounding around him, bringing his heart with it, and making him feel free.

Euan's clothing style, too, had relaxed. While he still favored vests, trousers, and dress shirts, he was now equally comfortable in jeans and a t-shirt, and he wore them often. What he never looked was sloppy, however, and even the jeans and t-shirts fit him well. He never understood the need to look as though he'd just rolled out of bed.

His first missions with Grace hadn't been difficult ones — or perhaps Grace simply made them look easy — and he'd quickly learned his part in this work. Not only was he to protect her, and act as her eyes and ears when she wasn't there, but he was always able to assist her by helping with the larger game. Sometimes that meant playing the villain to convince their target of a certain reaction. Other times, it meant his working in the background to help her engineer the proper outcome while she maintained a pretense of working for the other side. It was work he found he quite enjoyed, and together, they excelled at it. She'd already been one of The Council's best Watchers, and with the two of them together, this had only increased. It meant they were working constantly, and she had yet to be called on a mission where he couldn't join her. Grace was now fluent in Scots Gaelic, and it was the language they used at home so she might keep it up. It was also what they used to communicate while working. Usually, it ensured they wouldn't be understood, even if they were heard. He'd lost count of how many places and times they'd been in by now, but it didn't matter.

Beside him in the passenger seat, Grace took in the scenery as it went by, looking a bit like a film star in her dark sunglasses with her long golden hair. They were on their way to Oxford, as Grace had been asked to come down to deal with some legal matters regarding the scholarship she'd set up there. They could've taken the train, but Euan had wanted to make the drive and Grace had acquiesced. They weren't far away now, and the drive had been, thus far, uneventful.

Reaching out his hand, he gently took hers and she looked over at him with a smile. "What are ye thinking?"

"About how it's been a long time since I've been here. It feels like a lifetime ago, but it wasn't."

"I suppose it was, in a way."

"How do you figure?"

"Well, technically, ye died. That makes it another lifetime does it nae?"

"I guess it does in a weird way," Grace said.

Euan chuckled and lifted her hand, kissing it. "Probably has nae changed much."

"Not really, no."

"I am excited to go with ye, though. I get to see the university and the places where ye have spent so much time."

"I'm excited to show them to you. Turn here," she said as he took the exit she'd indicated.

Grace navigated them to the city center and the Old Bank Hotel, where she'd booked a room. When they arrived, Euan reluctantly handed his key fob to the valet and pulled the two overnight bags from the back before following Grace inside.

"Good afternoon, madame," said the clerk at the front desk as they approached. "Checking in?"

"Yes, a reservation under Grace Cameron."

"Ah, yes, we've been expecting you, Mrs. Cameron. You booked the Rooftop Bedroom."

"I did."

"ID and credit card please?" Grace handed them over to the clerk, who entered the information and then handed them back. "Here's your key. We hope you enjoy your stay."

"Thanks," Grace said, smiling as she took the key and headed for the elevator.

Once they reached the top floor, they stepped out and followed a long corridor to the very end. Opening the door, they stepped inside and shut it behind them, looking around. It was a single room, but well appointed. There was a desk to their left, the large bed to their right. Just past it was the bathroom. The real jewel of the room, however, was the view. This room had its own private terrace, and it looked out over the High Street, while directly in front of them was St. Mary's.

"Wow," Euan said, his voice softened by awe.

"At night this view is going to be worth every penny."

"I believe ye," he said, moving past her and setting the bags down on the bed. "It is worth it now."

Grace turned her back to the bed and dropped down onto it with a happy sigh, which made Euan laugh. "This is pretty comfortable."

"Aye?" he asked as he joined her on it. "Ooo, aye. But," he said as he rolled over onto his side and draped one leg over both of hers, "it is better because ye are on it."

"Is that so?"

"It is."

"Well, you can't do anything about it right now."

"Can I nae?"

"No," she said with a gentle laugh. "I have some places to be, remember?"

"Right."

"Going to get it over with first and then we can have a bit of fun. I can show you around."

Euan, however, didn't intend to make it that easy on her. Leaning over, he gave her a kiss that was anything but chaste. "Ye sure?" he whispered against her lips.

"You are evil."

"Will nae deny it."

"I have appointments though, unfortunately."

"Too bad," he said with a smile.

"I agree, but I have no choice now," she replied, sitting up and letting his leg slide away from her. "You're coming with me anyway."

"I am, I know," he said as he got up, and went to his bag.

Once they had both freshened up and changed clothes, they made their way to the solicitor's office where Grace was to meet with trustees and the university's solicitors. Euan remained reserved and quiet, as he was only there to accompany her and nothing more. He didn't know what, exactly, she was meant to do here.

"Mrs. Cameron, Mr. Cameron, a pleasure," the solicitor said. "Please do sit down. As you know, there are some legal matters to see to regarding the scholarship fund you wish to establish."

"Of course," Grace replied.

"It really is just a formality of filling out forms, but we need your witnessed signature. What is it that you wish to name this fund?"

"The Euan Cameron Scholarship for Continued Education."

Euan looked over at her, surprised, and she smiled at him.

"And the stipulations are that it's for an American student pursuing a degree in history, is that correct?"

"Or a Scottish one."

"I see," he replied, writing it down. "Very well, let's get to signing, shall we?"

"Why did ye name it after me?" Euan asked when the two of them emerged later and began the walk back to the hotel.

"The scholarship will help someone who wants more than anything to learn but can't afford to, just as happened to you. If I can keep even one person from experiencing that then I will, and it will have been worth every shilling I put into it."

Euan didn't know what to say. He knew she'd wanted to set up such a thing but not why. "I . . . Grace, that is . . ." he faltered, at a loss for words.

"If I could go back and make sure the young you continued his education, I would. This is the next best thing."

"Ye are the kindest of souls, do ye know that?"

"I try," she said before she stopped, her smile fading as she stared at the door of a pub.

"What is the matter?"

"I . . . my grandpa liked to come to this pub with me when he would visit."

"Oh," Euan said. He knew she missed them, and that this pained her to the point where she simply refused to speak of them. He didn't even know their names.

Grace closed her eyes, gave her head a small shake, and turned away from it. "Come on," she said as she started to walk again.

"Grace? Grace, is that you?" someone on the street called out.

Grace stiffened, sighed, and turned toward the voice, her expression becoming neutral. "Hi, Eric."

"It is! Wow! Look at you. You look amazing."

"Thank you."

"I haven't seen you since just before graduation."

"Yes, I went home, but you knew that."

"I do, I wanted to come with you."

Euan raised an eyebrow but said nothing.

"You did want to, but I wasn't interested in your doing so."

"You're still as gorgeous as you were, but there's something different about you," Eric said, ignoring the barb and taking her hand.

Grace pulled her hand out of his as soon as he touched it. "I'm a few years older, that's all."

"No, there's something else," he said, taking her hand again.

"She clearly does nae wish for ye to touch her," Euan said, his tone as cool as his expression when Grace once again pulled her hand away and stepped back toward Euan.

"Who are *you*, exactly?" Eric asked in irritation.

"Her husband," Euan said, the words firm.

Eric looked at Grace and something like anger slid across his face. "You got married? How long did you wait after you broke up with me?"

"A few years," Grace replied. "Not that it matters."

"Right, and you just happened to meet a Scot in America and get married. I knew you had to have been cheating on me."

"What? Eric don't start this again. I told you I wasn't, and I wasn't. We've only been—"

"Shut up, Grace," he hissed. "I can't believe you. You really were the whore I thought you were."

"What did ye just call her?" Euan asked, putting himself between Grace and Eric.

"You heard me."

"Euan, don't, it's not worth it. He's not worth it," Grace said, placing both hands on his chest as she stepped around him. This was more for Eric's protection than anything else, aware that Euan could do him some serious and permanent damage.

"Not worth it? Come on, Grace, let him. I can get some revenge on the guy who stole my girlfriend and my ticket to California."

Grace turned around and looked at him. "You're an idiot. You have *no* idea who he is and you're really asking for trouble if you keep goading him. He didn't steal me, I broke up with you, remember? I wasn't cheating on you at any point and he has nothing to do with it."

"It's why you didn't want me to see your phone that night."

"You saw it! Graham handed it to you after you slapped me, remember? There was nothing there!"

"Wait . . . what . . ." Euan began. "No, Grace get out of the way . . ."

"Euan, no. Eric, you really need to leave. I don't have anything else to say to you."

It was clear, however, that Eric wasn't about to let the opportunity to cause more discomfort slide. "What sort of dance does she make you do to get her into bed? She has all those weird hang ups after all. I know it was like pulling teeth for me."

"Maybe because ye were rubbish," Euan shot back. "It is nae a problem I have."

"Sure. Worth it once you get her there though, isn't it?"

"Stop," Grace said.

"Or what, Grace? What will you do? Nothing, just like you did the last time."

"Try it and find out," Grace said in a tone Euan had never heard her use before, and it gave him pause. He wondered if Eric would be smart enough to hear it and shut his mouth.

"Empty threats. Just come talk to me without this idiot," he said as he went to grab her hand again.

When Grace pulled her hand back before he could even touch it, he moved to grab her arm and she shoved his hand away. In the next moment it looked to Euan as though Eric had tried to either strike her or touch her face, and Grace blocked it with her arm before delivering a punishing punch to his jaw that sent him stumbling. Eric looked up at Grace in anger, making another move toward her, and she stepped back, grabbed his arm, twisted it viciously, and used it to slam him against the wall of the pub. Euan stared in shock.

"Not so empty now, are they," she hissed into his ear, grabbing hold of his hair, and using that grip to press his face hard into the wall. "Stay away from me, do you understand? If you come near me, I swear I will end you. You may have hit me once, but I'll be damned if I'll let you or anyone else do it again."

Grace stepped back and shoved him away from her before she stormed angrily away. Euan smiled in something like amused pride before he turned and followed her. It didn't take him long to catch up to her, his stride longer, but he could feel her fury within himself.

"Love," he said as he came up beside her. "Slow down."

Grace, however, said nothing and continued onward. It wasn't until they'd reached their room that she said anything, pulling the coat of her skirt suit off and flinging it angrily across the room. "Just . . . how . . . I can't . . ."

"Grace," Euan said, keeping his voice gentle as she paced the room like an agitated lioness. It was quite clear to him that when his wife was in this sort of a temper it was wise not to get near her, and he had no wish to have her turn that anger on him.

"How dare he! How dare he say any of that! I never did anything, never once, and I just . . ."

"Of course nae, but what he thinks does nae matter."

"He wanted to fight you! What an idiot! I should have just let you hit him."

"Ye did a fine job of that yerself, to be honest."

"Yeah, well, he always was pushy whenever I said no to him. I don't need to deal with it now."

"May I see yer hand?"

"Why?"

"Just want to be sure ye are nae injured."

Grace thrust it out, still furious, but not at him for asking. Euan examined it and there was no sign she'd broken anything, which meant his wife was far more versed in defending herself than he'd realized. Then again, they'd never been in a situation where she'd need to use such skills, even on a mission. There were the abrasions you'd expect, and her hand would likely be sore later, but he had a feeling she would take a moment to see Dr. Fraser for that.

"Why do men have to be like this? This is why I hated them."

Euan raised an eyebrow. "Clearly nae."

"You don't count."

"Oh? Last I checked, I am a man, unless ye know something I dinnae?"

"You're different," Grace said, ignoring his attempt at humor. "Not like anyone else. You're not pushy or a brute or cruel."

"Had I been I probably would have had it beaten out of me by the others."

"That's not the point!"

"Sorry."

"He only ever saw me as a meal ticket anyway and I'm so glad I got away from him."

"Grace, I have to ask ye, based on what I heard ye say a moment ago: did he ever force ye into his bed?"

Grace stopped, taken aback, and looked at him. "I . . . I don't think so?"

"Ye dinnae think so."

"I don't remember. I mean, not like held me down or anything, but he'd pester me sometimes until I just agreed to it so he'd leave me alone."

The hand not holding hers curled into a fist. "Then the answer to that is aye, he forced ye."

"No, I mean, it happens a lot, doesn't it? It isn't like the kind of force that would be a crime. Coercion, maybe, if you want to get technical."

"If ye did nae go into the encounter with yer whole heart and only endured it, then it might as well have been, though I do believe modern law would vehemently disagree with ye. I know we would have considered it to be forced, and he would have been made to pay for it."

"I don't really know what to say to that," Grace said, her voice quiet as her anger deflated. "I'm not sure I entirely disagree with what you're saying. Eric was the first and only person I was with. I thought that was what it was like, that you had to do it to make them happy even if you didn't necessarily want to."

"I am so sorry," he said. "It should never be that way."

"It isn't. Not with you."

"And it never will be, but ye know that. It should nae be that way with anyone."

"I wasn't even sure the first time," she admitted. "But then it was too late."

Euan frowned. "What does that mean?"

"I just . . . I was confused, you know? I didn't know what I felt, and I thought this was what happened and I . . . it just happened."

Euan closed his eyes for a long moment, his heart aching for her. There had never been a time in her life where the men who should have been good to her had been, and there was something so unfair about all of it.

"So, he forced ye into that, too, and in doing so he took away a moment that should have been so special to ye. There is no way he did nae know ye were unsure, Grace. He would have heard it in yer words, the tone of yer voice, how tense yer body likely was when he touched ye. He knew and he did it anyway because it was what *he* wanted. I never would have done that to ye. No one ever should."

"You didn't. You asked me if I wanted you to stop."

"How could I nae?"

"Can I just pretend he never happened? That it was with you instead?"

"Ye can do whatever ye wish and I will nae contradict ye. I want to erase it as much as ye do. I wish it *had* been me."

Grace stepped forward and rested her forehead against his chest. Euan knew this wasn't how she'd wanted this trip to go, but there were ghosts in this past and they would always find her, as they always found everyone. Euan ran a tender hand over her hair, and he felt the comfort slide over her like a blanket as she relaxed against him. He'd never hurt her, never do any of the things anyone else had. He loved her, truly loved her, in a way no one else did or could, and she knew it. He took every chance he could to show her.

"Ye should get that hand seen to, hm?"

"I suppose. Maybe I should wait to see if you need to come with me."

"Lass, what I would do to him would nae require any sort of healing for me. Blood comes off steel quite easily."

Grace looked up at him. "You'd stab him?"

"At the very least. Maybe give ye a go as well."

Grace smiled. "Lucky for him you don't have any weapons."

Euan's lips curled into a sly smile. "Nae that ye can see."

"What?"

"I am never without something. That is just laxity."

"Where?"

Euan took her hand, sliding it across his abdomen to his side, and then down, where her fingertips brushed the hilt of the sgian dubh he had concealed in his belt. She gasped and looked up at him, never having realized he'd been carrying one all this time.

"Nae the only one either, but the closest one."

"How did I not even notice?"

"Never had a reason to, did ye?"

"But, I mean, we've . . . and when I undressed you it was never . . ."

Euan laughed. "Think about it carefully: did ye take everything off or did I assist ye?"

Grace blinked. "Oh . . ."

"Exactly."

"So, you could've stabbed him."

"Could have, aye. Would have, probably nae. Dinnae feel like having to explain it to authorities. Besides, I have far better restraint than that."

"Shame."

Euan chuckled and then kissed her. "Now, let us get that hand seen to so we can have a nice supper and a dram on this lovely terrace this evening. After ye show me about, however. I am excited to see the libraries."

"I can do that."

"I know ye can. By the way, why have I nae seen ye do that before?"

"Do what?"

"Fight like that."

"Never had a reason to, did you?" she said, echoing his own words back to him with a teasing smile.

"Ohh, I see. Well, turns out ye are full of surprises."

"You have no idea."

"I almost assuredly dinnae, but I look forward to finding out."

Grace, however, wasn't the only one with secrets still to be discovered. Euan could only hope she never found out all of his, at least until he had a chance to come to terms with them himself.

Chapter 2

When they got home from Oxford, Euan decided to run a bath for Grace. He knew how she liked to relax after a long trip with a soak and that was an easy enough thing for him to accommodate. A relaxed wife was a good thing as far as he was concerned. The bath itself hadn't remained single occupancy for very long, however, and he rested there now with his back against the side of the tub and Grace's back against his chest. Her head rested on his shoulder; her eyes closed as he stroked her arm.

Grace groaned in irritation and Euan looked at her with concern. "What is it?"

Grace turned to look at him, puzzled. "What do you mean? You didn't get it?"

"Get what?"

"They have something for us."

"No," Euan replied. "I received naught."

He'd felt nothing and both had the same sinking feeling. A mission had finally come where Grace needed to go alone, and Euan sighed. It would've come eventually, he knew that, but it didn't mean he liked it. The time would, for Euan, pass more quickly than it would for Grace, but the waiting would still be unbearable for him.

"We should get out. Caia will be here any second."

Euan tightened his arms around her protectively. "I dinnae like this."

"Like what?"

"Ye going alone."

"I went alone before you."

"Aye, and ye have nae gone alone since. Why now?"

"I don't know. We were warned this could happen though."

"I should ask about it."

"No, you shouldn't. They wouldn't exclude you if there wasn't a good reason, Euan."

He nodded, knowing she was right but hating that she was. "Give me a proper kiss now because ye will nae be able to once Caia arrives."

Grace turned around to face him and gave him a long kiss. "Everything will be fine. I'll be back before you know it."

"Unless ye have already gone and come back, then no. I will know ye are gone."

"Euan, love," she whispered.

"We only just got home. The last mission we were on it was weeks before I saw ye again. When do we get a break to just stay in one place together?" Euan asked, not bothering to hide the irritation he knew she sensed from him anyway.

"We can ask for one when I get back but for now—"

"Ye have to go. Aye, I know."

"It will at least be faster for you than for me."

"Ye are nae making me feel better, love."

"Sorry."

Euan sighed and rested his forehead against hers. "It is nae ye. Come, let us get ye ready to go."

They were silent when Caia arrived and found Grace already dressed and ready to go. "I'm sorry, you two."

"It is nae yer fault, Caia. Ye dinnae give the assignments."

"No, I don't. If I did, I wouldn't split you up. Are you ready?"

Euan turned to Grace, who sat upon the bed. She suddenly looked frightened and upset, the same way he felt inside, and he couldn't tell if the feelings were his, hers, or both of theirs. To see those feelings manifested on her face knotted his stomach. She'd never looked this way before a mission. She was always calm, always confident. That she suddenly was otherwise didn't sit well with him and filled him with a sense of foreboding. She shouldn't go alone, and he felt it deep in his gut.

Reaching out, he cupped her face in his hand, smoothing his thumb over her cheek. "Ready as I shall ever be for this. Take care of yerself and we will take care of ye here. Ye come back to me, Watcher."

Grace managed a weak smile and settled herself on the bed. She wanted him near her as he always was, he could tell, but he couldn't be. He couldn't touch her when she was leaving lest it take him along. Caia and Euan pulled the curtains closed and heard Grace take a deep breath and release it before there was silence. Caia peeked inside the curtains to see Grace still and sleeping before she nodded to Euan. He crawled onto the bed beside her and studied her face. It was the first time he'd ever seen her this way. At least she looked alive.

"Come home safe to me," he whispered, reaching out to stroke her hair.

***

The scent of flowers brought Grace around, her eyes fluttering open, but she felt sick and closed them again. That wasn't normal for her, but she put it down to being nervous and working alone without the comfort of knowing her husband was somewhere near, and she missed him already. For the first time, she'd felt terrified of the darkness brought on by the closed curtains. Something had felt so wrong, she just couldn't say what. Whatever it was made her want to pull the curtains open and refuse to go, but she couldn't do that, and hadn't.

Grace forced herself to sit up, and after a moment, opened her eyes again. The world seemed to spin and blur but then righted itself. Grace looked around and found herself on a stone bench in a sunken garden. The smell of flowers made sense now. It was a beautiful place, a place she could spend hours reading in or sitting in with Euan if he were here.

Grace struggled to focus on the incoming briefing. France. She was in France, 1747. Though the information came in, it seemed slow and almost garbled, and Grace frowned. What would bring her here at this time? The mission itself finally appeared and Grace gasped. Prevent a third landing in Scotland orchestrated by the exiled chiefs. King Louis had shown no interest in it before, so it had never happened, but something had changed, and the resumption of war seemed imminent. Her target was the woman who held the ear of the king: Jeanne Antoinette Poisson, otherwise known to history and the world as Madame de Pompadour.

She looked down at her clothing to figure out how she was to approach things, because her station would determine what she could and couldn't do. Grace was delighted to find a beautiful sapphire blue and gold brocade dress. The stomacher itself was beautifully embroidered with an almost beige thread, the sleeves ending at her elbows with a large cuff and lace. The bodice fit closely but was comfortable and showed off her figure to its best advantage as it was meant to. Being of the upper class would certainly help matters.

Grace stood from the bench and fought the dizziness once more. She felt weak and her body ached. It usually didn't take her so long to recover from a transport.

"What is going on?" Grace whispered. She'd have to ask The Council when she tried to speak with them tonight. All she could do now was push through it.

There was a parasol in her hand, and she was thankful for it, raising it to shield her eyes from a sun that seemed far too bright. The sound of women's laughter came from nearby, and Grace followed it out of the sunken garden and onto a well-manicured path amidst a stunning larger garden. As she followed the path, it opened out onto a large clearing, and Grace soon realized it wasn't a clearing at all. It was a massive expanse of a vista. To her left was a long lawn and beyond it a body of water. To her right there were small hedge gardens, leading to a fountain and a set of stairs behind it. Looming large at the top of those stairs was the palace itself: Versailles. Grace had been here before but only in her own time, and she was awed to see it as it had been when it was a hub of political life, bustling with courtiers enjoying the spring weather. All the varying colors and textures were a feast for the eyes, and she could've remained here just watching all day. That was not, however, what she was here for. She made her way across the garden paths to the stairs and climbed them, though even that felt as though it took more effort than it should in a mission body, nearly running into someone as she reached the top.

"Oh! Please, pardon me, I am very sorry," Grace said, immediately dropping into French.

"You should truly be more careful, mademoiselle."

Grace couldn't hide her astonishment and quickly dropped into a deep curtsy. Standing before her was King Louis XV, thirty-seven years old and still handsome. He was tall, his presence commanding, and his gaze sharp. It was his mistress Grace was after, and this introduction would help her get to Madame.

"Your Majesty. Please forgive me. I was lost in my own thoughts."

Louis gave her the signal to rise, and she did so. With a gentle laugh, he gave a small, understanding, nod to her. "It is easy to do out here and I often do the same. I do think it was designed that way on purpose. It is a good place to go when you need to clear your mind. You are, of course, forgiven."

"Thank you, Your Majesty. I shall endeavor to be less distracted in the future lest I accidentally run into the point of a halberd instead of a forgiving king."

Louis laughed. "And a quick wit, too. Are you new to my court? I do not recall seeing you here before, mademoiselle . . . ?"

"Cameron, Your Majesty," Grace replied, lowering herself once more and then rising.

The king raised an eyebrow. "Cameron? Have you fled your own country, too? It seems we are becoming quite the destination for Scottish rebels."

"It seemed only right to follow my prince," Grace replied.

"Quite," the king replied, extending his hand to Grace. She placed hers atop his and he kissed it gently. "Your loyalty is to be commended. It is a great pleasure to have you here, Mademoiselle Cameron. If Scotland contains other beauties such as this, they are welcome to send them all here. We will take fine care of them."

Some of the other men with the king chuckled at the suggestion and Grace smiled. "I shall be sure to send word home forthwith so that your wish might be obeyed, and lovely young Scottish women shall be sent to you by the shipload. Perhaps a few of the Englishwomen, too, if they can pass muster."

Louis laughed again; a bit harder this time. "I do like the way you think. You remind me of the Marquise in that sense; always ready with an amusing answer. Have you met her?"

"No, Your Majesty. I have not yet had the privilege."

"I shall have to make that introduction as soon as I am able! I think she would find you pleasant and amusing. In the meantime, I believe we even now have some of your compatriots here."

"Compatriots, Your Majesty?"

"Yes, of course. Monsieur Cameron! I do believe I have found someone who may have once belonged to you."

The man to whom Louis called out turned around, and Grace's blood ran cold. Lochiel. Grace forced herself to relax and remember that this should be a time when he'd never met her, a different timeline. One where the battle had been lost but Euan was still dead.

She curtsied to him, but he frowned deeply. "*Ye*. What are ye doing here?" he asked in English, seeming to forget himself for a moment.

Grace fought the urge to panic when Lochiel recognized her. He wasn't supposed to recognize her. How was this possible? She realized then that they'd sent her to the same timeline. It happened, of course, but like this? So soon after all that had occurred?

Louis looked at Lochiel in puzzlement due to not only the change in tone but in language. "What greeting is this for one of your own?" he asked, moving to English himself.

Grace watched as Lochiel smoothed his expression with practiced ease. "Apologies, Yer Majesty, I was simply surprised to see her here. I had nae thought she had made it through the reprisals."

"How tragic that would have been. I shall leave you to speak and you may find out all about her journey. Until later, mademoiselle," Louis said as he kissed her hand again and she curtsied.

As the king walked past her and down the steps, Grace fought the urge to grab him and beg him not to leave her alone here. While doing so would never be her normal course of action, she felt unwell, so completely unlike herself and vulnerable that it was the only thing she could think of to do. Instead, she swallowed hard and looked at the man in front of her, whose countenance had gone back to anger. Beside him was the man she'd encountered at the loch when she first met Euan, the one who'd struck her. He was with several other men she didn't recognize, seeming to have been promoted with the deaths of his clansmen.

"What are ye doing here?"

"I . . ." Grace faltered for words. "Aileen sent me away when word of the British approach came. She told me to go to France and seek safety for it was no longer safe there."

"Euan's mother sent ye here, did she?"

"Yes," Grace replied. "I do not know what happened to her."

"Likely dead, like all of the others."

"I can only pray that is not so."

"Pray if ye wish, but it will nae bring the dead back. If it did, the four hundred men I lost would be alive now. Including Euan."

Grace winced and her eyes filled with tears. The image of him dead on the field was something that still haunted her. Her chest ached where the wound had once been, but far stronger than it ever had.

"Aye, Euan. Ye remember him, dinnae ye? The one on whose arm ye arrived at my home. The one who is dead because of ye."

"What? Because of me? I did not do anything!"

Lochiel stepped closer to her and grabbed her arm hard. "Oh aye, ye did. I suggest ye walk with me and I suggest ye do it calmly. We have some discussion due, ye and I."

As soon as he touched her, Grace felt as though the entire world had risen and then dropped, her stomach lurching. It made her feel even more unsteady, the briefing that was still trickling in abruptly ceasing. Her vision blurred and it made her dizzy again. She'd never felt this on a mission and didn't understand why she did now, even as the confidence and strength she normally had as a Watcher faded to nothing.

Lochiel turned and, still holding her arm, began walking back toward the palace. Though she didn't resist him, his pace was far too quick for Grace in this state, and he almost dragged her along, his men following them. As they went into the palace, the men surrounded her and Lochiel as if to shield her from view. They didn't want anyone to see her and that only unnerved her more. She could see nothing but their backs until the sound of marble and stone under her feet turned to the grit of the palace drive. In front of them was a carriage.

"Get in," Lochiel said as one of the men opened the door.

"I do not think—"

"I dinnae care what ye think. Get. In."

Shaking, Grace climbed inside and was shoved against one of the walls. Some of his men came inside with them and another climbed into the driver's seat.

"Lucky for me, I was just preparing to leave and had called

my carriage around, so we dinnae need to worry about someone seeing ye with us while we waited for it," he said to Grace. "Ye know where to go, lad," he called out to the driver

As the carriage jolted to a start, Grace looked at Lochiel and tried to discern what he might be thinking, but she found nothing there. "Where are we going?"

"To a place where no one will hear ye if ye scream and no one will overhear what is said," he replied, his gaze cold.

Something within Grace screamed at her to run where normally it would not. *"It is not right; you are not right! Something has gone wrong!"* Grace thought before she tried to lunge forward toward the carriage door to open it, only to be shoved back violently by one of the other men.

"I suggest ye dinnae try something so unwise again, lass. Next time they will nae be so kind."

"Help me! I need help! Get me out!" Grace pleaded to The Council, but she heard nothing and felt nothing, not even an acknowledgement that she'd been heard. It only reinforced her belief that something had gone horribly wrong.

The carriage picked up speed when it was clear of the palace and the woods raced by until it swung off the road and into the trees. When they stopped, the door swung open and Grace was pushed forward by the men inside and into the arms of the one who'd driven them. He shoved her against a tree while one of the others took a rope from the carriage. It was rough, the type of rope you would use to tie down the luggage of occupants, and it scraped Grace's skin raw as they tied it around her.

"Now that we are nae at risk of being overheard, who are ye?"

"Grace. Grace Cameron."

"Dinnae lie to me! Ye are nae a Cameron, no matter what ye said to the others."

"I am. Please, let me go, I can explain."

"I think ye are too dangerous to let go of, lass. That night, ye told us about the swampy ground and park walls at Drumossie. Ye told us exactly what would happen. How did ye know?"

"I had seen the ground. I told you so that night!"

"Ye are lying. If ye came from the Colonies ye would have come up from Glasgow, nae down from Inverness."

"The ship I came with went to Inverness instead. It had cargo to deliver there."

"Even if ye had seen the ground, as ye say, how did ye know exactly what would happen to our lines? How did ye know any of it?"

"I just—" Grace stammered, unable to formulate a quick answer to his question. It was never something she thought she'd have to explain.

"The better question is: how are ye here? I know damned well ye were nae at Achnacarry when Cornwallis came. Do ye know how? Because I was there, and I did nae see ye. Because my men saw ye at Drumossie. They saw ye try to stop Euan and saw ye run after him. The ones who survived told me ye had been there. Ye ran into the battle and yet, ye are alive."

Grace's heart felt as though it might pound out of her chest. She hadn't had time to think her story through, no time to think about how to maneuver around Lochiel and the others who may know her as she might've done if she'd not seen him right away.

"So, to me, that means one of two things. One, ye are a spy for the English and that is why they did nae shoot ye. Or, two, ye are a witch."

"What?" Grace looked at him in shock. A witch?

"Aye. Perhaps ye put a curse on us to cause us to fail. Ye saved yerself but left us to die. Perhaps ye are both. Let us see if witches can bleed."

Before Grace could say a word, one of Lochiel's men produced a knife and used it to place a deep cut on the inside of Grace's forearm as Grace screamed in pain. Within a few moments the realization hit her: pain. She could feel pain. How? The pain radiated up her arm and left Grace panting.

"Seems they can. Now, answer me. Which one are ye?"

"Neither! Please! Let me go!" Grace sobbed out.

"Ye are nae innocent so it must be one or the other. Why did ye curse us to failure? Was it because we did nae listen to ye? Did all of those men deserve to die because ye were angry?"

"I do not know what you are talking about! I did not want any of you to die and that is why I tried to warn you!"

"But how did ye know!" he shouted into her face. "How did ye know what to warn us about? Did ye see what was to come while doing some sort of spell?"

"No, it was a dream! I dreamt it and I tried to tell you what I saw! Please!"

"Now we are getting closer to the truth. So ye dreamt of the future, did ye lass? Then how did ye get to Drumossie unseen?"

"I stayed off the roads! I had to stop you and save Euan!"

"Save him! Ye killed him and everyone else with yer treachery and he lies rotting under that moor with the rest of my men! Dinnae act as though ye cared about him, though ye may have had him believing ye did. We did nae listen so ye told the English what we would do."

"No!"

"I am getting tired of yer games, lass. Now, ye tell me true or I will cut yer throat and leave ye for the animals."

Grace felt the point of the knife pressed just under her jaw. He was going to kill her.

Chapter 3

Euan had left the bed beside Grace and closed the curtains long ago because lying beside her would do no good. She wouldn't know he was there, and it wasn't as if his presence would help her mission in any way. His unhappiness about her going alone was still present, festering and eating at him like a nightmare he couldn't forget. He had a bad feeling about it, and something just felt off about the whole thing. He'd tried to make some sense of it while he'd been next to Grace, but it had only made things worse.

He shifted in the chair he'd taken residence in beside the bed, then stood up and left the room. Caia was working on something she couldn't tell him about, so conversation had been minimal, and it was just as well because he wasn't in the mood for it anyway. Euan walked down the hall to their bedroom but the sight of it empty only made him feel worse. Her things were here, but she wasn't. Her body was here, but she wasn't. *He* was here, but she wasn't.

Euan ran his fingers through his hair, feeling distressed. What was it that was bothering him so much? He felt so empty without her here, as though something that had been inside of him was now gone. He closed his eyes and tried to focus, tried to concentrate on what he was seeking: Grace. It was more than just her presence he sought, it was the part of her that lived in him, the link that forever tied them together. His eyes flew open as he realized that feeling was gone. *She* was gone. His heart felt like it would pound out of his chest as he hurried back to the room where Caia sat.

"Something is nae right," he said.

"What do you mean?" Caia asked as she set aside what she'd been doing.

"I cannae feel her. I can always . . ." he struggled to find a way to explain it. "There is this feeling of her always with me. I know if she is well or if she is nae, I can feel it, I just know. I cannae feel that now. I cannae feel her at all."

Caia frowned. "I haven't heard of any sort of link like that. Are you sure it's not just your worry?"

"No." Euan said, but paused as he suddenly doubted himself and what he felt even though he knew he was right. "At least I dinnae think so."

"Everything will be fine, Euan, you'll see. Grace worked alone for two years before she met you. This time won't be any different. I know it's difficult, I'm told the first time always is."

Caia's confidence did little to assuage his fears, and Euan went to the bed to look at Grace, her face untroubled and her breathing even. She would be fine. He had to believe that, but he knew he would be asking The Council to never do this again, to never split them. If they needed a lone Watcher, they could send someone else, but he couldn't do this again. Euan sat back down in the chair and tried to calm his mind. The darkness he'd encountered in the hallway told him that night had already come, and all he could do now was try to sleep.

The sound of a strangled gasp for air startled Euan awake. That was never a good sound. He knew that sound, had heard it more times than he'd ever wanted to. How long had he been sleeping? He glanced over at Caia, who seemed just as shocked and confused by the sound as he was before he leapt from the chair he'd been in and yanked open the curtains surrounding the bed.

"Grace?" Euan said, wary.

There came another of the same strangled sounds, but in the light, he could now clearly see her back arch from the bed and her body convulse. Euan jumped onto the bed and grabbed her.

"Caia!"

"Grace! Grace, wake up! Grace!" Caia shouted as she gave Grace a shot of something in her arm, but when it didn't work, she looked terrified. "Dr. Fraser! Abort the mission! Pull her out!"

Grace's body bucked again in Euan's arms and she struggled to breathe. "Grace, love, please wake up. Come on, lass, please ye must wake up! Grace!"

Euan couldn't control the panic he felt as Grace didn't respond to any of the measures being taken to try and wake her. He had no idea what was going on, but whatever it was, he knew this wasn't supposed to be happening. This was the first time they'd sent her anywhere without him and this is what happened? Grace's body went limp in his arms and Euan looked at Caia frantically.

"I don't . . . this . . . I've never seen this!"

"Help her! Do something! GRACE!" Euan shouted as he shook her and got no response.

The door to the room opened and, instead of Aileen, it was a person neither Euan nor Caia could've expected.

"Councilwoman!" Caia cried out in shock at the sudden appearance of the head of The Council. The Councilmembers rarely came to the past unless they were working themselves. This was *not* a good sign.

The Councilwoman ran to the bed and looked at Grace, then looked at Euan. "They can't get her out."

"What?"

"That's what you're seeing. We're trying to get her out and we can't!"

"What in the hell do ye mean ye cannae get her out?"

"Something has gone wrong, but we don't know what. This has never happened, and it wasn't in anything we saw. She asked for help but when we tried to pull her out it wasn't working!"

Euan looked at Rochford with a horrified expression. Grace was trapped wherever they'd sent her, and she'd been asking for help. What he'd witnessed was Grace's body reacting to The Council's unsuccessful attempts to bring her back.

"What have ye done . . ."

"Euan, we have to send you. It's the only thing we can think of even though it's against all protocol. We need you to go find out what's happening and try to bring her back."

"Answer my question! What have ye done!" Euan shouted at her. "Where did she go!"

"France. 1747. The exiled chiefs are trying to convince the French king to stage a third landing and a resumption of the war to depose the Hanover king. If it goes as it should, he'll ignore it and have no taste for it. Something has changed to show he'll accept it this time. Grace went to make sure he doesn't."

1747. Of course. That's why he couldn't go. It was in his former lifetime, a time when he was supposed to be dead. To send him would break protocol in one of the most serious ways they could, but clearly the situation was bad enough to warrant doing so.

"It should nae matter. She was only in one timeline for anyone to recognize her, so any other line should nae matter. Why would it cause this?" Euan watched Rochford's face go pale. "No. No, ye could nae have been so foolish as to send her to the same one and nae someone else. Tell me ye did nae do something so stupid!"

"We've done it before, and it has never been a problem. Watchers go to the same timelines all the time, the same places. The recognition often helps."

Euan felt sick. She'd likely be recognized, and they'd done it on purpose.

"How many of them tried to stop a war? How many tried to change history by telling the ones in charge how to win?" Euan replied through clenched teeth.

"None, but that shouldn't matter. The manner in which she met you shouldn't make a difference."

"So ye think it is wise to take a woman who tried to help them, a woman they did nae listen to, and put her in a position to be recognized by them when they are looking for someone to blame for their failure?"

"Even if they did, they can't—"

"Send me. Send me now."

Euan hurried from the bed and wasted no time in changing clothes as Rochford explained what would happen before returning to The Council to make sure the assignment was set up. Grace would be his target, allowing him to easily track and find her, and his mission would be to make sure she completed hers. He tried to remain calm but found it difficult. Grace was in trouble somewhere and he had no idea what was happening to her. Why had she called for help? Grace had never needed to do so before. She always had it under control, and the knowledge that it was somehow so far out of that control that she'd called for a near immediate extraction was terrifying. Euan dropped back onto the bed and looked over at Grace beside him. Taking her hand, he kissed it, then kept a tight hold on it.

"I am coming for ye, love. Hold on," he whispered.

Caia drew the curtains and Euan closed his eyes before she'd even finished. The familiar sensation came, and he opened his eyes to find himself in the woods. Before he could even concentrate on what The Council was sending him, a carriage sped past on the road just beyond the trees. Grace. She was in that carriage; he could feel it thanks to the targeting. He scrambled up and grabbed the horse that was there waiting for him, thankful that The Council had at least thought of that. Euan swung into the saddle and immediately urged the horse into a full gallop. If they continued on, he'd be able to overtake them, but if they stopped before he caught up, all he could do was follow his sense of Grace to find her when they stopped.

A woman's scream rang out through the trees, chilling

Euan to the core. Pulling the horse to a stop and dismounting, he walked slowly into the trees in order to keep his footfalls silent, though he could hear Grace crying.

"I am getting tired of yer games, lass. Now, ye tell me true or I will cut yer throat and leave ye for the animals."

"I swear to you, I am telling the truth! I am not a witch and I am not a spy; I am just someone who tried to help you!"

"Then if ye are well and truly one of mine, a Cameron, I have the right to do what I am about to do. I dinnae care what ye insist, I know this is down to ye, at least some of it. It is time to avenge some of my men and make sure ye cannae do this again. Kill her."

"I would nae do that. It would be quite unwise of ye."

The man with the blade froze in his movement and the other men turned slowly to look at who'd joined them. It was a voice as familiar to all of them as their own, and Euan watched as the color drained from their faces even as Grace sobbed in relief.

"Euan," Lochiel whispered. "How . . ."

"Lochiel," Euan said without bothering to offer him any sort of deference. "Let her go."

"Ye are dead. This is impossible."

"Clearly, I am nae, as ye can see me standing here. I will ask ye again: let my wife go."

"Wife?"

"Aye, *wife*. She has naught to do with any of this."

"She cursed us to failure! She is a witch and needs to pay so she cannae do this again!"

"She did nae do anything of the sort. We failed because the prince could nae command the army by the end and did nae listen to those who could. Ye know that as well as anyone. We did nae need witchcraft to fail."

Lochiel looked at him, curious. "How are ye here, Euan? Where did ye come from?"

"The same place ye did. From the battlefield. The same

one ye were rescued from, I was rescued from. By her." Not a lie but not the full truth either. Euan had no intention of telling him any of that.

"Nae the question I asked ye," Lochiel said before he looked at Grace and then back to Euan. "How could she even do such? How could she do it without meeting her own end?"

"I saw ye leave with her, and though I could nae get to her in time to stop ye, it was easy for me to track ye. As for the rest, how do ye know she was nae wounded for her efforts? Have ye even asked her? Did it ever occur to ye that some of us who were wounded may have lived? She was hurt but she cared for me and kept me alive. Once we were well enough to travel, I was forced to come here rather than be hunted like a dog by Cumberland's men. A Cameron officer and, nae only that, but the one with a bounty on his head. Would nae that have been a prize?"

Euan watched, his face impassive, as his words began doing their work, untangling the knot of suspicion, anger, and grief.

"She just said she dreamt of the battle. How is that nae witchcraft?"

"She is nae a witch, I can promise ye that. Perhaps God tried to warn ye. She would nae be the first Cameron woman to have a dream that would save her chief's life, would she?"

Lochiel blinked at the reference to an old clan legend, and then looked at Grace again. "When did ye marry her?"

"The night before we left. I found the priest and did it quickly. I wanted something to come back to, and she was it. Did ye nae say that night that it seemed I might be the husband she had come to seek? Turns out ye were far more prescient then ye knew. If God sent her a warning to give us, is it any wonder she came to Drumossie to try to stop us? Due to hubris and foolishness, her vision came to pass, and we were slaughtered like cattle."

"It was too late to stop. We had gone so far already."

"Aye, we had. Ye are right, and that is why it did nae work. It came too late. I know ye tried to make another stand."

"Aye, we did. But we were vastly outnumbered, and I faced losing the rest of my men, so we fled."

"Ye fled. Ye fled with the prince and the other chiefs to save yer necks while ye left the rest of us to suffer and die for yer treason. Ye are cowards, all of ye."

Lochiel's face turned red with rage. "How dare ye!"

"How dare I? Look at ye. Ye are well fed, ye are healed of yer wounds, in fine clothes at court with a king while even now yer people are starving and being shipped to the Colonies against their will! Why? Because ye ran instead of facing yer death as ye asked all of us to do."

"I charged those lines just as ye did! I took fire, took injury. I was ready to die just as ye were that day, alongside my men. I did nae stay to hang, that is true, but I cannae avenge my men and my clan when I am dead, and someone had to make sure the prince got out of Scotland safely. Ye dinnae want to make an enemy of me, lad."

"No, I dinnae, ye are right. I want to live a quiet, peaceful life in safety with my wife. Ye can have yer anger and I can have mine."

Lochiel looked away from Euan for a long moment before he nodded. "Ye are right. Ye are bound to be angry about what happened, just as I am. Just as we all are. For that reason, I will forgive yer insult. I have always liked ye, Euan, ye know that. It was why I did all that I could for ye and made ye an officer."

"Let her go."

"Nae yet. We are nae the only ones here. The others fled too and are here even now, petitioning the king to let us regroup and stage another landing, this time with the full French army behind us. Ye should join us, lad. Ye have a keen mind for it and yer help was always invaluable."

"No. I have no interest in such a thing. It does nae matter how many soldiers ye have if the one ye fight for cannae lead ye without infighting."

"He would nae be in command this time. He would remain here until we sent for him. Until Scotland was ours."

Euan shook his head. "My fighting days are behind me now. As I said to ye, I just want to enjoy what remains of my life."

"I can order ye."

"No, ye cannae. We are nae in Scotland any longer or in Achnacarry. I am no longer yers to command, Lochiel."

Euan fought the urge to tell him that he was commanded by something larger now, something beyond anything Lochiel could imagine. Euan's duty to him had ceased the day he'd run straight toward a line of government forces by his order.

"Ye will feel foolish for nae joining us when we succeed, and ye will come crawling back to me to return home."

"If it happens, ye are welcome to make me suffer for it before ye allow me to return."

"How do ye know I will let ye return?"

"Ye will need me, just as ye always have, and I am far too valuable to ye to leave me by the wayside. Besides, there are no more men. Perhaps by then I will be ready to fight again."

Lochiel smiled wryly. "Aye. Ye are right. I know ye will return, Euan. Ye cannae keep a warrior from a battle for long, especially one of yer caliber. Untie the lass."

Euan walked across the clearing, getting to Grace just as they dropped the rope. She fell into his arms but remained silent. "Thank ye. I am sure I will be seeing ye about court."

"Aye, ye will. Be careful of it, Euan. Ye can trust no one. Dinnae fear me telling anyone ye are nae noble. If anyone has earned such a new start, it would be ye. Ye were always a good man and I always knew I could count on ye. Hopefully soon I can again."

Euan nodded, though the idea that this man felt Euan needed his warnings about the French court after all he'd been put through here was laughable. Euan knew far more about the workings of this place than any of the men here could ever dream of. Lochiel motioned to his men and they all got back into the carriage they had come in, departing and finally leaving Euan alone with Grace.

Chapter 4

When he was sure they were alone, Euan sat Grace down and grabbed underneath her skirt to find her petticoat. He tore a strip from it and wrapped it tight around Grace's still bleeding arm. It enraged him that they'd hurt her, but at the same time he couldn't understand why she wasn't already healing from this.

"Euan . . ." she said, her voice weak.

"Aye, I am here, love. I came for ye and ye are safe."

"How? You cannot be here!"

"It was an emergency. They had no choice but to send me when they could nae get ye out."

"But they could have sent someone else," she countered, her mind seeming unable to register Euan's telling her they'd been unable to pull her out.

"There was no one else, and if ye think I would let anyone else come after ye when ye are in danger ye are mad."

"I called for help. They did not answer me."

"Aye, they did and that is why I am here. They tried to pull ye out, but it was nae working. It was a horrible thing to watch."

"Euan, something is wrong. Very wrong."

"I know, but I dinnae know what it is and neither do they."

Grace looked down at her bandaged arm. "It is not healing. I feel . . ."

"Shhh, easy now."

"No. Euan, I . . . I am not a Watcher here."

"What?"

"It is all gone. I can feel pain. I can feel fear. I feel weaker, almost as if I am . . ."

"As if ye are really here," he finished in a soft voice.

"Yes."

"I feel it still and I dinnae understand why ye cannae. I feel fine."

"I felt so ill when I arrived. The briefing came in so slowly and I had trouble focusing. It is gone entirely now."

Gone entirely. Whatever had happened had made Grace as real as anyone here and that meant extreme danger. "We need to get ye out of here immediately."

"The only way is to finish the mission."

Euan released a heavy sigh. "I thought ye would say that. And, though I disagree and think they could send another, I know ye will nae stand for it, so I will be here to help ye finish it." He stood up, bringing her with him and steadying her on her feet. "Let us get out of these woods and get ye someplace we can better treat that cut. I will have to stitch it closed for ye."

Grace looked up at him before turning and putting her arms around him, hugging him tightly. It was an embrace Euan returned with silent thanks to every deity he could think of. He'd been so close to losing her. A moment longer and they would've killed her, he knew that, because Lochiel had been serious about his accusations. They never should've sent Grace to do this mission. The Council didn't understand what it could be like here. How could they when they were so far removed from it?

"I love ye," he whispered. "I will always come for ye. I will nae allow them to part us again."

"I love you. I know this is against all of the rules, but I am glad you came."

Euan stroked her back. "Perhaps it is best I am here. I know these politics the best of any of us. I know the players. At least this time I get to be with ye as yer husband. About damned time."

Grace laughed, though it was weak, and Euan walked her back to the road to where the horse was waiting. He lifted her up first and then got in the saddle behind her, the position keeping his arms around her in case she fell. Grace rested her head against his shoulder as he started them back down the road toward the palace and the town beyond it. His briefing told him they had lodgings in a townhouse near the palace. Grace had been meant to stay there on her own, but now they both would. Euan knew this area, the palace and the surrounding woods, better than he'd ever want to admit to anyone in his new life, because doing so would lead to questions he had no desire to answer yet.

"It is a beautiful dress ye are wearing. The blue makes yer eyes more striking," he said after a long silence.

"I quite like it, too."

"Tell me what has happened so far. How did ye get here?"

"I ran into the king. Quite literally. We had a pleasant conversation and he offered to introduce me to my target. Then he called Lochiel over."

"And it all went wrong from there."

"Yes. Once the king was out of sight, Lochiel dragged me into the carriage, and that was how we ended up here. I called for help in the carriage."

"At home, all we saw was ye struggle to breathe and yer body act like someone was pulling ye, but we could nae wake ye. Councilwoman Rochford herself came to tell us that The Council could nae reach ye and I had to go."

"She came?" Grace asked, shocked. "The Council never comes!"

"This was an exception it seems."

"I am so tired," she whispered.

The words struck a chord of fear in Euan. The only fear he ever felt now, at least when he was working, was when it came to Grace's safety. "Tired?"

"I just want to sleep."

That she would say such a thing only deepened his concern. She was right; whatever made them what they were was no longer with Grace. She was as human as Lochiel had been, and that frightened him. Euan didn't want to think about what could happen because of it.

"If ye wish a rest ye should have one. I will wake ye when we arrive," he said, though there was no response from Grace, who was already asleep.

When they arrived back in town, Euan gave her a gentle shake to wake her and she sat up. Carrying an unconscious lady into town would bring quite a bit of suspicion, and that was the last thing they needed right now. Euan turned the horse into the small stable yard of the townhouse and a young boy ran up to assist him.

"Bonjour Monsieur Cameron. Did you enjoy your ride with Madame?"

"Aye, thank ye, I did," Euan replied in French without a thought. He was glad he had no need of The Council's assistance when it came to speaking this particular language; he could handle that perfectly well on his own while sticking to English or Gaelic with Grace.

Before, it would have shocked him that anyone knew who he was, much less people he'd never seen before. That they should greet him as though they'd just seen him would only make it worse, but he was used to all of this by now. This was how it worked on missions like this one. They were inserted as though they'd always been there, so that any household staff or people serving them knew who they were, so as to help them blend in. He wasn't sure how The Council did it, but he'd long ago given up asking those sorts of questions.

Euan slid from the saddle and helped Grace down. "Let us see to yer arm, love."

"Will you be needing your horse again today, monsieur?"

"No, I will nae, thank ye lad."

The boy nodded and led the horse off as Euan helped Grace

into the house. It was beautifully appointed with large, bright rooms. There were carpets on the wooden floors and various paintings on the walls. If they had to be here a while, at least they could spend it in a bit of luxury. A woman came out to greet them but looked shocked as she saw the state Grace was in.

"Madame has injured herself. I need ye to bring a bottle of spirits, a needle, and thread upstairs."

"Shall I fetch the surgeon, monsieur?"

"No," Euan said. "There is no need, I can take care of this myself. I have had my fair share of this work after battles."

The woman nodded and hurried off to get the items he'd requested as Euan walked Grace to the stairs and up. He opened one of the double doors to the room he knew was theirs and shut it behind them.

Grace looked around and then nodded in approval. "This will do nicely. Much better than our last mission accommodation."

Euan laughed. "Aye, that is the truth. I did nae know London could smell so wretched in the summer."

"Well, there is a basic sanitation issue. I am sure that Paris is not any better."

"It is nae," Euan replied offhandedly.

Grace looked at him, her expression curious. "How do you know?"

"That is what Lochiel told me," he replied, smoothly covering his mistake. "I am glad we dinnae have to find out for ourselves."

Grace turned to him, a wry smile on her lips. "Were you not just grousing about when we would get to spend time together in one place?"

Euan shot her a vexed look. "This is nae what I had in mind, love."

"We can always make the best of it," Grace replied as she made her way to the wardrobe to look at the clothing inside. It was well stocked with what they'd need for an extended period if it were necessary, though Euan hoped it wouldn't be.

Shutting the wardrobe door, she studied herself in the looking glass. Per usual, her normal appearance was toned down a bit and she didn't look quite so healthy as she normally did. Her hair color remained mostly the same, though it was hard to tell with the powder on it, and it was done up in a more elaborate style. Her deep blue eyes also remained, but her skin was paler and he couldn't be sure if that was The Council's doing, or if it was whatever was happening to her.

"Aye, we can and should. Who knows if we will be so fortunate as to be able to publicly be together next time. Enter," Euan called out as a knock sounded at the door and the woman from earlier entered the room with a tray.

"Thank ye," he said as she set it down on a table and left. "Come, sit ye down."

Grace surveyed the items with a wary eye but came to the table and sat down. "Euan, are you sure we should not send for a doctor?"

"A doctor is nae a doctor here, *leannan*. He is far more likely to kill ye than I am; a fact I know ye are keenly aware of." Euan picked up the bottle and looked at it before nodding and setting it in front of her. "Whisky. Good. Start drinking."

"What?" Grace asked in shock.

"Drink it so ye dinnae feel what I am about to do."

Grace looked horrified and he couldn't really blame her. This wasn't how things were done in her time.

"If ye want to feel the needle then be my guest. If ye dinnae, then by all means . . ." he said, gesturing toward the bottle.

Grace reached out without another word and grabbed the bottle, taking a swig from it and then coughing. "I will have to go back to the palace tomorrow," she wheezed out.

"Aye. Though I suggest we work this from two angles: ye work with yer target and leave the men to me. I can talk to them and perhaps get them all to agree to step back."

"It is worth trying," Grace conceded as she took another drink.

"It may get us out of here more quickly. Stand up."

Grace pushed herself up from the table and swayed a bit, the whisky already working on her, not entirely a surprise in her already weakened state. "Oh."

Euan chuckled and turned her so that she was almost sitting on the table before he carefully began to unpin her bodice from the stomacher. He set it aside and then helped her to slide the bodice from her shoulders. The skirts followed and all of it was laid out on the bed to be sent down to wash the blood from it.

"This is my favorite part," Euan whispered in her ear as he turned her around so that her hands were braced on the table.

"What is?"

"This," he whispered once again as he began to loosen the spiral lace on the back of the stays.

Grace shivered. "You are evil."

"Aye. I can always make it worse."

"Can you?"

"Is that a challenge, love?"

"Maybe."

Euan grinned and leaned over to kiss her neck even as he unlaced her. His teeth then grazed her shoulders as he worked his way along them to kiss the back of her neck. Grace inhaled sharply before he pulled away from her.

"Arms up," he instructed and pulled the stays over her head and off when she did so. "Take another drink."

Grace sat down and did as he asked while Euan remained behind her and reached over her shoulder to unwrap her arm, glad to see that the bleeding seemed to have tapered off somewhat. He took a deep breath and released it in silence, not looking forward to what he was about to do. Euan stroked her cheek before he suddenly clamped a hand over her mouth. Just as she was about to struggle, he grabbed the bottle from her and poured whisky over the cut. He both heard and felt her gasp in pain before she screamed into his hand. Euan winced, knowing firsthand just how much it hurt. She screamed again into his palm as he poured a little more, and he felt her body shaking with sobs. These screams were why he'd covered her mouth. There was no need to bring any of the household running in to assist her.

"Shhh, lass, I know. I am sorry for hurting ye," he said as he removed his hand from over her mouth. "Try to breathe."

Grace rested her head on the table on top of her other arm, sobbing. Euan walked around to the other side of the table and picked up the needle from the tray. He lifted the small piece of metal to the flame of a candle until it glowed red. This would ensure it was at least somewhat clean.

"No . . . no, Euan . . . please . . ." Grace stammered as she caught sight of the needle.

"Grace, I must. Ye cannae walk around this way," he replied as he threaded the needle.

Grace tried to pull back as he grabbed her arm. "Yes, I can. It will heal. The Council will fix everything. Please let go!"

"Grace," Euan said, his tone firm as she tried to pull away before using his strength to pin her arm to the table. "They cannae fix this because ye are nae yerself. They cannae reach ye and ye are nae invincible now. If I dinnae sew this up it *will* get infected and it *will* kill ye. We dinnae know what was on the blade they used."

Euan watched as Grace did her best to calm her panic, turning her head away and gripping the edge of the table with her other hand in what he knew would be a futile attempt to steel herself. As the needle pierced her skin and she felt the thread being dragged through, she buried her face in her arm and cried out.

"Good lass, that is the way. I will be as quick as I can."

For Grace, it wouldn't be quick enough, and he understood the feeling well. However, he managed to close the cut on Grace's arm both quickly and neatly. If a scar developed it would be minimal, but he wondered if it would matter. Would it show up on her body back home or would it be gone when they left here and she was able to reconnect with The Council? He hated that he even had to do it in the first place, hated that he had to be the cause of any pain to her. Worse was knowing precisely what everything felt like because he'd needed to have it done to him or had done it to himself.

That the whisky had done its work was both good and troubling. If things were as they should be it shouldn't have affected her, but it had. It was yet more proof of what she'd said: she was not a Watcher here and something was terribly wrong. If someone wanted her dead, she would be. She'd need to be extremely careful in all of her moves now and would need to use her wits and education instead of her ability if she wanted to complete her mission. He'd need to watch her carefully, almost like a Guardian. She could die but he couldn't, and he wouldn't let that go to waste if he had to protect her.

To his dismay, Grace wanted to sleep again when he'd finished. He wasn't concerned only because the nights were usually their time together when they were on a mission, though that certainly didn't help, but because she shouldn't need to sleep. There was a fear eating at Euan that one of these times she simply wouldn't wake up. It was the same feeling he'd experienced at Culloden, the one that had told him to pull Grace back from that ghost of himself. That feeling frightened him the most because it had been right, which meant there was a good possibility this one was, too.

Euan sat on the bed with Grace's head in his lap. She'd done this for him once; sat awake in the night to guard him, and he'd do the same for her now. He stroked her hair as she slept and tried to clear his mind of all of this. He needed to focus on the task at hand and he needed to contact The Council. It was always a strange thing to do. It was all mental, a sort of telepathy, and he always felt a bit doubtful of the responses. What if he was imagining them? He never had been, of course. Euan let the back of his head rest against the wall and closed his eyes.

He let his breathing even out and deepen, let that clear his mind of other thoughts, and then reached out to them.

"Councilwoman Rochford."

"Euan, thank goodness!" The sound of her relief in hearing from him was very plain. *"Were you able to find her?"*

"Aye, I found her, and she is with me now. Thank ye for the horse."

"You're quite welcome. What news?"

"It is a good thing ye sent me. She would be dead now if I had nae come."

There was silence for a long moment.

"What do you mean she would be dead?"

"I know why you could nae pull her out. She is nae a Watcher here. Something has happened and she is as normal here as I was when ye sent her to me. She can bleed, feel pain, feel fear. She needs sleep, drink, food. She said she felt ill when she arrived, that the briefing came in slowly and muddled, before it was gone entirely."

"How . . ."

"I dinnae know. What I do know is that ye made a huge mistake sending her here. Lochiel is here and, as I feared, he recognized her. He called her a witch and was about to kill her when I found her. He blamed her for our defeat, called it witchcraft. Perhaps ye are too far removed to understand what it is like here. Superstition is strong and ye sent a woman who had been seen at a battle and then vanished after trying to warn them. What did ye think they would believe when they watched with horror as her warnings came true?"

"If things were normal it wouldn't have mattered."

"If things were normal it would only confirm their suspicions when she did nae die after they cut her throat. How would she be able to complete her mission with these men shouting to everyone that she is a witch and nae to listen to her? She could nae complete it if she was imprisoned."

Euan heard Rochford sigh.

"That's true."

"How is it that none of the future Watchers came back to warn ye against this?"

"An excellent question."

"It does nae matter now. I have her and will keep her safe. We will

finish the mission and that will hopefully allow us to return. I still cannae feel her with me."

"Feel her?"

"I cannae explain it well. There is something I feel, something of her that is always with me. It is how I know if she needs me, how I know if she is all right. That is gone now. I cannae feel it and I could nae once she had left. Caia said it was nae something she had heard of."

"And she'd be right. There's a link, of course there is, but not a link like that. We'll need to research it."

Euan felt a sense of dread curl around him as he suddenly remembered a detail he hadn't even consciously noticed. It was so small he hadn't thought anything of it.

"Her mark is gone."

"No, that's impossible!"

The note of panic did not make him feel better.

"It is nae there, Councilwoman. I just realized it was gone when I stitched the cut on her arm."

Euan kept his eyes closed but reached out to find Grace's left wrist, running his finger across the inside of it. His heart sank when it confirmed what he already knew.

"I cannae feel it on her wrist when normally I could. It is nae there."

"Is yours?"

Euan reached out and ran the fingers of his right hand over his left wrist, easily finding the slightly raised surface of the symbol that marked him as a Companion. *"Aye."*

"This is . . . none of this makes any sense!"

"Ye have time to figure it out. We have work to do still. I will keep her safe until we can return."

"Thank you, Euan. Good luck and we'll let you know what we've found when you contact us next."

Euan opened his eyes, ending the contact between them. He looked down, praying he was wrong, but he wasn't. The Watcher's mark was gone, and he debated for a moment as to whether he should point it out to her when she woke. She hadn't noticed, which was curious to him. No, he shouldn't tell her. It wouldn't help her and would only throw her even more off balance. She would turn her mind to trying to find out what was happening to her rather than trying to do what she was sent here for. It was his task to protect her, and he'd take this part on himself.

Chapter 5

When Grace woke up, her head and body ached terribly. It wasn't the feeling she'd have if she had a hangover from the whisky, she hadn't had that much, but something more than that. It felt almost as though she had the flu, and it made her not want to get up. Maybe she didn't have to. Maybe Euan would bring her tea and come cuddle her in bed until she felt better. They had plenty of shows to catch up on and they could make a day of binge watching them together. Why had she been drinking whisky anyway? Well, at least as much as she had.

Grace groaned and buried her face in a pillow. She felt so awful and she only wanted it to stop. Her arm hurt, but she couldn't remember why. She pushed herself up despite her reluctance to do so and opened her eyes. She didn't recognize this place. Where was she? It was so dark she could hardly see, but there was a candle burning, a small pinpoint of light in the darkness. Grace slid out of bed and walked toward it.

"Euan?" she called out as she picked up the candle and tried to look around. The flame seemed to make no difference, the darkness remaining just as heavy.

Had they lost power in a storm? It wouldn't be the first time. Grace shuffled forward, free hand out in front of her, until her fingertips touched a wall. She frowned as she slid her fingers across it; it didn't feel like a wall she knew. It certainly wasn't the ones they had at home, they were smooth plaster, but this wall had a strange texture, like fabric.

"Euan? Where are you?"

"Grace," he said as he suddenly stepped out of the blackness and in front of the candle.

Grace screamed in shock and almost dropped it, then took a deep breath. "Christ! Do not scare me like that! What is going on? Did we lose power?"

Euan didn't answer, looking at her in silence. It was only then that she noticed his face was dirty, there was blood on it. From behind him, more men suddenly stepped into the meager light, all of them with the same faraway look. Grace gasped and took a step back, but they followed her forward. In the flickering light, the ones she could see all had pure black eyes, no white to be seen.

"Euan, what is wrong with you?" she asked, her voice small and quavering with fear.

"Grace!"

Her name shouted in a familiar voice got her to turn around, only to find Euan behind her. This one looked like the one she knew. He was in their bedroom at home, but where was she if not there? Why were there two of them? She turned to look back and the men were still there, Euan at their head, all of them staring at her. With a whimper of fear, she turned and tried to run for the safety of that other room, only to run into a wall of glass in front of her. Grace cried out in shock and pain before shaking it off.

"No!" she shouted as she pounded on it. "Euan help me! Please!"

"Grace!" he screamed as he pounded and kicked at the partition between them. "Grace!"

"Euan!" There was terror in her voice when she shouted his name and, when she turned to look back and saw the men still advancing on her, she screamed and resumed pounding on the wall between them. "EUAN, PLEASE!"

Caia and Rochford joined Euan now, looking dismayed and confused even as he desperately tried to break down what was between them to reach her. She could feel those other men getting closer, but there was nowhere for her to go. The false Euan was suddenly there, his hands on her waist, drawing her back against him.

"No! No!" Grace sobbed out as she struggled against him, watching the faces on the other side of the wall go white with fear before Euan attacked the wall with even more desperation. "HELP ME!" She didn't recognize the sound of her own voice now.

"They cannae help ye. No one can. They cannae stop us now. Welcome back, lass."

The voice, so familiar but so cold, only added to her terror before a hand shot forward and covered her mouth. She screamed against it but there was no sound, the blackness consuming it even as it consumed the light. The candle dropped to the floor and went out as she fought to pull forward and away. There was nothing but their laughter as a multitude of hands dragged her down into the dark.

Chapter 6

War. It was what they were good at, what they'd always been good at. Every war in the past had been their doing. War meant profit and profit meant happy people. Well, some people. They'd once been present across all of the timelines, working with impunity, but then The Council came. People turned away from war, and The Council found a way to control everything, limiting their profit and their pleasure, something they found unacceptable. They'd tried once to destroy them openly, but The Council sent the damned Cameron Watcher to stop them. The Cameron Watcher was the one who found a way to shut them out of the timelines entirely, relegating them to operation only in the divergent spaces of a timeline, the spaces where there was tension between one path and another. Those were the spaces The Council couldn't control, the spaces where it was easy to hide. It was there where they could try to force the choices that would open the timelines to them once more, where they could poke and prod until they found a weakness. They hadn't found one yet, but they would. They had to.

The Council operating now, the one sending Watchers now, wasn't The Council they'd tried to destroy. That was this Council's future and thus it was safer to stay where they were as yet unknown. Confinement to the divergences meant they couldn't physically do harm. They couldn't hand someone a weapon they could use to murder someone and start a war, though they'd done that once to great success; 1914-1918 had been very good years indeed.

No, they had to be cleverer than that. They were now the whispers in the wind, the "visions" from God, the voices in someone's head. This Council called them "timeline ghosts," but that was naive. Let them believe that, it allowed them to pick off Watchers who were too new to know better. The fewer Watchers there were, the easier it was for them. They knew that a divergence would bring a Watcher and that was where they could watch and wait.

All the Watcher lines were dangerous to them, of course, but there was one they hated the most: the Camerons. Not only had it been one of them who had trapped them, but it was always the Camerons who led the others to fight against their enemies. War was so foreign to The Council that they didn't know how to fight one, but the Camerons did. The Cameron Watcher came from a long line of warriors, it was in her blood, and she'd fought back with a ferocity that none of them expected.

They avoided the Cameron Watchers in any divergence now and at any time if they could. To go against them wasn't a chance they could take, not yet. There had been a moment where they'd almost gotten one of them entirely by accident before someone had yanked her away from them at the last second. It was only later that they realized who it had been: the Mother. The first Cameron Watcher from whom all else would come. It was her Companion who'd stopped her, the warrior whose blood and spirit would be alive in the one who would defeat them. Had they caught her, had she touched them, they could've ended it all right there, in that very moment. It would've destroyed everything the future Council had done. Without her, there would be no others, and the one who fought them would never exist.

They'd taken refuge in this current divergence, this place where they could try to influence a new war. The men who had come to speak to this king wanted revenge, bloodshed, and more war. It was the perfect opportunity. They haunted the dreams of these men, infecting them with visions of glory that would never come. Anything to get them to beg for assistance to restart the conflict. A Watcher had, of course, come; they'd expected that. What was not expected was *who* they sent. It was a stroke of luck and a rare mistake by The Council. They had sent *her*.

To send her here so close to her own death in this timeline had made her weak and vulnerable, but it was a weakness she could've recovered from if given time. Her link to The Council had been shaky as it fought against the disturbance her presence created. She was supposed to be dead and yet her energy was here again, very much alive. It was sheer luck that they'd been there whispering to Lochiel at the very moment he'd seen her. The second he touched her it had grounded her forcefully to the timeline, the convergence of energies from two people who had shared the same event: someone very much alive touching someone who should be dead. It had severed her link to The Council entirely and stripped her of anything that made her a Watcher. It had given them an opening to attach to her as all of the energies mixed, including their own. She was helpless.

It had been they who'd told Lochiel she was a witch, a spy, worthy of death. He'd been moments from killing her, moments from delivering them a great triumph, but then *he* had shown up. Once again, he'd snatched her back from them at the last moment, but it was too late. They had their opening now and it was just a matter of time. Without her link she was nothing. She was as human as anyone else and they would take advantage. They already had. They could exploit the rift created by her presence here to pull her into the divergence as she slept. In the divergence they were stronger. It was there where they could take her memories from her in what would seem like a nightmare to her, one that she wouldn't remember having when she woke.

This first time had been glorious. Her fear when they'd welcomed her back to her death in the images of those who'd died with her was beautiful. Her terror as they'd told her that no one could help her before they yanked all that she was into the blackness of forgetting had been perfection. It had been so easy, though it had required many of them to work together. Every time they pulled her in, they could take more. All they needed to do was to erase everything except that moment where she'd died in this timeline. When it was all she had left, she would willingly come to them, willingly surrender, and willingly die. All she needed to do was touch them of her own will because they couldn't force her. They couldn't touch her themselves in the physical world, though in the divergence they could. It was how they could extract things from her but, unfortunately, they couldn't use it to kill her there. Her surrender had to be her choice. The key was her Companion. He would always be the one who drew her until they erased him entirely. In that final moment she would go to him, drawn by the link they shared even if she couldn't remember it, and when she died so would he. The Camerons would be eliminated from the future.

In this first pull they'd taken everything from her that had existed before she'd met him. If anyone asked her about her family, about her friends, about her life she would find nothing. It was now time to chip away at what was left, and what was left was him. Their link was proving stronger than expected, stronger but not unbreakable. They were patient. They could take it away, little by little, memory by memory, until it was gone. The longer she remained here the closer she got to her destruction, and those who would protect her had no idea.

She belonged to them now.

Chapter 7

Grace opened her eyes to sunlight streaming in through a window, her heart racing. She felt afraid, but of what? There was something there, something just beyond remembering, but she was not inclined to try to find it. She groaned a little, wincing against the brightness of the light. Her head throbbed and she put a hand to her forehead, but she relaxed as she felt a gentle kiss on her hand. Euan. She smiled and looked up to see him smiling down at her.

"Good morning to ye, love. How do ye feel?"

"My head hurts, my arm hurts, and I feel like I could sleep all day."

"I am sure it is a bit disconcerting on yer body to be here without all yer normal help."

Yes, of course that was it, but why did she not have it again? "I still do not understand."

"Nor I. Nor does The Council. They had discovered naught when I spoke to them last night," he replied as he gently stroked her hair. "They will get it sorted. Meanwhile, ye and I will do our jobs."

Grace closed her eyes; it was more comfortable that way for the moment. "I suppose this means I ought to get up and get dressed."

"Nae yet. It is still early."

Grace pushed herself into a sitting position but covered her eyes as a wave of nausea swept over her.

"Are ye all right?"

Grace took a deep breath, letting it pass before she opened her eyes. "Just felt ill for a moment. How early is it?"

Euan's concern was clear on his face, but he didn't press her. "I dinnae know, maybe about seven or so. The court will nae be up yet so there is no sense going there."

Grace moved closer to him and then straddled his lap, flashing a wicked smile. "Plenty of time then."

"For?"

"For you to help me get rid of this headache."

"Would ye like me to get ye some tea?" he asked.

"No," she replied, even as she knew he was teasing her, lifting one hand to draw her fingertips across her collarbone and down to the tie of the shift. She looked down and pulled it slowly as she looked back up at him through her lashes while gently biting her lower lip.

It was unfair, cheating, and she knew that. She knew what it did to him and just when to use it, and just like all of the other times, it didn't fail to elicit the precise reaction she wanted from him. Euan pulled her hard against him as the shift slid halfway down her arms and buried his face against her shoulder before he nipped it and followed it with a kiss. Grace dropped her head back with a pleasured sigh, sliding her fingers into his hair. The reaction from her caused his hands to flatten against her back for a moment before he smoothed them down and took the shift with it, leaving it around her hips. As he lavished attention on her now exposed skin, she took a sharp breath in, her hands tightening in his hair for a moment.

Taking his hands from her back, he cupped her cheeks and brought her face down to his to kiss her as she dropped her hands from his hair to slide them under the nightshirt he'd changed into when she was sleeping. He obliged her when she pulled away from his kiss to lift it over his head and toss it aside so that she might feel his skin against hers. When she took what she wanted without allowing him the control, he dropped his head back against the wall with a loud groan, and it made her smile. She knew him so well in this way now, knew what he needed, what he wanted, and she felt him grab her hips without even thinking, though he made no attempt to direct her movements.

Grace brought her lips back to his only for a moment before she broke it to let go of a groan, and she brought her hand down hard on the wall beside his head, giving herself even more leverage. When he swore softly and involuntarily, she smiled, enjoying pulling such a reaction from him. That triumph was brief, however, because the end she'd sought took over, her head dropping back as she cried out and his own was smothered against her shoulder.

There was nothing said, no movement made other than her sliding her arms around his neck, and then pressing her lips to his in a soft kiss before she rested her cheek against the top of his head. Euan wrapped his arms around her and held her close to him as she tried to catch her breath. There was no need to bother with anything else at the moment. All of it could wait.

***

Afterward, there had still been at least two hours to kill before they could get to work, and they made use of every second of them. Grace had eaten a small meal, and Euan had changed the bandages on her arm while they'd discussed the strategy for the day. She now stood still as she was pinned into her gown for the day. It was just as beautiful as the other one had been, ornate without being gaudy. Instead of blue it was an emerald green covered with a delicate gold brocade design. The stomacher matched it, the abundant lace at the end of the sleeves adding to the richness of the look. Euan watched her in the mirror as he slipped his frock coat onto his shoulders. Whatever had plagued her earlier seemed gone now and he was thankful for it. It was so hard to see her struggle.

When her dress was pinned, Grace held her arms out at her sides as the maid slipped the long gloves onto her hands. They were fashionable but had the added bonus of covering her arm, so she needn't explain her injury. She then sat down upon a small bench before a dressing table as the young woman fastened a necklace around her throat and then picked up a hat, placing it on Grace's head.

"There, madame, you are ready!" the maid said as she finished pinning her hat.

"Thank you," Grace responded as she stood. "Are you ready?" she asked Euan.

"Aye, ready."

"Then let us away into the den once more."

Euan smiled and offered his arm, which she happily took. They went down the stairs and out of the front doors to where a carriage waited. It was not far to the palace, but it wouldn't do for a lady in a dress like Grace's to walk through the dirty streets. Euan helped Grace in and then followed behind her.

"Do you think he will be there?" Grace asked, switching her speech to Gaelic so that no one could understand them if they were overheard.

"Lochiel? Likely," Euan replied as the door shut and the carriage pulled away, and he saw Grace stiffen. "He will nae hurt ye now."

"But he wanted to."

"Aye, he wanted to, but I prevented it and would again if he tried. Ye are safe from him now."

"No, I am not," Grace said in almost a whisper.

Euan looked at her, puzzled by her reaction. "Of course ye are."

She blinked and looked at him. "Of course I am what?"

"Safe from Lochiel."

"Oh, yes of course I am. He would not dare go against you now. You told him an incredibly good story."

Euan's puzzlement turned to complete confusion. "But ye just said . . ."

"I did not say anything," she replied, looking at him as though he were mad.

Euan opened his mouth to challenge her but stopped himself when he realized she genuinely believed she hadn't said anything. "Maybe it was someone outside."

Grace shrugged and turned her eyes to the window. "I am glad one of us was able to think on our feet about what to tell him and how to get out of that situation," she said.

"I told the truth," Euan said. "Just nae all of it."

"I am just glad you arrived when you did."

"As am I."

"At least we have a story to stick to, one that makes sense."

Euan gave her hand a gentle squeeze. "What shall we say about yer arm if anyone notices the bulk beneath one glove?"

"Riding accident?"

"That will work," he said. "Ye were thrown and cut yerself on something on the way down."

"The knife I keep for safety when I ride."

"Oh, that is a good one," he said with a chuckle. "Clever of ye."

"Of course, that could change based on whether or not Lochiel has said anything."

"Why would he? I am nae sure the king would look favorably upon a man dragging a woman from his court, driving her out to the woods, and then trying to kill her."

"He could have made some other excuse if he was seen with me."

"We shall worry about that if it happens, but I can almost promise ye he said naught."

The concern in her expression didn't diminish, so he lifted her hand and kissed it, which brought her eyes back to him.

"Grace," he whispered. "I will nae let him, or anyone else, harm ye. Ye are my target this mission and ye know what that gives me leave to do if I feel I must. Trust that I will do it before I ever let them harm ye again."

Grace nodded, and she squeezed his hand in return as the carriage pulled into the forecourt of the palace. When they came to a stop, a footman opened the door and Euan stepped out first before holding out his hand to Grace. She placed her hand in his and stepped down gingerly before she took his arm and walked inside.

Euan forced himself to not show his discomfort at walking into this place once more. He'd been here before, resided here for quite some time, and there was a sense of familiarity that needled him in a way that made him uncomfortable. He wanted to tell her he'd been here before, wished he could explain everything that had happened to him in this place and why he hated it even as he found beauty in it. Perhaps he would when the mission was over. The memories were supremely unpleasant, and he'd spent the years after his return to Scotland trying to forget it but failing miserably. His eyes scanned the faces of those they passed, and he wondered if he'd see anyone he recognized, because that could prove quite problematic.

Despite this, he still found the palace beautiful and it was now filled with people, all of them jockeying for some sort of position in court. He was thankful that it was something he needn't bother with because it likely would've driven him out of his mind. Grace's sudden resistance brought him out of his thoughts and caused him to look back at her before following her gaze to see Lochiel.

"Ah, Euan, there ye are. I was wondering if ye would come today."

"Lochiel," Euan said with the respectful bow he'd neglected the previous day as Grace curtsied.

"And ye have brought yer wife, I see. It is a shame I did nae know ye married her or perhaps I would nae have responded with such surprise when I saw her here."

"Apologies, Lochiel, but we were a wee bit busy with fighting a war. I did nae feel the need to trouble ye with something so small at such a time."

Lochiel laughed. "Aye, that was true, lad. Ye remember most of these men I would wager."

"Aye, indeed, I do. It is good to see ye again, Lord Murray, Mr. MacDonald," Euan replied with another bow.

"I did nae expect to see ye again, Euan Cameron, but it is a blessing that we have," Lord Murray replied. "All of us who gather here can return to take our country back from those bastards."

"Aye," Lochiel replied. "Though Euan says his days as a soldier are done."

"Surely nae," Murray replied. "Ye were as fine an officer as I have seen, Euan. A good mind for strategy and an eye for tactics. Why would ye nae want to serve yer country now?"

"I thank ye for the compliments, my lord, but I feel I have seen enough war to last me a lifetime. I was lucky to escape with my life, and I dinnae know that I would wish to endanger it again for something I am nae certain would work."

"Nae certain would work? Why would it nae?"

Before Euan could reply, the doors behind Lochiel, Murray, and MacDonald opened. "The king will see you now."

The three men nodded and Lochiel turned to Euan. "Come along, Euan. Ye can at least meet the king for all yer trouble."

Euan gave a small nod and followed them inside with Grace still on his arm, the doors shutting behind them. The room was vast, with tables and maps spread out upon it. At least one of those maps Euan recognized as Scotland.

"Good afternoon, gentlemen," the king said as they entered. "Ah! Mademoiselle Cameron as well! How good it is to see you again. I will admit we do not often find a female face here. Who is the lucky young man who has the pleasure of escorting you today?"

Grace curtsied as the men bowed. "Your Majesty. This is

my husband, Captain Euan Cameron," she replied in French.

"Husband! You did not say anything about a husband yesterday."

"It would be rude to correct a king, Your Majesty, and you did not ask."

"Touché, madame, touché. Welcome to my court, Captain Cameron. You are lucky to have married madame already, or you may have found her stolen from you here."

The other men chuckled, as did Euan. Though he'd known the king wouldn't remember him — he had no reason to — Euan was thankful to see his assumption confirmed. "Aye, Yer Majesty, I am lucky indeed to have claimed such a fine bride. I thank ye for yer welcome."

Euan's perfect French brought a raised eyebrow from the king. "Well, well. An educated young man at that. Perhaps, madame, you should worry about losing your husband here. The ladies would be quite fond of a pretty young man with tales he can whisper to them of dangers and hardships as he beds them."

Grace's hand tightened for a moment on Euan's arm, a movement no one else would see. "They are certainly welcome to try, Your Majesty, but they will fail."

"You are quite certain of your hold on him. Young men will be young men, madame."

"Wherever he goes, I know he will return to me in the end."

The king offered a wry smile. "We always do return to the one who holds our heart even if our needs take us elsewhere."

The men laughed again, and Grace smiled, though Euan knew it was forced. He also knew Grace was well aware he'd never do such a thing, so it was easier for her to dismiss it. His needs were fully met by the very same person who held his heart and he would want it no other way.

"It would take quite a woman indeed to pull me into such an affair," Euan replied.

"Ah, we shall see, shall we not? This is not Scotland and there are many more to choose from," the king said with a small laugh. "However, let us give Madame Cameron a reprieve from the topics of men. I promised her an introduction and she shall have it." He looked over at one of the men standing near him. "Take her to Madame."

Chapter 8

As Grace followed the man on the long path to the royal apartments, her thoughts remained with Euan. She hated to leave him there with those men, though she knew this introduction was the link she needed to her target. He would be fine because he knew the game and how to play it, but she knew it must be difficult to be in their presence once more. It certainly would be unlikely to help with the dreams that still sometimes tormented him. When they stopped at a large set of doors the man knocked and, a short time later, a young woman came to answer it.

"The king sends Madame Cameron for an introduction to the Marquise."

The young woman nodded and shut the door, only to return a few moments later to open the door wider to allow Grace to enter.

"Thank you," she said.

"Come with me, Madame," the young woman said before she led Grace through to a sitting room. "Wait here."

Grace looked around her, taking all of it in. These rooms, of course, were no longer open to the public in her own time. The walls were covered in silk damask between panels of shining dark wood, and the same fabric covered the settee and chairs, while the wood of the tables matched the wood on the walls. Fine rugs were spread out upon the floors, and natural light from the windows filled the room. She studied the paintings on the walls, the intricate designs of the candle sconces, and the varying other small details that always made historical rooms fascinating to her.

When the door opened and another woman entered, Grace curtsied to her. She was pretty, though not striking, with a delicate frame. Her clothes were, of course, of the highest fashion. She studied Grace with an almost detached air of curiosity before she spoke.

"Please, rise. I understand your name is Madame Cameron?"

"Yes," Grace replied. "The king thought we might get along, so he sent me to meet you while he tries to lure my husband into war."

The woman laughed and shook her head. "Ah, men. They only ever have two things on their minds: fighting and fucking. I am Jeanne, Marquise de Pompadour, and mistress to the king. Please, sit."

Grace could not help but laugh at the unexpectedly coarse language from a woman so high in status and who looked as refined as Jeanne did. "My name is Grace Cameron," Grace said as she sat down. "And, yes, usually that is correct."

"No title?"

"No, madame. We have only recently arrived from Scotland."

"Scotland! I think you are the first lady from that country I have met, though I have met the men. You have an excellent command of the French language. Was your husband a clan chief in the rebellion?"

"Thankfully not. He was an officer in Lochiel's Cameron regiment."

"Ah, Lochiel, yes. An interesting character."

"You could say that."

"It does not seem you are overly fond of him."

"My husband nearly died under his command and we had to go into exile. I am not entirely sure I have forgiven him for it."

"I am sorry to hear it. Not that you have not forgiven him — I do not think I would either — but that you were driven from your home and nearly lost your husband. It is clear to me already that you care for him a great deal."

"More than that. I love him," Grace replied, almost to herself.

"Love? What a fortunate thing for you. Not many women can say the same."

"No, they cannot. I am quite fortunate indeed." Grace said, smiling as she came back to the present.

"The chiefs are pushing for another campaign in Scotland, I understand."

"Yes, they are. They seem to believe the outcome would be different if they only had more men."

"But you do not think so."

"No. I think it is a foolish dream now. There is no one left in Scotland to rally. Those clans loyal to the Stuarts have been devastated. Even now many remain imprisoned for their part in it, awaiting transportation or death."

Jeanne looked at her curiously. "You say they are trying to bring your husband into the new plan. Why would they need him?"

"He was an officer, a captain. He knew the men, the problems, the mistakes. He is a young man where the chiefs are not. His perspective and his assistance would be invaluable. Perhaps they believe he could rally the young back to the Stuart banner."

"Do you think he could?"

"If he desired it, yes, but he does not. As he has told them, he wants only a quiet life now. His days of war are behind him."

"It does not mean they will not try, however. I am not sure the days of war are truly behind any man once they have fought, no matter what they want to believe." Jeanne sighed in something akin to irritation. "The king is, for whatever reason, considering their proposal most seriously."

"You do not seem to be in favor of it. You have his ear, could you not simply direct him otherwise?"

She laughed. "You make it seem as though I am not trying."

"I did not mean to imply such a thing."

"I did not think you did. I counsel him against it, and they come to him to argue for it as soon as I am gone. I tend to agree with you; twice is enough and the Stuarts are better left to themselves. They do not have the support they would need even in their own country."

"How may I be of assistance in this? We have the same goal of preventing the men we love from yet another needless war. Mine to yet another war for the Stuarts and yours to opening another front when he is still at war with Austria."

Jeanne looked at Grace, her interest piqued. "You seem well versed in such matters, Madame Cameron."

"A natural state when one's husband is a soldier, is it not? War seems to be a frequent topic of conversation."

Her lips spread into a smile and she nodded to Grace. "Too true, madame, though with a king it is not always war."

"I must needs take your word for it, for I have never had the pleasure of much conversation with a king." A complete falsehood, but it rolled off Grace's tongue with practiced ease.

"I believe you would handle yourself quite well. Clearly you said something to the king that pleased him enough to send you here."

"He made a quip about Scottish women coming here for the men to take care of, and I told him I would see to his request forthwith and even throw a few English into the bargain."

Jeanne laughed. "I am sure they would love it if you managed it. An excellent parry and it is clear why he sent you."

"I am glad for it, for I find I have no company here in France."

"I would be happy for you to join mine if it pleases you. I know what it is to be lonely, madame."

"Even when you should not be. Even when you are surrounded by hundreds of people."

"Precisely, for the false love and friendship of hundreds cannot make up for the true love and friendship of one. Tell me of Scotland."

Grace smiled and closed her eyes, picturing it in her mind.

"Scotland. There are mountains and glens, rivers and lochs. All of it so vividly green. There are times when you can watch the fog roll down from the mountains like some great, celestial blanket to cover the glens and nothing seems to move. It is beautiful there, a place where I always found the greatest peace, but that peace is gone now."

A flash of a face behind her closed eyes startled her. The sight of Euan dead upon Culloden moor. His eyes opened and he smiled at her, but the smile became malevolent and he jumped at her. Grace cried out and jumped up from the chair she'd been sitting in before a sharp pain in her chest sent her to her knees.

"Madame!"

The feeling was so familiar, so strong, that she swore if she looked down, she would see the point of the bayonet again. Her entire body ached, suddenly feeling wounds that were no longer there. Grace clutched her chest and tried to breathe, knowing full well it was an anxiety attack and nothing more, but the knowledge didn't make it easier.

"I shall have your husband fetched here!" Jeanne said as she stood and made for the door to call someone.

"No," Grace managed to pant out, holding up her hand. "Thank you. I will be all right after a moment. I still remember it."

"Remember what?"

"The final battle."

Jeanne looked at her in amazement. "You were there!"

Grace nodded and pulled herself back up, returning to her seat even though her entire body was shaking.

"If it does not trouble you too much, would you tell me about it?" Jeanne asked as she came back to her seat.

Grace took a moment, trying to catch her breath. To speak of it would be difficult, but it would also give her a valuable insight into just how awful another war could be. "It was the final battle on Drumossie moor near Culloden House. I had only just married my husband the night before he left to march north. I had a dream of how terribly it would all turn out and I went to seek him. I wanted to stop him."

"Of course, for you would not want to become a widow so soon."

"Yes. I found him, begged him not to go." Grace's hands tightened around her skirts involuntarily. "He went anyway, for he had a duty to his men. I ran after him."

"You ran after him into battle! You are mad or brave or both!"

"He would say both," Grace replied, her smile weak, before going on. "It was difficult to see. There was so much smoke from the guns and cannons. I could hear the balls, the cannon shrapnel, colliding with the bodies around me as they screamed in excruciating pain and dropped to the ground. I found him just as . . ." Grace trailed off, remembering that moment with perfect clarity. She couldn't tell the truth. "Just as a ball hit him. I saw him fall and then I felt such terrible pain because I was hit, too."

"Mon Dieu," Jeanne said with a horrified gasp.

"He saw me, and we managed to get away together. We hid as best we could and took care of each other until we got well. We were lucky. So many were not."

"I am surprised he left the field with his men still there."

"He had no choice when he realized I was there and hurt. I think he also realized it was a lost cause and he would die there, just as I had told him, and he could not and would not let me die there beside him." Grace looked up at Jeanne with tears in her eyes. "War is horrible, Madame. Blood and fear; screams of pain and terror. You can smell the blood, there is so much of it. They die in agony, crying out for help from their mothers or their wives. Half of our men never left that place. The other half were hunted down afterward by the government forces."

A tear slid down Jeanne's cheek as she listened to Grace describe something she had only ever read about. "They know all of this and yet they still wage war."

"They are not always the ones to fight it, so they don't understand what it is really like. The chiefs here do, for they charged in alongside their men, but kings certainly do not. They don't understand the things they are asking others to do and experience. Kings sleep at night in the comfort of their warm beds, eating fine food, even as they demand other men sleep upon the ground and eat only enough oats or biscuits to make sure they do not collapse. A king will die old in his bed, not upon the ground pleading for mercy as the blood drains from his body and he cries out for his mother to save him, so he does not die alone."

"No, they do not, and perhaps that is why it is easy for them to see the men as nothing more than pawns to be moved, as they do the little figures I see on the maps. I am sorry, truly sorry, for what you have suffered. I cannot imagine having experienced such a thing."

"Before I did it, neither could I."

Jeanne chuckled and dabbed the moisture away with a handkerchief. "Even in such a somber moment you can find a way to amuse."

"I think finding humor in it is the only way to truly move past it."

"Such a thing is true far more than it ever should be, and I feel women know that far better than anyone else. Tragedies and injustices are often heaped upon us with no care for what such things might do to our hearts and minds."

"As though we are not people as they are, but dolls."

"I see you have also lived a life with such experiences. It is my hope that one day women will not suffer in such ways. I will press the king to abandon these plans, you have my word, madame. Though, you may need to speak to him yourself. If you can speak to him as you just did to me, it may turn his head enough to wrest his ear from the others."

"I will do whatever I must."

"In the meantime, you simply must spend time with us

here. I am sure they will keep your husband quite busy and that will leave you all alone."

The door to the sitting room opened and the young woman from earlier stepped inside. "Madame, the husband of Madame Cameron has come to fetch her."

"That was quick," Jeanne said in mild surprise. "Send him in. I would like to see this mythical man for myself, the one who would inspire a woman to run into battle after him."

The young woman nodded, then returned with Euan, and Grace realized she'd hardly looked at him today, *truly* looked at him. He looked extraordinary in the outfit he wore, made of sapphire blue silk with silver embroidery, his dark hair tied back with a matching silk ribbon. It made the blue of his eyes seem even more intense, and the suit was tailored to him perfectly, the close fit showing off the broadness of his shoulders and chest, as well as his trim torso. He seemed to fill the room, fashionable as it was with its delicate furniture, and tower over the women in it. You couldn't miss his presence. Jeanne stared at him, eyes wide and mouth slightly agape. She had never seen anyone who quite looked like him, that much was clear.

"Mon Dieu," she whispered.

Euan smiled and bowed to her. "Marquise. A pleasure to meet ye at last."

"The pleasure is *absolutely* all mine, Monsieur Cameron. Your lovely wife has been telling me all about your homeland and the horrors of war."

Euan crossed the room to take Grace's hand and kiss it. "Of anyone, she would know."

"I can certainly see why you charged into battle after him, madame," Jeanne said, her smile becoming sly.

Euan raised an eyebrow and looked at Grace. "I would prefer it was nae a feat she repeated or had needed to perform in the first place."

"I am sure you do not. Did they get you to agree to join them, monsieur?"

Euan laughed. "No, and they will nae, though nae for lack of trying. I have had enough of war."

"Well then, it seems that leaves only one thing left on your mind."

Grace laughed before she could stop herself and Jeanne grinned, though Euan looked confused.

"I have many things on my mind, madame, and most of them are nae pleasant at the moment, unfortunately."

Jeanne gave him a quizzical look. "Do sit down, monsieur, and take a moment to regain at least some bit of pleasantry. I know those buzzards can be tiresome, I have been listening to them squawk for months. At least you speak lovely French."

Euan sat down in a chair beside Grace and chuckled. "That is a good way to describe them at the moment, aye."

"You have a great interest in stopping them for someone who will not fight."

"I have an interest because it is my countrymen who will fight, die, and suffer even further for the treason against the Hanover king led by the men now here begging your king for another chance."

"And they have done enough of that already."

"Aye, they have."

"It is a miracle you survived it."

"More than ye realize, madame. It is a miracle any of us did."

"Truly?"

Euan nodded but said nothing, and Grace could tell he was trying to suppress the memories he wanted to remain buried. "If it was nae for my wife I would be dead now. What she did was beyond anything anyone could have asked of her, especially me."

"Yes, she was telling me all about the battle and how you were both injured."

Euan looked at Grace, knowing full well how difficult it was for her to speak of it. "I will nae put myself in such danger a second time, nor ever again put her in such a position as she found herself that day."

"When you married her the night before you departed, did you believe you would return?"

"No," Euan answered with blunt honesty. "I did nae."

There was a small intake of breath from Grace, one only he would hear, and he gave her hand a gentle squeeze.

"But, if I was nae to return, I knew she would be provided for as my wife if we were victorious. If nae, I would be there to meet her when the English surely sent her on to me."

"You do not mean to say they would have executed her, do you?"

"Oh, aye, they would have. Her, my mother, and anyone else tied to me. I was an officer, madame, I would have been given no quarter and neither would they had our positions been reversed."

"Barbarians! Women and children should always be off limits!"

"Usually they are, and Highland Code would call for it, but the English government forces would nae have abided by it. Remember, their goal is to crush a rebellion, and there is no better way to make sure a people dinnae rise again than to meet their survivors with as much brutality as ye can offer. They have done so, and if the chiefs are so foolish as to try again it will be even worse. Though I am nae sure there is much more they could take from us. We have naught left."

Jeanne shook her head gently. "I have told Madame Cameron that I would do all I could to stop the king from agreeing to such a plan. The Stuart prince is a broken man, and quite honestly, so indecisive now as to be unfit to run a country."

"I cannae say I dinnae agree with ye."

"I would much rather they put you in charge, monsieur. You seem a fair man, just and brave as well as calm and rational. Just the type of man needed to put the country back together again. If the king does go through with this, perhaps he should venture to put you upon the throne instead of the Stuart prince."

Euan smiled. "I thank ye for such a gracious compliment, but I have no interest in such a thing, nor the patience for the politics that go with it."

"I think you do not give yourself enough credit."

"And I think ye need to spend more time in my company before ye are so sure of it," Euan replied with a wry smile that made Jeanne laugh.

"Do you think I should worry about him, madame?" Grace asked.

"In what way?"

"The king told me I might lose my husband to the temptations of the French court. I wonder if I should truly worry."

Jeanne clicked her tongue in amusement. "They can certainly try, and they will, but they would have better luck at getting into bed with the Holy Roman Emperor than they would with your husband. That much is clear."

Grace laughed and so did Euan. The mental image was quite a comical one.

"Aye, they would. I have no need of any other. My wife keeps me perfectly happy in all ways and there is naught they could offer me that would tempt me from her."

"As I said, it is perfectly clear to me and should be to them if they are not simple. It does not mean they will not try for the sport of it."

"They are welcome to their attempts," Euan said.

"I am so glad you came to join us, monsieur, and I am very pleased the king so graciously made an introduction to me of your wife. I will be most happy to entertain the both of you. There is to be a ball soon and the both of you must come as my guests. I insist upon it."

"Then how can we say no?" Euan replied. "And I am glad to see that my darling Grace has found a friend here at last."

Jeanne smiled and stood, which alerted Grace and Euan

to do the same. "I will warn the both of you of one thing: be careful in your attempts to stop this madness. The chiefs seem to be pursuing this with a fervor beyond anything I have seen before, and they will not take kindly to interference, countrymen or no."

"Thank ye for the warning, madame," Euan said, bowing to her as Grace curtsied. Jeanne nodded, and then swept from the room.

Chapter 9

After leaving the Marquise's apartments, they decided to take a walk in the expansive gardens the palace offered. There was a need to be outdoors, a need to find respite from the court and its glittering, manipulative denizens, and just be in each other's company. It would also allow them to compare notes on their separate conversations. Euan walked slowly along one of the paths, Grace's arm in his.

"She is an interesting character," Euan said when they were well away from the palace, switching to Gaelic now, but careful even here in case any of the chiefs or their men were about.

"Yes, but I like her. She speaks plainly and I can see why the king favors her. She must be a relief from all of those around him who tell him what they think he wants to hear."

"I can imagine she would be. I cannae comprehend trying to navigate that and think for myself. I am glad I have no need to."

Grace rested her head against Euan's arm near the shoulder as they walked. "I do not think I have told you how handsome you look today."

"Ye have nae, but I appreciate the compliment whenever it comes. Ye look beautiful in these dresses, but then ye always do."

"I am sure there are fashions that do not favor me."

"I have yet to have seen any and we have been many, many places."

Grace smiled. "I am glad you are here because it makes this so much easier. I never realized how lonely it could be until now."

"I think ye knew just how lonely it was but ye dinnae wish to remember."

"Do I? Perhaps not. I cannot seem to think of it now. I really cannot remember a time when you were not with me."

"That is strange. Ye had just over two years of work on yer own before ye even met me."

"It does not matter. You are here now and that is what counts."

Euan stroked her hand on his arm. "Are ye feeling any better?"

"Some, though I am still so tired. I feel as though all I want to do is sleep, but there is no time for that."

"Ye must remember that ye need sleep here. Ye cannae do as ye normally would."

"Please do not remind me," Grace said, her tone dejected.

"Someone must and, of anyone, I know how ye can be when ye are working."

Grace nudged him with an elbow, and he smiled. "Not as though you are not the very same. How did it go with the king?"

Euan sighed. "I mostly listened. I want to know what their plans are, what they are thinking, what the resources on offer may be. It is the best way for me to tailor my approach to the problem."

"Is it already so organized as that?"

"Aye. At least to the point that they have an idea of how many men they might need and what forces there may be to assist."

"I am surprised the king is even willing to discuss it while he is still at war with Austria."

"He was at war with them when he helped before. There is no reason he would let that stop him this time."

"You and I both know there are not enough forces left in Scotland to muster."

"They seem to believe there are, no matter what I say."

"Such denial would lead to another loss."

"Aye, it would. All I can do is try to make the king see what a waste of his resources such a course of action would be."

"Perhaps personal experience is best. Tell him what you saw, what you felt and experienced."

"That will be my last resort. I dinnae like to speak of it, ye know that. I am surprised the marquise was able to convince *ye* to do so."

"Whether I truly wished to or not is irrelevant. She is my target, and my job is to get her to successfully intercede. If that means I must speak of things which I would rather not, then that is what I must do. Sometimes the best route is to appeal to emotion." Grace didn't feel the need to mention the part where she'd experienced a panic attack, as she knew it would only worry him. There had been something else too, something that had spurred it, but she couldn't recall what that was now.

"I cannae say I disagree with ye, though I am nae sure emotion would win with the men. They are singularly focused on this and I dinnae know why yet," he replied. "These are beautiful gardens. I could spend hours here just walking in them with ye, enjoying the flowers and the mild weather. Perhaps one of these afternoons we can sit beneath one of these trees and just eat, talk, and enjoy each other's company. We are rather at our leisure here."

Grace didn't miss the intentional switch of topic. Though Euan had been helped by his visit to the Cognitive Specialist from The Council, it was still something he had no desire to speak of if he could help it. They weren't pleasant memories for him, and still had the power to stir up emotions he wanted no part of. "That sounds like a lovely idea."

"Tell me, what did the marquise mean when she said I had only one thing left on my mind?"

Grace couldn't help but laugh; she'd known he'd ask eventually. "She had earlier said that men had only two things on their minds: fighting and fucking. Given that you no longer had a desire for war, that left only the other."

Euan's eyes widened. "She said that?"

"Exactly that."

Euan's lips twisted into a wry smile. "Well, she is nae wrong, I will give her that."

"Euan!"

"Ach, ye know it to be true enough. Dinnae act as though ye are somehow scandalized by the suggestion."

"You have far more than those things on your mind."

"Though that is true most times, it is nae always so, and sometimes one leads to the other. I will admit to rather enjoying it when it does."

Grace stopped walking as she began to laugh, turning to bury her face in his shoulder, which only drew him into the same sort of laughter.

"You have experience with this?" Grace asked, through her amusement.

"A little. Ye dinnae?"

"No!"

"That is a shame. Perhaps I need to pick a fight with ye so ye can learn," he said, grinning.

"It will have to be another time when we are home and away from all of this. I am not sure I could handle a fight with you right now, in play or no," Grace replied, her voice becoming distant and troubled.

Euan's laughter ceased and he frowned. "Love, it would nae be that way. I would never say anything to hurt ye," he said as he stroked her cheek. "Why would ye think so?"

"I do not know. I do not know anything anymore."

"What?"

"I cannot think clearly. I try to remember things, but I cannot. The only thing I can remember is you."

"Naught? That cannae be. Ye are only tired. Watch, I will prove it to ye. What is yer mam's name?"

Grace searched to find an answer that should easily come to her. Her mother. Did she have a mother? She couldn't conjure any memories of her. What did she look like? "I cannot remember. Do I have a mother?"

"What do ye mean, do ye have a mother? Of course ye do."

"I cannot remember her just now, or what she looks like or sounds like. I cannot remember her face. Does she look like me?"

Euan looked at her with grave concern. "What about yer friend. The first one I met. What is her name?"

"What friend?"

"Vanessa. What about Vanessa?"

Grace shook her head. "I do not remember anyone with that name. Are you sure I have a friend named Vanessa? Euan, are you trying to trick me into correcting you? I do not really have friends, just you."

"Grace, tell me about yer grandmother. The one who was a Watcher like ye," Euan said, his voice pained as he seemed to have to force the words from his lips.

"A Watcher like me," Grace repeated in a soft voice as she looked down, desperately digging for something, anything, to answer his question and finding nothing but empty blackness. She should know this if her grandmother was a Watcher. Had she been? She looked up at him, frightened, and shook her head. "Euan, I cannot. I cannot remember!"

Grace watched as something like fear came over Euan's countenance. "Tell me what ye do remember. What is the first thing ye remember?"

"You. Your smile when you helped me walk after Duncan shot me."

Euan stared at her in stunned silence for a moment. "Nae yer training, yer first meeting with The Council? What about yer stepfather?"

Grace shook her head. "Nothing . . . there is nothing! Euan, there is nothing!" The note of terror in her voice was unmistakable. She had a life before him, of course she had, it was impossible not to have. Why could she not remember any of it?

"Shhh . . . it will be all right. Perhaps it is just another effect of whatever has happened here. It will come back when we set it right again."

Grace buried her face in her hands and Euan pulled her close. It felt like something so much worse than that, but she couldn't explain it. "What if we cannot?"

"We will," he said with firm conviction. "Grace ye must trust in The Council and in me. We will find out what is happening, and we will fix it."

"What if I forget—"

Euan stopped her from saying any more with a gentle finger against her lips. "Dinnae say it. Dinnae say that, for I will never let that happen." Grace nodded and Euan kissed her. "Please, I need ye to believe me."

"I do. I have to."

The rest of the day was spent at court and they'd dined there in the evening at the marquise's invitation, and the decadence was astonishing. It was one thing to read about it and another thing entirely to experience it for yourself. Euan did his best to avoid getting dragged into yet more conversation about war, Scottish or otherwise, and instead turned himself to entertaining not only his wife but the marquise and other ladies with stories and bawdy songs.

Grace was so exhausted by the time they returned to their lodgings that the maid hardly had her undressed before she'd fallen into bed. It felt as though she'd barely closed her eyes before she was dragged roughly from the bed. In confusion, she cried out in shock.

"Get up," Euan hissed.

"What? What is going on?" Head aching, she found it exceedingly difficult to focus and even harder to stand without swaying.

"Ye are leaving."

"But the mission . . ."

"I dinnae need ye to complete it. Ye are only in the way here, as useless as ye are."

"Useless?"

"Ye have no ability here. Ye can do naught, help naught. If ye are nae here as a Watcher ye are useless."

Grace gasped. "Why would you say that? There are plenty of things I can do just as myself! We discussed this and you agreed!"

"Because it is true, and it is time I was honest with ye."

"Honest. Euan, what in the hell is this about?"

"Shut yer mouth!" he shouted at her as he yanked her around in front of him by the arm he still held. "All ye can do is talk at me; tell me what to think and do and believe. I am done with it! I can do it without ye."

Grace flinched as he shouted at her. It made her head hurt more and brought her to tears. "Please, stop! You are hurting me," she whispered.

"Good, it is about time someone did. Stop yer crying, ye stupid woman! I told ye that ye were worthless did I nae? Ye are weak, ye are naught to me or anyone else," he seethed as he squeezed her arm so hard that she yelped in pain.

"Euan, please!" He'd never spoken to her this way, not even when he was angry.

"Shut yer mouth!" This time is was a bellow and it brought a sob from Grace. "I regret coming here and I regret tying myself to ye. I dinnae love ye, Grace. I never have."

"No!" She shook her head and tried to pull back from him, but he squeezed tighter and dragged her closer to him.

"Oh, aye. Ye played yer part and saved my life but ye have served yer purpose. I can exist without ye now and I shall. Ye can continue on yer own and continue to fail — just as ye did with me."

The sting of his accusation was acute. "You promised not to—"

"To leave?" Euan asked, cutting her off before laughing, a sound as cold and as dark as he was in this moment. "I would tell ye whatever I needed to in order to get into yer bed." He yanked her against him and pressed his cheek to hers so he could whisper in her ear. "And oh, it was sweet. Sweet how much ye loved me, how much ye wanted me to love ye. Sweet to achieve such a victory over one who had made it her mission to never love anyone."

Grace began to cry harder. Every word he spoke cut deeply. He'd never loved her. "Stop it! Please!"

Euan shoved her away from him, causing her to stumble backward. Before she could look at him, he struck her and sent her spinning onto the bed. In the next moment she felt his weight against her back, pressing her into the bed, her scream smothered in the blankets.

"Perhaps yer stepfather was right. Ye are too stupid to understand anything but this."

The strike only made it harder to think, to focus. Everything hurt. What had happened? This was not the Euan she knew. He would never do this to her. This was wrong, all of it was wrong.

"Do ye like pain, Grace?"

"No," she sobbed out against the mattress.

"Oh, I think ye do," he said as he grabbed her hair and pulled her up, bringing a shriek of pain from her. "And I think I like to cause it."

He shoved her face first against a wall, still holding her hair, pinning her with his body. With his free hand, he grabbed her injured arm and dug his fingers into the wound. Grace screamed in agony as she felt his fingers sink into the cut skin, the threads snapping and allowing the gash to reopen as she fought to get away from him. The action only made him laugh harder before he threw her onto the floor, where she curled up in a crying heap.

"Why are you doing this?"

Euan squatted down and grasped her chin in his hand, forcing her to look at him. "Because I hate ye and I am tired of trying to hide it. I am joining the chiefs and going back to Scotland. Ye can do whatever pleases ye, but ye will nae come with me."

"If you die then—"

"So will ye, aye. Do ye think that troubles me? Stop fooling yerself, Grace."

"Euan—"

"Dinnae speak to me. Ye have naught to say that I want to hear," he snarled as he shoved her face away.

Grace sobbed as he stood and started to walk toward the door. "Please do not do this. I am your wife!"

He stopped and turned back to her. "I no longer have a wife," he replied coldly as she stared in horror, walking out and slamming the door behind him.

Grace woke with a start, sitting up in bed. It brought with it the familiar nausea and she gripped her head in her hands at the ache that still resided there but felt amplified now. Again, there was something there, something just out of her reach. Something she should remember but couldn't. All she knew was that there was a pain in her heart so strong that it physically hurt. She quickly found herself overwhelmed in tears she couldn't explain.

"Love? Why do ye cry?" Euan asked in a gentle voice as he sat down on the bed beside her.

"I am not sure," she answered.

"Do ye feel unwell again?"

Grace nodded. "My head hurts so much," she whispered. "How long have I been sleeping?"

"Hours now," he replied as he reached out and brushed some of her hair from her face.

Hours. It hadn't felt that long. "I think something is very wrong."

"Aye, but we already knew that."

"No, something more than that but I do not know what."

"Ye dinnae think it is all down to the lost connection to The Council?"

"It could be." Grace said in a heavy sigh. "I do not know anything anymore. I feel so unsure that I cannot even trust myself."

"I am worried for ye, lass. This is nae like ye. It is the opposite of everything ye are. I dinnae think I have ever seen ye so off balance, nae even when ye came for me."

"I am worried for me too," she admitted.

Euan reached out to draw Grace into his arms and kissed the top of her head. "I love ye, and I promise we will find out what is happening to ye. We will get ye out of here and back home where ye can be yerself again."

"What if I no longer know what that is? I cannot remember so much; what if it never comes back? What if I forget who I am? What if I already have?"

"Ye must have faith in yerself and in The Council, as I said to ye this afternoon. Ye know they are working hard on this and trying to figure out how to help ye," he replied as he stroked her hair. "I will nae let ye go without a fight."

Grace cried against his shoulder. The pain, the illness, the exhaustion — all were taking their toll on her. She wanted it to be over.

***

Euan continued to stroke her hair until she fell asleep again, because there was nothing else he *could* do. He was at a loss, but he knew they had to finish this mission as quickly as they could. How much longer could she last this way? Once he was sure she was asleep, he left the room in order to brief The Council. He sat down in a chair near the fire in the sitting room and let himself relax. It felt as though he'd hardly been there a moment before The Council was with him.

"Hello, Euan," said the familiar voice of the Councilwoman.

"Good evening to ye."

"How's it all going?"

"Nae well. Grace is struggling terribly. She is tired all of the time, has a constant ache in her head, but there is something worse than that."

"Worse?"

"She has forgotten everything in her life that came before me. She

cannae remember the name of her mother, her grandmother, her friend. She does nae remember her first meeting with ye, her training, none of it. It is all gone."

"What? How can that be?"

"Yer guess is as good as mine, but I know she is terrified. She does nae trust herself now. I have never seen her this way and I dinnae know how much longer we can put her through this."

"Are you asking to abort your mission?"

"Nae yet, but if this gets worse ye may need to send a Guardian to bring her home and another Watcher to take her place. I will nae put her in any more risk than I have to."

"The fear would be that bringing her back would not only not help but make things worse. We have no idea what's happened to her, and without that understanding there's always the possibility that any transport of her in this state could do her more harm."

"That is something we can address if the time comes. Have ye found anything out?"

"Not yet, but we have not given up."

"Grace made contact with the marquise and has befriended her. The marquise has said she will do all she can to stop the king. I made contact with the king in the company of the chiefs. The plan is much farther along than I expected."

"That must be why it was flagged."

"Aye. I will do my best to continue my work from inside that circle."

"Of course you will. Please let us know if you discover anything else or if she gets worse."

"*I will,*" Euan replied as he opened his eyes again. They had no answers, nothing to help them.

He rubbed his face with his hands and stood up. He hated that he was so ineffectual in helping her in this, and he hated to see her this way. He wanted to protect her, but from what? She was right to be afraid of what was happening to her. It frightened him to watch his normally confident wife become a shell of herself, someone who second guessed every move, every word. Whatever this was, he wouldn't allow it to take her from him. He'd promised her he wouldn't let her go without a fight and he wouldn't, even though he was entirely unsure of what he was fighting against.

Euan returned to the room and undressed, climbing into bed beside Grace. He may not need to sleep, but he could be there with her all the same, holding her and letting her know that he was with her even as he prayed that he could somehow deliver her from this.

Chapter 10

Grace opened her eyes to a darkened room but closed them again as another wave of nausea swept over her. After taking a few deep breaths, the sensation passed, or at least as much as it was going to. It was her constant companion since she'd come here, and she was hoping they'd soon figure out what was causing this so it could end. She hated being queasy. She sat up and stretched, trying to ignore the pounding in her skull that seemed to be the twin of the nausea.

"Euan?" she called out. He wasn't beside her, but that didn't surprise her. He didn't have to sleep, and it didn't mean he needed to be right by her side while she did.

There was no answer and she pushed back the blankets, turning and swinging her legs over the side of the bed. When she stood, she placed her hands on the mattress to steady herself and, when she felt as though she could do so, walked farther into the room. "Euan?"

"Euan is nae here."

Grace jumped at the voice, both unfamiliar and not. No one else should be here. "Who is that?"

The sound of a match being struck, the sizzle as the sulfur caught after being pulled through the phosphorus paper, reached her ears before the tiny flame was lowered to the lamp on the table. It rose to life and illuminated a man sitting at the same table; a man she recognized.

"Oh, I think ye know quite well who I am judging by the look on yer face."

"Duncan," she whispered. "How did you get here? You are—"

"Dead? No, I was one of the lucky ones and I came with Lochiel. When I heard Euan had come back, well, I had to see for myself. Then I find out he married some strange woman and no longer wanted to fight. That had to be a lie and, as it turns out, it was."

"A lie? What do you mean?"

Duncan laughed. "Ah, lass, ye did nae really think he loved ye did ye? A man like Euan does nae tie himself to one person and be happy. No, he saw ye as an opportunity and he took it."

"An opportunity," Grace repeated before she shook her head. "Get out."

"Or what? Ye will make me? I doubt that, and if ye think Euan will be along to save ye then ye are quite mistaken."

"I do not need him to save me. I can save myself."

"Can ye? That is nae what I heard. Ye are unwell, ye cannae even think much less defend yerself."

"Get. Out."

"No. We are nae finished speaking."

"Yes, we are."

"No, we are nae!" Duncan shouted as he stood up and slammed his large hand down on the table. "We are done when I say we are!"

Grace flinched even though she tried not to, the shout ringing in her ears and making her head throb.

"Aye, that is what I thought. Ye cannae handle loud noises, can ye? I will be sure to keep that in mind."

Grace knew that he didn't mean to do so in any way that would benefit her. "What do you want," she asked, her tone flat.

"It is nae about what I want lass. I was sent on a task by my captain, so here I am."

"Your captain?"

"Aye. Euan has resumed his position with Lochiel and is there even now."

Grace's eyes widened for a moment. "No, he is not, he would not."

"But he did. As I said, he does nae love ye. Ye were a means to an end."

"What end was that?"

"Survival. Now that he has done so and has rejoined his clan, he has no need of ye or pretending he gives a shite about ye."

Grace's heart ached, as though there were some truth in what he said, as though Euan had said so himself, but she'd forgotten. She squeezed her eyes shut for a moment before she opened them again and glared daggers at Duncan. "You are a liar!" Grace shouted before she moved to cross the room to the door.

Duncan moved quickly and shoved her backwards, sending Grace stumbling, though she remained upright and looked at him in shock.

"Where do ye think ye are going?"

"To find him!"

"Oh, no, I dinnae think so. He wants naught to do with ye. No, it all ends here."

"Like hell it does."

In that moment, several other men stepped out of the darkness behind Duncan, all of them staring at her. Grace gasped and took a step back. This was bad. Very bad. Even if she were healthy, she couldn't get past that many and without a mission body she wasn't about to try.

"It does, and we are here to make sure of it."

"None of you belong here and I want you to leave. If he has something to say to me, he needs to come say it himself."

"Ye are speaking strongly for a woman who cannae do anything about our presence here. Now, let me tell ye what I am sent here to say."

"No."

"Yer marriage is a lie," Duncan said, ignoring her. "As I said, he was with ye to survive, that purpose has been served, and now he has left ye. He has countrymen and clansmen to avenge and he does nae need ye in the way."

"In the way!"

"Aye! Just as ye were at Drumossie when ye cried and pleaded and pulled at him."

"And saved his life doing so!"

"More like he saw sense as the tides were turning and saw ye as his way out."

Grace shook her head. "No, you are lying, and you need to go. This is all Lochiel, I know it is! Euan loves me! Get out!"

Duncan lashed out and slapped Grace hard, though the blow didn't send her to the floor. The pain was sharp, and she looked up at him in anger, though the sting brought tears to her eyes. "Would a man that loved ye give me leave to do that?"

"No, and when he finds out—"

"He knows! He told me to do it! Get it through yer head!"

"And you need to get it through yours that I know you are lying!"

Duncan struck her again, this time on the other side, and Grace's vision swam. She hadn't been able to react fast enough, not with the way she was and not with the haze from the first slap. This time, she landed hard on the floor, but pushed herself onto her hands and knees, trying to recover her thoughts. Before she could, Duncan was beside her, and he grabbed her hair at the base of her neck, yanking her face up to look into his.

"Do ye want to know what he was doing before I came here? He was doing the king's mistress," Duncan said with a laugh. "And when I left it sounded as though she was quite enjoying herself. To think, that used to be ye."

Grace angrily tried to shove him away from her, but he shook her by the hair he still held, and Grace yelped in pain.

"Now, now, play nice."

"Get off of me!"

Duncan dragged her up from the floor and turned her to

face the other men, who were all smiling in the same dark way Duncan was. "Now lads, am I telling the truth?"

"Aye," one said. "He certainly was doing that, but he had been with a few of her ladies already."

"He told me he often does it when he is away from ye at any point. As many as he can get before he goes back to ye because ye bore him. Ye cannae give him what he needs, is what he said," said another.

"No one can," said a third. "Nae a lad like Euan," he finished as he laughed.

"Shut your mouths you lying filth!" Grace shouted and they all laughed.

"Ye lying filth," the third man said in a high, mocking voice that made them laugh again.

"Ye see?" Duncan said, turning Grace back to face him. "He does nae want ye. Us, on the other hand," he said, stroking her cheek.

Grace turned her head and bit his hand as hard as she could and he cried out in shock, releasing her. Turning, Grace made a run for the door, only to be grabbed by one of the others and shoved back toward Duncan, who now looked furious. His hand, however, had no wound and Grace couldn't tell if that was real or imagined.

"Ye stupid bitch," he growled as he caught her. "We were trying to do this nicely but, oh no, nae ye. Ye have to make it har." Duncan shoved her backward toward the others and one of them caught her.

"You thought it would be easy?"

Duncan's smile was dark and menacing. "I will admit I like a bit of fight in a lass."

Grace noticed the gleam of silver in the lamplight and struggled to get away from the many hands that now held her. Duncan grabbed her injured arm and ripped the bandaging from it before he lifted the dirk and reopened the cut there, deeper this time. Grace screamed, the pain burning hot and bringing her to tears.

"Ye see? It did nae have to be like this. Ye could have just accepted it."

"No!" Grace sobbed out.

"Ye know, as I left, I heard him say *'mo leannan bòidheach'* to the mistress before the door closed. That did get a moan from her."

Grace's breath caught. My beautiful lover. He said that to her often. Her chest tightened as though someone were squeezing it, and she began to cry harder now. It was true.

"Ah, there it is, the piece of truth that made ye see the light," he said with a smile. "Did he say that to ye before he bedded ye? I promise he was thinking of someone else in order to get the job done."

Grace struggled to get away from them again, but it was weaker now, a combination of tears, exhaustion, and blood loss. When Duncan grabbed her other arm, she tried to pull it away from him, but he cut that one too, the same as the other. Grace's scream of pain echoed off the walls and it seemed to delight Duncan.

"I think we are done here, lads," he said as he stepped back, but then paused. "Oh no, there is one other thing. This?" he said, holding up her left hand, which was now slick with blood from her bleeding arm. "Ye dinnae need this any longer," he sneered as he grabbed her ring and ripped it from her finger, the blood helping it come off more easily but still painfully, and Grace cried out.

"No! You cannot have it!"

"Too late," he said with the same dark smile as he held it up in his fingers. "It belongs to me now and I will show it to him as proof we completed our task. It will make excellent balls for a rifle, perhaps one he will use to rid himself of ye for good. Would nae that be poetic?"

Duncan walked past her and the man holding her shoved her to the floor before they all turned and walked away, their laughter trailing behind him as Grace cried hysterically.

***

Once outside the door, the image of Duncan faded and left another man in his place, the same happening with the other men who'd been with him. A malicious smile crept across his lips as he looked down at her wedding ring in the palm of his hand. Memories of a wedding, of love pledged, all gone.

The young man walked through the darkened halls after dismissing the others, a smile on his face. It was all going according to plan. He, of course, needed to report to Command and let them know where things stood, but it wouldn't be long now. The doors to the chambers that Command occupied opened and he walked inside, bowing to the black-suited men seated there.

"Commander. I have a status update on our current . . . project," he said.

"Proceed, Sergeant Forbes," said the older man sitting at the center of the table.

"All is going to plan. The Cameron Watcher is getting weaker with each contact we make, but today was a significant incursion."

"In what way?"

"We had her almost the entire night and we were able to take the last several months of her memories of him. She still recalls meeting him, saving him, and The Council joining them. We left her at their planning to go away somewhere."

"Very good. It's smart to take your time with this and you're doing well."

"I have something even better. May I approach?"

"Of course."

Forbes walked forward, extending his closed hand before placing it on the table and opening it. "Her wedding ring. We took it from her when we took the memory of their marriage. She would have no need of it now we told her."

The Commander laughed. "Well done, Forbes. How did you take it?"

"We used the images of the men from his own regiment to corner her. I ripped it from her finger before we left her."

"Why his men and not him?"

"I used him the first time, and my feeling was that if I used his image again in such a situation she might resist me the next time I appeared as him even if she didn't realize why."

The Commander nodded. "Excellent work. However, I would now like you to hold off on further action."

Forbes frowned. "But, sir, we are so close—"

"Yes, we are. Leave her alone for a couple of days. Let her start to feel well again, to perhaps feel as though this is over and she has stabilized. Let them both believe it. It may lower his guard and it will make the final push and our victory that much sweeter."

Forbes smiled, an air of malevolence even in something that shouldn't be. "Yes, sir."

Chapter 11

The following morning, Grace was so ill and in so much pain that Euan didn't dare make her get up. There was certainly no question of her not going out today when she could barely move. He made sure all the curtains remained drawn because the light hurt her eyes and intensified her headache, and once again he changed the bandages on her arm. That, at least, seemed to be healing well. He then held her as the nausea finally pushed her past the point of being able to control it. He'd seen her ill, but it had never been like this, not even close. It was as though he were relegated to watching her die little by little, every moment, and he felt helpless.

"Love, I am nae going to court today and will stay with ye. Ye need someone here."

"No," she said in a whisper. "We have a job to do and it cannot be done if you are sitting here babysitting me and watching me sleep. Go."

"It is nae babysitting ye, it is making sure ye dinnae get worse," he protested.

"Euan, one of us has to go and the only one of us who can right now is you. It is not up for debate. Go."

Euan grumbled and got up, his conditioning making it difficult to resist an order from what was essentially his commanding officer. He dressed himself for court, having no interest in dealing with a valet right now when he could take care of it on his own. By the time he'd dressed and returned to say goodbye to her, she was already asleep.

He decided not to take a carriage to the palace, preferring to go on horseback instead. To ride in a carriage alone would only serve to remind him that she wasn't here and was, instead, only getting worse. Euan shook off the thought as best he could, though the thought certainly didn't help his mood. When he arrived at the palace, he asked for a message to be sent to Madame to let her know that Grace was unwell and not at court, but that he'd call upon her later himself if it so pleased her.

"Captain Cameron, the king and the others would like to see you," one of the king's pages said.

"Did they have ye waiting for me to arrive?" Euan asked, only half joking.

"Yes, they did, Captain. Please, follow me."

Something about the fact that he was being waited for didn't sit well with him, but he followed the man all the same, because if the king called, you went. The man led him through to an area away from the general rooms reserved for the courtiers. These were the chambers for the politicians and strategists, and these rooms were where the true running of the kingdom was done. He'd been in them many times, and all of them were while he was plotting the deaths of thousands.

The man opened a door and bowed to Euan. "Captain."

"Merci," Euan replied, walking inside as the door was shut behind him.

On the table before him was a map of Scotland and England, and as Euan approached it, he could see areas marked upon it. Places where they'd won, places where they'd been defeated. He frowned and smoothed his hand over it, trying to distinguish what they were doing here. Also marked were the territories of all the clans, the names of those who had been loyal to the Hanover king circled.

"They will be who we must get rid of first."

Euan turned to see Lochiel watching him, along with some of his men, Murray, and the others. "Get rid of? How do ye mean?"

"They are traitors to their country, lad, to their people. Those chiefs must be eliminated, and the command of their men taken," Lochiel said.

"Ye cannae simply murder the head of a clan and expect his men to follow ye loyally into battle."

"They will nae have a choice. If we kill the chief, they belong to us and must do as we say."

"Ye are speaking madness," Euan said as he looked back at the map. "The chiefs have sons to follow them who would never break ranks with their fathers on this, and the men of these clans would rather die than follow ye into battle against the English. The Grants, the Campbells, the MacLeods, the Munros." He shook his head. "They will nae follow ye, I can promise ye."

"If they would rather die, we can arrange that," Murray said.

"And then? Ye would murder yer own countrymen and make enemies of the rest?"

"If they are smart, they will fall in line so they can be recognized properly by their true king," Lochiel replied. "Especially when they see themselves outnumbered by the French forces, along with the Prussians and the Spanish."

Euan felt his blood run cold. "Ye have secured the support of the Prussians?"

"Aye. Ye are seeing the way of it now, are ye nae lad? This *will* come to pass and there is naught the English can do to stop us this time."

"Ye should join us, Euan," Murray said. "There could be great rewards in it for ye if ye do."

"No," Euan replied.

"Ye are being foolish," Lochiel replied.

"I am keeping to what I told ye. I am done with war. There is naught to be gained from it and anything ye offered me would be tainted with the deaths of more of our own," Euan said, gesturing to the map.

"Do ye nae wish to avenge the death of the men of yer

clan? The ones ye fought beside and lived beside? The ones ye commanded? What of Duncan? What of Iain or Malcolm?"

"Enough," Euan said, the mention of his fallen friends instantly raising his hackles.

One of Lochiel's men looked at him in disgust. "The ones ye abandoned to save yer own skin," he said.

Euan made sure to check his immediate response, which was rage. He wanted to grab the fool and pound his face until it could no longer sneer, this same man who'd once slapped Grace for doing nothing more than speaking to him in a way he didn't like.

"I did nae abandon my men. I marched into battle with them. I watched them die beside me," Euan said through clenched teeth. "I saw them blown to pieces by cannons and cleaned those pieces off my own clothing. I saw them fall when shot and heard them scream in agony as they were run through by bayonets. How *dare* ye accuse me of such a thing."

"Yet ye are here and they are there, dead and buried."

"The same could be said for ye," Euan replied, his voice now deadly calm. "Where were ye while yer clansmen died? I dinnae recall seeing ye on the front lines with us at Drumossie."

"Just because ye did nae see me does nae mean I was nae there."

"Lies," Euan hissed. "I would have known if ye were there. I know what company ye were with and I know who yer captain was. Ye were nae there and ye know ye were nae. Saying ye were may work with those who were nae there, but *I* was. Ye skulked off back home rather than fight, and that is why ye are here now, benefitting off the backs of yer dead kin with a promotion." He then smiled, his expression dark. "Even my wife had more courage than ye. She was out on the battlefield too, charging with the men of her clan. Ye know, the place ye were nae."

Euan heard the gasp from the others and the man stood up quickly. "Are ye calling me a coward?"

"More than calling ye one. I am telling ye that ye are one,

and the only reason ye are angry is because ye know damned well it is true and so does Lochiel, though he has no choice but to employ ye since ye are one of the only ones left. It is about time someone called ye on it, aye?"

"I will kill ye for such a slander!"

"Ye are more than welcome to try," Euan said as he gestured to the door.

"Lochiel, I request yer permission to challenge him for his slight to my honor."

"Granted, as it must be," Lochiel said, though Euan could see the doubt in his features at the sanity of this man for challenging Euan in any way.

Euan smiled and turned to the door, opening it and walking out. "Show us to the gardens, would ye?" he asked one of the men standing there. The young man nodded, and they followed him.

As they reached the gardens, Euan kept walking until he found a wide-open space. As a Watcher's Companion, he had no reason to fear being killed, but even if it were possible, he wouldn't have worried about it anyway. He knew his own skill, knew what he could do, and he'd not let himself get out of practice, though he wished he had his own blade with him. It was, unfortunately, in the future where the rest of the things he'd had on him at Culloden were.

The general demeanor of the men caused people to stop and look at them, but Euan didn't care. He pulled the frock coat off and tossed it aside, not looking or caring where it landed. If Grace were here, she'd be trying to stop him, to check his baser urges, but she wasn't and that meant bad things for his opponent. He turned around to face the men who had been following him.

"Is this location agreeable to ye?"

"Aye."

"Euan," Lochiel said. "Are ye sure ye want to do this?"

"Oh, aye. He was nae the only one slighted."

Lochiel nodded and drew his own broadsword before he handed it to Euan. "Ye will be in need of this then."

Euan nodded. "Thank ye," he said as he took a few practice swings with it to make sure he could move properly. When he was satisfied, he looked at the man across from him. "Shall we?"

The man immediately charged at Euan to try and get him off balance, which Euan sidestepped. It was quickly followed by a strike straight down at Euan's head, and he quickly blocked it, using the basket to shove the blade clear of himself before he turned it and brought it back down toward the man's shoulder. Euan's strike was blocked, but he put force into shoving it toward his opponent, forcing the man to push back before he stumbled away to regroup.

The fight had now drawn a crowd, but Euan didn't notice them; he was watching the man across from him intently. Euan then brought his blade forward in a swipe toward his opponent's side, which almost landed and would've been a ghastly killing blow if it had. He didn't wait for the man to counter, bringing the sword back up to strike diagonally at his neck. The man got his blade up just fast enough, then shoved Euan's blade away with it.

Euan stepped back, both men circling each other and attempting to not only consider the next attack but to catch a breath. It was his opponent who now took the initiative and moved forward, trying to send a slice across Euan's midsection. Euan stepped back even as the man attempted an immediate thrust. As the momentum took him past Euan, Euan turned around to keep his eye on him, and could see that he was already getting tired.

The man spun around, his expression furious. He tried a feint, attempting to hide a thrust in what would look like a bid to take a diagonal hack at Euan. Euan stepped back and grabbed his arm, simultaneously pulling him forward with his non-weapon hand while sticking out the elbow of his other arm and yanking the man's face right into it. There was a gasp from the crowd as Euan's elbow connected with the man's nose and caused him to drop his blade. Euan kicked it away, where it would be difficult for him to recover it without incurring significant exposure to an attack from Euan.

As he recovered his senses, the man pulled a dirk from his belt and charged at Euan despite the blood running down his face. As Euan caught his wrist, he turned into his opponent's body, dragging the man's arm over his shoulder, before using his momentum to swing him up and over, throwing him to the ground. He slammed into the grass with astonishing force, knocking the air from his lungs even as Euan, who still held his wrist, twisted it and yanked the dirk free. Euan immediately placed the tip of the broadsword blade at the man's throat.

With the dirk clutched in his hand, everything in Euan screamed at him to plunge the sword forward and end this man's life for all of his insults and transgressions. For his cowardice, for his cravenness in daring to attach himself to Lochiel as though his skill had saved his life instead of his spinelessness. The urge to kill him for Grace to avenge his crimes against her was almost overpowering. For cutting her arm open with the same knife Euan now held, for his intention to murder her with it, for even laying a hand upon her that first time at the loch.

Just as Euan started to move to do just that, a voice shouted at him. "Hold!"

Euan caught himself and stepped back, looking up to see the king standing there, and he bowed. "Yer Majesty."

"What is the meaning of this, Captain Cameron?" the king demanded, his eyes glittering with anger.

"He called me out, Yer Majesty. Accused me of abandoning my men. I was simply answering his slight."

"Is this true, Lochiel?"

"Aye, Yer Majesty. My man did call out Euan as he says."

"I should put them both in prison for this!"

Euan knew it was best to say nothing. Dueling was illegal

here and he was well aware of it, but he hadn't really cared. He wasn't sure he cared now, either.

"I apologize to ye, Yer Majesty," Lochiel said. "This is the way such disputes are settled in Scotland."

"This is not Scotland!" the king shouted before he regained control of himself. "However, it is my prerogative to excuse such a lapse in judgment this time. If it happens again, they shall both be sent to prison for thirty days," the king said before he looked at Euan. "Well fought, Captain. You can take yourself away from war, but it seems you cannot take the war from within you."

"Yer Majesty, I have no wish to—"

"Enough. Let us return to the chamber where we were meant to meet. Therein we will wait and give Captain Cameron a moment to freshen up. Your man should see the surgeon, Lochiel."

"Aye, Yer Majesty," Lochiel replied.

The king turned and headed back toward the palace, while Lochiel looked at Euan. "I knew ye could nae stay away long, lad. Ye have nae lost a step, have ye?" His laughter had a note of darkness behind it that Euan didn't recall having ever been there before. "It feels good, does it nae? Ye wanted to kill him. Another moment and ye would have. Ye are a soldier through and through, Euan. Killing is what ye are good at."

Euan couldn't respond as Lochiel took his sword back and re-sheathed it. Some of the king's men helped Lochiel's man up to escort him to the palace surgeon, all of them leaving Euan standing there alone. Turning away, he picked up his coat and started walking back to the palace. Lochiel was right. It had felt good, but Euan knew that behind all of it was his anger at what was happening to Grace and his own feelings of helplessness. He knew damned well that he'd goaded the man on purpose to draw him into a fight because that was what *he* needed. What *he* wanted. Killing *was* what he was good at, Lochiel wasn't wrong in saying so. It was what had kept him alive through the entire campaign. It was one of the reasons why he'd been an officer, why they wanted him with them even now. They wanted to use him, harness him to kill his own countrymen, just as they'd done the first time. If he'd survived and fled with these men, if Grace hadn't been there or if she'd not chosen him as her Companion, would he already be in agreement with them on yet another landing? It was a question he couldn't truly answer because those two lives were so vastly different. The one thing he did know was that he wouldn't join them now and nothing he'd felt during these moments would change that.

When he got back inside, he was led to an antechamber where he could clean himself up. Euan took a moment to sit and try to collect his thoughts as well as calm down. His heart was still pounding and his anger still pumping with it. He breathed deeply until he felt sufficiently calm, then stood to unbutton his waistcoat and pull his shirt off. Wetting a towel, he gave himself a quick wipe down before he looked at his shirt. There was blood all over the sleeve, but at least it wasn't his own and there was nothing to be done about it now anyway.

Euan untied his hair, picking up a comb and running it through. After he pulled his shirt back on, he re-combed his hair and tied it once more. The waistcoat went back on and was buttoned, then covered by the frock coat. As he looked at himself in the mirror, his heart ached for his wife, and he wished more than anything that she was here right now. Swallowing hard, he shook it off before he stepped out of the room. The same man from earlier showed Euan back into the chamber where the others were already in discussion, and they looked up when he entered.

"Apologies for delaying our meeting," Euan said with a bow.

"Lochiel and Murray were speaking of their plan to get the clans to their side," the king said.

"I assume they dinnae just mean those who fought for the Stuarts last time."

"Of course nae," Lochiel replied. "I already told ye what we planned to do."

Euan shook his head. "It is a foolish plan and it will nae work. Ye know as well as I do that it does nae work that way, or at least I thought ye did. Do ye think that if someone murdered ye that we Cameron men would have fought for him?"

"I was nae a traitor."

"Ye did nae answer my question. Aye or no."

"No, ye would have avenged me."

"Aye, and what makes you think these men will nae do the same?"

"I will nae be there yet."

"What? Then how do ye plan on doing this?"

"Mercenaries."

Euan stared at him in shock. "Then they could nae blame ye."

"Precisely. The chiefs would be replaced with their heirs, young men looking for guidance. We will come to give it to them, and they and their men will follow us."

"I think ye greatly underestimate the sons of these men, and ye know as well as I do that they would nae go against what their fathers stood for."

"It worked with ye did it nae?"

Euan felt as though he'd been punched in the gut. Deep down he'd known all along that this was true, that Lochiel had used his desire for a father figure to mold him into what he'd wanted Euan to be. To hear it spoken in such a way, however, was another thing entirely.

"Yer Majesty, please excuse me. I promised Madame I would call on her to give my wife's regrets. She is very unwell today and was unable to come to court."

The king nodded, his expression holding something like pity for Euan. "Of course. Please give her my regards and my good wishes to your wife for her recovery."

"Thank ye," Euan replied before he bowed and left the room. "I am to go to Madame, with the king's permission," Euan told the young man waiting outside the door.

As he was led that way, he tried to get his emotions under

control. What he truly wanted was to leave and go back to Grace. Even if she was sleeping, he could still find comfort in her presence and, better yet, he wouldn't be *here*. It should be strange, how tied to her he was, but to him it felt normal. Of anyone, she understood him, and she would understand how everything said today had been a staggering blow.

Euan was admitted into Jeanne's private sitting room, where he'd met with her and with Grace only the day before. He sat down in the chair she'd occupied and buried his face in his hands for a moment, drinking in the silence. When he heard the doors open, he stood and bowed to Jeanne as she entered. "Madame."

"Captain Cameron," she replied, offering her hand to him. "To what do I owe the pleasure of seeing you?"

Euan took her hand and kissed it. "I am sorry that it is only to tell ye that my wife is quite ill and was unable to come today, but asked that I deliver her regrets to ye personally."

"Ill?"

"She has nae been well for several days, but today has been the worst of it."

Jeanne frowned. "She was not entirely well yesterday. She had a moment where she said she felt pain in her chest, and she remembered the battle. I wanted to send for you, but she asked me not to."

Euan was unable to stop himself from sighing heavily and sat down on the settee even though Jeanne remained standing. He couldn't tell her why Grace's chest would pain her with those memories, but it had never happened before. At least not that she'd told him. "She is still greatly affected by it."

Jeanne sat down on the settee beside him with a concerned expression. "May I call you by your name?"

"Aye, of course ye may," Euan replied.

"What has happened, Euan? You are not the same person that was here yesterday."

"I dinnae know what is wrong with my wife, only that

something is. I feel as though she is dying but I cannae say why. I am unable to help her, and I am at a loss."

"We could send the king's private surgeon to her. Perhaps he could help?"

"No, I know he could nae. None of us can. I need to get her home."

"To Scotland?"

"Aye, but nae to—" Euan stopped himself. He couldn't tell her the truth. Grace had told him what she was when they met, but he'd never known her to tell anyone else. He had a feeling it was because they'd already known her for what she was, so she'd had no need for pretenses. Jeanne had no idea.

"Not to what?"

"Nae to a place where there will only be more war and bloodshed. I dinnae think she would make it through it all again."

"Nor would you."

"For an entirely different reason."

"Because you feel this time you would die?"

"I dinnae just think so, I know I would, and so would everyone else."

"What have you heard?"

"They now have the support of the Prussians and the Spanish for a third landing. They have a plan for how they would overcome the resistance of the clans who remained loyal to Hanover."

"Mon Dieu," Jeanne whispered. "But of course, they *would* have their support. They are already our allies in Austria so it would not take much to divert some of them to help with a Scottish landing. Especially if they were promised land or spoils in Scotland and England."

"They cannae do this. They are so focused on going forward that they are nae considering whether they should, whether the cost is truly worth it. They want to murder the chiefs of the loyalist clans, install the heirs, and then manipulate those young men into following them."

"Would that even work?"

"Honestly, I dinnae think so. Those men, I know them. The fathers and their sons. I have met them all before and there is nae a one of them who is interested in the return of a Stuart king. The sons are nae as malleable as the chiefs seem to believe they would be. They would be surrounded by counsel from their own clan and would have no need for the word of anyone else. They would lead their clans in the same ways their fathers had."

"I tried to discuss this with the king last night, but he had no desire to speak about it with me after having had those men in his ear all day. I need to find a way to speak to him about it in the morning before he sees them."

"It will be difficult for ye to get through them to his ear."

"Perhaps, but I will, and I will need Madame Cameron's help."

"I dinnae know if she can help ye as she is and, if she were here, she would tell ye to call her Grace."

"If she is well enough then we will try it. She needs to speak with the king herself. He needs to hear from her what it was like. He hears of the military cost but not the cost to those left to go on without the men."

"There is a last resort."

"What is that?"

"I cannae tell ye that now but be assured that I have a plan should I need it."

Jeanne's eyes went wide. "Let us hope it does not come to that."

"I hope it does nae."

"You are quite the talk of court this morning," she said, changing the subject.

"I am nae surprised. There was a bit of an incident."

Jeanne laughed. "Is that what you would call it? And here I thought it was called a duel."

Euan shrugged, offering a small smile. "May have been."

Jeanne only laughed more. "We all saw you; you know.

From the windows. We saw the whole of it. You were quite impressive."

"I should be, or I would nae be here now. Who is 'we'?"

"Some of the young ladies sitting with me. They were all astonished by you, and then you took off your coat. You would have thought you had taken everything off the way they acted. It seems you do still have two things on your mind after all."

Euan smiled. "As I said to my wife yesterday, one often leads to the other does it nae?"

Jeanne laughed. "Oh, how right you are. I should have known she would tell you."

"Ye should have known I would ask," Euan said with a smile before it faded. "We keep no secrets," he said, his voice going quiet. "We are entirely open to each other, as we have always been."

Jeanne's expression softened and lost any of its previous merriment. "You love her so much," she said. "I cannot comprehend such a feeling. It is beyond any I have felt. I love the king but not in the way you love her. It is a rare thing, this type of love."

"She is the entire reason I am alive. I would nae be here if nae for her, and I will never forget it. I will never forget her dress, red with blood, her skin stained with it. Her hair was no longer the golden color it was but a sick shade of crimson. It was the most horrific thing I have ever seen and I cannae ever be rid of the image."

"You have seen your friends die beside you but even those were not as traumatic to you as that moment? It only proves what I said."

"My friends went to battle fully aware of what they faced and what the possibilities were. She did nae. As horrible as their deaths were, they were nae unexpected."

"You fear her loss now, this person who is as much a part of you as you are to yourself."

"More than anything," Euan replied, the words whispered past the lump in his throat. "I cannae—" It was a thought he couldn't finish. He wouldn't have to live without her, at least he had that.

"Shhh," Jeanne said, covering one of his hands with her own. "Do not speak the words or even think them. You must believe she will come out of this."

Euan nodded, but said nothing else.

"You should go home to her," Jeanne said. "I will tell the king why you are not with us this evening, though our table will be far less merry without you."

"Thank ye," Euan said, standing before bowing and kissing her hand.

Once out of her rooms, he departed the palace as quickly as he could. He wanted nothing more than to be away from there, away from Lochiel and the words they'd all spoken. He was off the horse nearly before it had stopped moving and hurried into the house.

When he got to the top of the stairs, he slowed and entered the room quietly. "Grace?"

"Here," he heard her say in a quiet voice.

She sat in the light of the setting sun, wrapped in a robe. She looked pale, but she smiled when she saw him. It relieved him to see her awake and he hurried forward without thinking, kneeling in front of her and kissing her hands, before sitting with his back to her and putting his head in her lap.

Grace reached out and stroked his hair. "What is wrong?"

"Where do I even begin," he replied, his voice gentle and quiet.

"Wherever you need to."

Euan lifted his head and reached up behind him to take her hand. He kissed it, and as he pulled back, he noticed something that made his heart feel as though it had stopped. He hadn't noticed it the first time. "Love, where is yer ring?"

"What ring?"

He turned to look at her with a frown. "Yer wedding ring. Where is it?"

She shook her head, confused. "You have not given me one. You said that as soon as you found one you wanted to give me you would. Besides, even if you had, you know we wouldn't wear them while working anyway."

Euan glanced down at his own hand, just to be sure, even though he could feel the ring on his finger. He knew she'd been wearing it yesterday. "Grace, I did. I gave it to ye when I married ye in— no . . . no . . ."

"What are you talking about? Euan, we have not gotten married. Not really. Not yet."

Euan stood up quickly and turned around, feeling like he wanted to scream. "Ye remember naught about Edinburgh?"

"No? We have not even been there yet."

"What about Achnacarry . . . the lodge . . ."

Grace shook her head. "I only remember Achnacarry from when I went to the party with you."

Euan knelt again and put his hands on her arms. "Grace: do ye remember going back to Drumossie? Do ye remember seeing the spectre there?"

"No."

"What do ye remember. What is the last thing ye remember?"

"I . . . we went to buy clothes for you and your mother. We are going to Scotland soon."

"But ye dinnae remember having gone?"

Grace shook her head.

"You dinnae remember standing across from me in a church in Edinburgh? Where I put a ring just like this one on yer finger?" He held up his own hand.

"No," Grace said, her voice wavering as tears filled her eyes. "Euan, please stop. This is not funny."

"I am nae trying to be! Grace, I married ye. I married ye in Edinburgh. We have already been to Scotland; we bought a house there. We have lived there for almost a year! How do ye nae remember?"

Euan watched her expression grow panicked as she tried

to search for a memory of anything he said and came up with nothing.

"I do not remember any of that at all."

He stood up, his heart feeling like it was shattering as he backed away from her. "This cannae be happening."

Grace stood up and reached out her hand to him, but he turned away from her and walked toward the door. "Euan, wait!"

Euan heard her call after him, but he couldn't stop. He couldn't be around her in this moment. She had forgotten their marriage and the loss of those memories had taken his wife with them.

Chapter 12

Euan retreated to the study to contact The Council and inform them that things had, indeed, gotten worse. That she'd forgotten their marriage was such a severe blow that even The Council hurt for him. They couldn't apologize enough, but apologies did nothing, meant nothing, and he didn't want them. Apologies wouldn't give her back those memories, memories that were now his alone. Apologies wouldn't save her.

If he could get drunk in a mission body, now would've been the moment he chose to do so. Drinking so much whisky that he passed out and couldn't think about any of this sounded very appealing, but he also knew it would still be there when he woke up. At least he'd be blessedly free of it for a while. Closing his eyes, he let his head fall against the back of the chair, and when he heard the door open, he knew it was her. He'd known she wouldn't leave him to himself for long. She knew him too well for that, even with those memories gone. To leave him alone was to leave him to wallow in his head and let his thoughts tear at him.

"Euan," she said, her voice soft as she slipped a hand onto his shoulder. "I am sorry."

He reached up and covered her hand with one of his own. "For what? Ye cannae control this."

"For forgetting. I would never want to," she replied in Gaelic before he realized he'd immediately answered her in it. It was so common when they worked together it was no longer a conscious choice. At least she still had that in her memory somehow.

"I know, but that does nae make it hurt any less."

Grace came around and slid onto his lap, and he wrapped his arms around her, holding her protectively as she rested her head on his shoulder. "Tell me about it. Tell me what you remember. Maybe I will remember, too."

"We went to Edinburgh to sign the deeds and transfer the money for the lodge in Achnacarry. We made an entire day of it, and I showed ye around the parts of the city I remembered from my time there. I saw some rings in a shop window and went to see if they had any with my clan on them and they did. I bought them and hid them in my pocket."

"That sounds like something you would do."

"How do ye mean?"

"Sneaky."

"Ah, well, that is something ye have called me more than once."

Grace laughed. "Go on."

"I told ye there was a church I wanted to see, and we went there. It was grand and beautiful, ye were so taken by the glass. I asked ye to marry me, and ye laughed at me and told me we were already married. I told ye I meant truly, because ye wanted to, nae because we had a piece of paper. Ye agreed and the priest did it right there."

"Was I happy?"

The question cut him like a knife. "Aye," he whispered.

"I wish I could remember it."

"So do I."

"I do not want to forget you, but it seems like I will." she whispered to him. "Euan, I am afraid."

Euan held her a little tighter and rested his cheek against the top of her head. "So am I. We must get ye out of here. They will need to send someone else."

"No," she said, much to his surprise.

"What?" he said, pushing her up so he could look at her.

"We have to finish the mission, Euan."

He shook his head. "Grace, we cannae. Ye are dying here!"

"I know."

"Then ye know we have to get ye away from here so we can try to find out what is going on."

"You asked me once if I would still do my duty even if it meant my death. I told you I would, and this is no different."

"No! This *is* different! Damn it, Grace! Ye have already died once and that is enough! They cannae bring ye back this time because we will both be dead!"

"In the service of something we both believe in. In our duty to make things right."

"*Please*. Dinnae do this." He understood now how she must've felt the entire time she'd been trying to convince him to stay back. The pain, the frustration, the anger when the person you loved knew what was coming and continued anyway.

Grace rested her forehead against his. "I must," she whispered, echoing his own words and actions back to him.

Euan couldn't help the sob those words drew from him as it touched a place so deep, so raw, that it could still bring him instantly back to that moment when he'd held her as she begged him not to go. The moment when he'd been unable to stop himself from kissing her because the pull was too strong, overwhelming all else, and she'd become part of him. He knew he wouldn't change her mind, knew that if the situations were reversed, he'd do the same. He had. It wasn't his own death he feared, though he knew it would come, but hers. He feared watching her die slowly, watching her suffer. How long would it take after she'd died for him to follow? How long would he have to feel that pain before it was, mercifully, taken away from him?

"We may be able to complete this before it happens."

"We will have to because I am nae going to let ye die here. Nae again."

"Tell me what happened today," she said, wiping tears from his cheeks.

"I met with Lochiel and the others. It did nae go well."

"Why?"

"I goaded one of his men, the one ye met at the loch that time, into a fight by telling him he was a coward. He had accused me of such, of abandoning my men."

"Euan."

"I know, I know, and had ye been there I would nae have done it. I could hear ye in my head, I knew what ye would say, but I did nae care. I wanted to fight someone, I wanted to act on all that I feel now."

"I cannot say that I blame you. Did you just punch him?"

"Ah. No."

"Euan, what did you do."

"Broadsword."

"What! You killed him?"

"No, of course nae! I mean, I was tempted, but I did nae. The king stopped us."

"Was he injured?"

"I broke his nose, that is for certain. I cannae speak to anything else."

Grace laughed, even though he knew she was irritated with him for getting into such a situation to begin with. "That is all, hm?"

"Better than dead, I would wager."

"Definitely."

Euan smiled, the first time he felt like he'd truly done so all day. "I rather wish ye could have seen it."

"Me too, honestly."

"The rest of it did nae go so well either. The plans are far more advanced than I imagined."

"How so?"

"They have secured the support of both Prussia and Spain, who have agreed to lend forces to the landing if it goes forward."

Grace's eyes widened. She remembered enough to know that this was a bad thing. "Oh no."

"Aye. Lochiel plans to send mercenaries ahead to murder the clan chiefs who were loyal to the Hanovers. He believes this will allow him to control the sons and thus their forces as well."

"Why would they? They saw what happened the last time."

"Precisely. The sons will resist him, as they should. The sons of the chiefs he wants to do away with, I know those lads and know them well. I have met them before, gotten drunk with them, celebrated with them before war made us enemies, and there is nae a one of them who would follow Lochiel."

"Has he sent the mercenaries?"

"Nae yet, but if I sense he is about to, I will write ahead to warn them. I will nae let this happen."

"I am honestly surprised that he thinks such a thing would work, that these young men would follow him just because their fathers were dead."

"When I said the same, he said, 'it worked on ye did it nae?'" It still hurt him to even say it.

Grace gasped. "What an awful thing to have said!"

"It is true, no matter how awful it might be. Without a father of my own I sought one elsewhere. He made me feel as though I had found it but, really, he simply used those feelings to mold me into what he desired: a soldier who would follow him without question."

Grace stroked his cheek before kissing him. "Whatever he tried; you are so much more than that."

"I was nae until ye."

"No. You always have been, even if you did not let anyone else see it. Do not let what he said bother you."

"It is more than that. He told me that killing was what I did best. That I was a soldier and always would be. He asked me if it had felt good to fight that idiot and, God help me, it did. It *is* what I am good at, I had to be, I was trained to be."

Grace frowned. "Stop it. Do not let him tell you what you

are, Euan, and do not let him define you. You have given up enough of your life to those machinations and it is time to put an end to it. It felt good to fight that man because you needed a release, not because it is the only thing you can do. Make him pay for what he said but do it by stopping him from destroying Scotland. Show him what a true soldier can do."

Euan smiled at her. She was right, of course. No one could tell him what he was or wasn't, at least not anymore. "Make him pay for what he said. Do it using my mind, instead of my body and a weapon."

"Yes! You can do it, you have so many times before. I do not know how I know that, but I do. I can feel it."

"I have, ye are right."

"Then we know what we must do."

"Aye. I spoke to Madame; she is working to get the king to hear her and feels ye may need to speak to him yerself."

Grace nodded. "Then I had better do it before I forget anything I could tell him."

Chapter 13

When Grace woke the next morning, it was clear she was feeling better than she had since she'd arrived. Gone were the headache, nausea, and exhaustion, and it seemed as though she'd finally gotten a night's rest. It made Euan relieved beyond words to see her at least somewhat back to the way he always knew her to be. The summons from the king came in the early hours of the morning: he wished to see Madame Cameron in a few hours' time. They dressed and got into the carriage after a small morning meal — during which Euan had taken the time to reacquaint her with the facts she'd need about the rising and both of their experiences with it — and Euan was happy to see that there seemed to be no fear or concern on her face. She knew what she had to do, what she had to say, and that kept her secure.

When they arrived, he stepped out and helped Grace down, tucking her arm under his as they walked inside. When the page came to meet Grace, Euan stopped her from immediately going.

"Ye be careful. Good luck, my love."

Grace nodded, and he kissed her hand before she departed, watching her disappear behind the doors.

"Euan!"

Hearing his name called, Euan stopped and turned around to see Lochiel approaching him. His jaw tightened, and so did his fists, but he bowed. "Good day to ye, Lochiel."

"Is yer wife feeling better?"

Euan wanted to ask why he cared since he'd tried to murder her but refrained. "Aye. She is with the king now. He requested to see her."

"Alone?"

"Aye."

"Are ye nae worried about that, lad?"

"Should I be?"

"He does have a bit of a reputation for interludes with the wives of others."

"I am very certain I dinnae have to fear on that account."

"Ye assume she would have a choice."

Euan's stomach tightened, but he dismissed the thought. "What can I do for ye?"

"I just wished to apologize for what happened between us yesterday. There were things said that should nae have been."

"Which? The part where ye plotted murder against yer own, or where ye told me killing was all I was good at, or perhaps the part where ye admitted ye used my need for a father to yer own ends."

"I am nae sorry for the first, and that is still a plan being discussed but has nae been decided. The king has requested we nae meet on the matter until after the ball. The second, it is partial truth though it is nae all ye are good at. Ye have a keen mind, Euan, ye always have. I would have recommended ye for a spot on the king's council had we won. I still will if ye join us."

"I have no need of such a position." A spot on the king's council. Someone else had offered that to him once, and much more, in exchange for his participation in their plans. He'd declined it then, too.

"Ye may nae now, but ye should think carefully before ye decline. A mind like yers is well suited to strategy, to the long game. It was yer brilliant work that helped us come out on top more than once. It is nae meant to be consigned to a farmer in the arse end of France."

"If it is as ye say, why would I wish to turn it on my own?"

"Ye already did, Euan. Ye fought those clans who came out against us, or are ye forgetting that?"

"I have nae forgotten and never will. I cannae. I cannae forget standing across from lads I had known all my life and looking them in the eyes as I ended their lives. How could anyone forget? It is why I want no part of any new landing. Why do ye? Have ye nae seen enough of it? I know I have, and I will nae murder those few of us that are left."

"This is yer wife's doing. Ye were nae so sentimental before she arrived."

"Ye are wrong. I was, but I was more concerned with what ye thought of me than I should have been, too conditioned by my training and what ye put me through, and I kept it from yer sight. It is no longer something I need trouble myself with."

"I was proud of ye, lad. Proud of how ye fought for yer country and yer clan. I could nae have been prouder of ye if ye were my own son."

"That is nae what ye said yesterday, and 'proud' is certainly nae a word ye ever uttered to me before now."

"What I said was in anger at yer attempts to counter me. To me, ye are still one of my men, whether ye believe yerself to be or nae."

Euan shook his head. "No, yer anger made ye speak truth. Ye told me exactly what ye had done, and ye were nae sorry for it. Ye still are nae, even though ye now think it may be wise to try and convince me otherwise."

"I took care of ye, Euan. I raised ye when yer father died. I gave ye purpose and the guidance yer mother could nae give ye. I paid to educate ye. Ye can at least be more grateful."

Euan felt his temper rising. The insinuation that he should be grateful for the things Lochiel had put him through, for the manipulation and the lies, for all that had been stolen from him, infuriated him. Grateful for a purpose he'd been given no choice in? A purpose he'd long since stopped wanting by the time Grace had shown up? "Grateful? Grateful for what? For ye taking a boy and training him to become the unquestioning, unflinching officer ye wanted him to be? For sending me away from my home, my mother, and my friends to a place where I knew no one and could be tortured and broken only to be rebuilt into what *ye* desired? Did ye ever ask me what I wanted? I dinnae recall ye doing so. Everything ye did and said, all of it was to get me to follow ye, and I did. Blindly, because I had naught else. Just as ye wanted."

"Ye think ye could have become anything without me? Anything but a simple, uneducated farmer on my land? I saw promise in ye and made sure ye followed it!"

"I might have been happy that way, just as my family had been for generations. I will always be thankful for the education ye gave me, because now I can use it to question ye. I can use it to make sure ye dinnae succeed here and ye will nae. I swear it to ye."

Lochiel stiffened, his face reddening. "How dare ye," he hissed. "All I have done for ye and this is how ye will repay me? By working against me?"

"Working against ye for my country," Euan replied. "And I will never be sorry for it."

"As I said before, ye dinnae wish to make an enemy of me, lad."

"Oh, I think I do, for ye have already made an enemy of me."

Lochiel pulled back, the answer unexpected. Euan knew Lochiel was aware of what he'd been trained to do and that he understood making an enemy of someone with that training would be bloody.

"Is it war ye want, lad? Are ye sure?"

"It is clearly what ye want, and if ye bring it to my door ye can be sure I will end it."

"Ye dinnae know what ye are saying."

"I do. I will repeat myself for ye: it is war between us."

Euan turned his back on the man before he could answer and walked away from him. His heart was pounding so hard he swore others could hear it, the blood rushing in his ears to drown out all other sound, but it wasn't out of fear. It was anger, pure and white hot. Euan kept up his pace until he found himself alone enough to let his guard down and screamed in rage. How could he have ever followed this man so blindly? How could he have seen him as a father? No more. If it was war Lochiel wanted, then it was war he'd get, and Euan wouldn't lose.

Pacing, he tried to calm himself. He'd need to think strategically now. Every move, every word. All of it would need to be deliberate, even more than it already was every day of his life. There was no doubt they'd go after Grace and Euan needed to make sure she'd be safe. She was far too vulnerable here the way she was. Unless she was with Madame, he'd need to have her always with him. Food. They could poison her food and drink. She couldn't eat or drink here at the palace and must take her meals at home — though even there, he'd need to taste it all first. If it were tampered with, he'd feel it, and that would save her. The last resort he'd mentioned to Jeanne would need to be readied; he'd send letters of warning to the clans of the plots against them. If he and Grace didn't succeed here, dispatching those letters would be the last thing he did. For now, he needed to go back to the palace and make sure he was there when Grace came from her meeting with the king so that no one else got to her first.

***

As Grace left the Watching Chamber, they didn't go where Grace imagined they would, and instead, stepped out into what seemed to be a private garden. The page left her, and Grace looked around with a smile. It was a beautiful garden, well-manicured like the others and filled with varying flowers. Grace went to one of the rose bushes, admiring the white roses that adorned it.

"Beautiful, no?"

Grace turned and curtsied. "Indeed, Your Majesty."

"Would you like one?"

"I would, thank you. That is very kind."

The king smiled and gestured to the page accompanying him. The young man cut one for Grace and handed it to her before the king dismissed him.

"Did you know that white roses are the emblem of the Jacobites? They are a particular sort only found in Scotland," Grace said.

"I did not!"

"Now you do," Grace said, smiling.

"I was very sorry indeed to hear that you were unwell, madame."

"It seems to have been temporary. I feel much better now."

"That is good to hear. I think Captain Cameron was a bit lost without you yesterday. Please, walk with me."

Grace fell into step beside him. "Yes, he told me about the little . . . incident . . . he had."

The king laughed. "You could not have chosen a milder description! He was moments from killing the man and likely would have if I had not stopped him. Though, between you and me, he could not have chosen a better man to go after. I have disliked him since the moment I met him."

Grace chuckled. "My husband is not one to take insults lightly, and I am sure the man was well aware of it."

"He is an interesting man, your husband. It is hard to tell what he is thinking or feeling most times. A soldier who would kill a man for an insult, yet kind and gentle when it comes to women and those not of his own level."

"I will not deny it. It is part of what drew me to him."

"Is that so? Madame mentioned the two of you married the night before he left for that final battle."

"Yes, we did," Grace said, thankful for the primer on their story from Euan this morning. "We both felt he would not return, so why wait?"

"But if he would not return, then why bother?"

Grace looked at him with curiosity. "Because I loved him and I wanted to be his wife, even if it was only for a moment."

Remember me as ye said ye would. Soon enough, ye will be the only one alive who does. The memory of those words sent a pain through her so sharp it made her want to cry.

The king frowned. "Are you well, madame? You look pained."

"Yes, I am fine, thank you. I was simply remembering what he said to me before he left."

"Which was?"

"To remember him, because soon I would be the only one alive who did."

"How was he so sure he would not return?"

"I dreamt that he would not return, that none of them would."

"And that is why, as Madame told me, you decided to go there yourself to stop him?"

"Yes. I had to do what I could. I could not just let him die."

"What of the danger to yourself?"

"I did not think of it."

They walked in silence for a few moments before the king spoke again. "Lochiel, Murray, and the others want to try again, but I am sure you know that."

"Yes, but you should not listen to them. They only want revenge for their own pride, not because it is what is best for the country."

"Pride is not something your people lack."

"No, it is not, but that does not mean it always leads to the right thing."

"True. Although it is unconventional, I do want to know what you think. You have the curious position of having been there but not as a combatant."

"What would you like to know?"

"Were the people truly out in force for it?"

"Not that I saw, and certainly not in England. While many common Scots supported it, there were not enough to make up for the ones who did not. The prince ordered the Camerons to Drumossie even though they had taken leave of him after Stirling, so I think even Lochiel was wary."

"But he went anyway."

"Of course, for they had gone too far to stop. What would he say to the prince? 'No, thank ye, I dinnae think I will,'" Grace said, doing her best impersonation of Lochiel, which made the king laugh. "Would you have taken that sort of an answer?"

"No, most certainly not."

"It was the same here."

"Tell me what you saw at the battle."

"I saw a disorganized army with low morale. I saw them engage Cumberland upon unsuitable ground that because they had to fight where they'd fallen in exhaustion. I saw a leader who had become so dispirited by infighting that he could not lead while his advisors bickered. I saw orders ignored, advantage unpressed, supplies of everything depleted."

"It would be different with a more organized army."

"Such as the Prussians and the Spanish?"

The king looked at her, surprised.

"Yes, he told me. Your Majesty, those men are not at all familiar with Scotland and certainly not with the Highlands. It is a different world there, a different terrain and climate, and it is dangerous for those who are not prepared."

"The men who lead them will be familiar with all of it."

"Oh? Will you put a chief at the head of each regiment? There are not enough of them for that. Another officer? Where will those officers come from? Not to mention the difficulty of maintaining consistent supply lines."

"Lochiel believes he can get the loyalists to his side by eliminating their leadership and replacing it with his own."

"You cannot honestly believe that such a thing would work?"

"Do you not think so?"

"As my husband said yesterday, there is not a one of them

who would organize under Lochiel, Murray, or any of the others. They are in a good position due to their loyalty and they would not sacrifice that. Besides, there would still not be enough chiefs to lead men in unfamiliar territory even if it miraculously succeeded."

"Perhaps not. What of the battle itself? I am told you were injured?"

Grace winced. "I was. I did go and I did try to stop him. I went so far as to try to pull him from the line of his men. Of course, that did not work. He bid me farewell and walked away."

"To what he was sure would be his death?"

"Yes," Grace replied, her voice strained.

"That is bravery."

"Or foolishness."

"Perhaps both. What did you do?"

"Ran after him. All I wanted was to stop him. I thought if I could just pull him down, we could get away and keep under the fire, but it was not so. We both took fire and were lucky to live through it. We hid, moving constantly to avoid sweeps by Cumberland's men looking to catch survivors, and when we were healed, we waited for our opportunity to get here."

"I am sorry a lady needed to see such a thing."

"I am sorry that anyone does."

"I have been to the front but never so close to the battle."

"It is a horrible thing, as I told Madame. There is so much blood, and the smoke from cannons and rifles is so thick you cannot see. There are screams of war, of rage, of fear and agony. There is a scent I cannot even begin to describe. The sound lead balls make when they enter a body is horrific, as are the sounds the men themselves make when they are hit. Those that do not die immediately lay screaming in agony, screaming for God to save them. What I will always remember are the screams."

The king blanched. "It is no wonder, perhaps, that Captain Cameron has no desire to see the field of battle again."

"It should not be. Most anyone who has lived through

such things would not wish to experience it again. The Cameron regiment lost half of their men that day, and amongst his company were his friends, those he had known his whole life. He saw them die even as he lived, and he feels tremendous guilt over it."

"Anyone would, I should imagine. What happened afterward? We have heard dispatches, of course, and accounts from the others, but you were there long after they were gone."

Grace once again silently thanked Euan for having the foresight to re-arm her with the facts. "Cumberland's retribution was swift and merciless. Anyone suspected of being a Jacobite was killed, even women and children. Homes were burned, livestock taken, and they were thrown out into the snow to die of exposure and hunger. Anywhere in a 50-mile radius of Inverness became a smoking wasteland. Any men who survived the battle were hunted down and shot if they were lucky, beaten and tortured to death if they were not. Some were transported to the colonies, and they would be considered the lucky ones. All of their weapons have been taken and they are banned from carrying them. Not only that, but they are forbidden from wearing Highland dress."

The King stopped and looked at her. "They are no longer armed?"

"No. The government forces made sure of it. Swords, guns, artillery . . . all of it gone."

"Then how does Lochiel expect them to fight?"

"How does he expect them to fight when they have been so depleted of men and resources, regardless of access to weapons? When they are starving because their economy has collapsed, they are unable to grow food, and there are not enough men to rebuild or bring in what crops they can grow?"

"Mon Dieu, this is not what I was told!"

"Your Majesty, I implore you, listen to Euan. Ask him. Ask him what he thinks and whether he believes there is a chance of success in this, about whether his countrymen will fight again. Ask if they want the Stuarts now that it has cost them so dearly. Euan does not want his country destroyed any more than it already has been."

The king sighed and then nodded. "Thank you, Madame Cameron, for your counsel. I will take it under great consideration."

Grace curtsied as the king left. She could only hope she had done enough as she followed the page out of the garden. She sighed in relief when she saw Euan waiting for her as she came back into the Watching Chamber. Smiling, she made her way to him, and he embraced her.

"Did he harm ye in any way?" The question whispered in her ear so no one would hear.

Grace looked up at him, confused by the question. "No. Why would he?"

"There was mention that he tends to require some sort of recompense for his time."

"Well, he did not require it of me, so you need not worry. I am fine."

"That is a relief. I would hate to have to kill him. Regicide is always such a messy business."

Grace laughed and embraced him again, not really worried about what anyone might think of it. "Yes, there is no need for such drastic measures."

"Did it go well?"

"I think so. I told him what I could. The refresher you gave me this morning was perfect. You are a genius."

A mind like yers is well suited to strategy, to the long game. Euan closed his eyes and shoved the memory away. "I am glad it served ye well."

"I would not have been able to answer some of his questions without it."

"Let us hope that soon ye will nae need such a thing and ye will nae lose more than ye already have. Come, I need to speak with ye where no one will hear."

"Why?"

"Please."

The look on his face told Grace it was not a request. "Very well."

Euan took her hand and walked outside to the gardens. He was silent until, once again, he was sure they were alone. "I need ye to be careful now."

"Careful?"

"Lochiel tried again to get me to join him and once again it did nae go well. We are against each other now and he knows it. I will nae put it past him to come after ye to try to bring me to heel." Euan produced a sgian dubh from his boot and handed it to her. "Keep this with ye and use it on anyone who tries to do ye harm."

"Euan—"

"Grace, do it and dinnae try to argue with me. This is a fight I am familiar with, and I know what those who engage in such things will try. I will try to keep ye with me as much as I can, but it does nae hurt for ye to be prepared."

Grace took the blade from his hand and slipped it into one of the small slits in her over-gown and thus into the pockets tied over her petticoats to align with it. "Do you really think he would try to hurt me?"

"More than think. I know he will. It is only a matter of time, and the longer we are here the more danger ye are in. Ye cannae eat or drink here at the palace. Anything and everything is suspect, and I will taste yer food at home." He reached out and stroked her cheek. "Ye are the most important thing in all the world to me and he knows it. If ye want to strike at a man, ye take what he loves. Do ye understand?"

"A blood feud."

"Aye. A blood feud within his own clan. I know he is dead here within a year, but that is far longer than I care to have to outlast him."

"He is?"

"Aye, he is. Another reason the landing is foolish, but I cannae tell them that. He will start a war and nae live to suffer the defeat and the devastation it would bring."

"No, of course you cannot tell him, but I am sure you wish you could."

"Aye," Euan said, chuckling before he kissed her forehead. "I am sorry for this. I imagine this is why they dinnae send us back to our own lifetimes: there can be too many demons to fight."

"I am not worried. I know you, and you will not let him beat you."

"No, I will nae. He helped make me what I am, and he was happy to set that monster upon others. Now he will see what happens when the full weight of that is brought to bear against *him*."

"I am not sure I have ever seen you this way."

Euan gave her a half smile. "No, you have nae, and I hoped ye never would. There was a reason I survived the campaign as long as I did. Even when ye and I worked together and I had to use these skills, ye never saw them. This is what I do, and I am good at it."

Grace studied him, her expression a mix of curiosity and wariness. "Why did you not want me to?"

"I think I am nae the man ye know when I must turn my mind to such things. When all ye must do is win, and all ye can do is work to outmaneuver yer opponent, whoever they may be, ye cannae think about who else might be hurt."

She nodded and then looked away from him. "I wish it was not like this. If I was as I should be, none of this would have happened. You would not be here, and you would not need to face any of this."

Euan reached out and turned her face back to him. "Ye are nae at fault in this. Ye did nae choose for this to happen to ye, and I would face this a million times to keep ye safe, love. What I need ye to do is stay concerned about yerself."

"I will stay vigilant."

"Good. We dinnae have to be back at court until the ball. The king has suspended all counsel on this matter until afterward. It may be best to keep away from here unless we are sent for. We are safest at home."

"Shall we go now?"

"Ye are nae to meet with Madame?"

"No, she has not sent for me and the king did not mention it."

"I have need of her assistance. Can ye take her a letter from me?"

"Now?"

"No, next week. Aye now," Euan said, chuckling as she gave him an annoyed look even as he pulled it from his pocket. "I wrote it while I waited for ye."

Grace plucked it from his fingers in faux irritation and gave a playful roll of her eyes before she tucked it away in the same pocket as the knife. Leaning up, she kissed him and stepped away to leave.

"Grace."

She stopped and turned to look at him over her shoulder.

"As soon as ye give it to her and get a response, come to the forecourt. I will be waiting for ye. I love ye."

"And I love you," she replied, giving him a wink before she departed.

Grace made her way back to the palace, her demeanor calm and untroubled. She knew Euan was there with her, watching her to make sure she got there safely even if she couldn't see him. Once inside, she threaded her way through the crowd to the doors that led beyond the Watching Chamber.

"Madame Cameron to see the Marquise. It is urgent," she said to the page. The young man bowed and disappeared within.

"Ye tell yer husband to stop interfering with Lochiel's plans," a voice whispered in her ear as Grace felt the point of a knife against her lower back. "Or he shall find out what grief truly is when I cut yer throat."

"Are you quite sure this is a game you want to play?" Grace replied without turning around, even as she discreetly slipped her hand into her pocket.

"I dinnae fear him. I know him, and he will do naught so that ye are safe."

"It is not him you need to worry about," Grace said, a small smile crossing her lips as she heard the man gasp when the tip of the sgian dubh she now held was pressed against his groin. "How long do you think you will live when I shove this in, hm?"

"I would kill ye before ye could."

"Somehow I doubt that. You seem to forget who you are dealing with, and that is foolish indeed. Not only did I survive a battle, but I am a Cameron wife. *Euan's* wife. I suggest you leave me be unless you wish to find out whether or not I will actually do it, though I promise you I will, and I will quite enjoy watching you bleed out all over these lovely marble floors."

Grace felt him step away from her and, she was certain, fade back into the crowd. She kept the knife in her hand, tucked between the folds of her skirt, until the page returned to allow her inside. Once the door was shut behind her, Grace allowed herself a triumphant smile before she followed the young page, returning the sgian dubh to her pocket.

She'd barely knocked when the door opened. "Come in, madame."

Grace walked inside and was taken to the sitting room, where Jeanne was already waiting. "Madame Cameron! I did not expect to see you."

Grace curtsied. "I know, and I beg your forgiveness for my intrusion. I wanted to thank you for setting up my meeting with the king. I was happy to tell him everything I could."

Jeanne smiled. "We have the same aim. I am glad he met with you."

"There is more."

When Jeanne raised an eyebrow, Grace stepped closer.

"I have a letter for you from Captain Cameron."

"Why so secretive?"

"I am sure he explains in the letter. He asked me to bring it to you for him and get a response," Grace replied as she pulled it from her pocket and passed it to Jeanne.

Jeanne unfolded the letter and read through it before nodding. "Tell him yes, I can assist him with what he asks. I will send a royal courier when it is done."

"Thank you," Grace replied with another curtsy. "I shall see you at the ball."

"You are keeping away from court until then?"

"Yes, at his request."

"He is wise to do so, and I think you know it too. I shall see you at the ball."

Grace curtsied again and left, the page walking her back out. She had the sgian dubh hidden in her hand once more as she made her way through the crowds and into the forecourt where Euan waited for her, as promised.

"What did she say?"

"She said yes. She will send someone when it is done."

Euan's smile was wicked as he took Grace's hand and kissed it before helping her into the carriage.

Chapter 14

When they arrived back at their lodgings, Euan sent Grace upstairs while he stayed down to give instructions to the staff about who he and Grace would see, and who would need to be sent away without being let in, along with the descriptions of which people would require the servants to notify him immediately if they were seen anywhere near. Afterward, Euan headed upstairs, almost relieved to know he'd have this time alone with his wife. It might be the last they had if his plan didn't work. The thought made him stop where he was as it took his breath away. Placing a hand on the wall, he closed his eyes. No, he couldn't think this way. He needed to believe that they'd get out of here before that happened. With a shake of his head, he continued up. Grace had already kicked off her shoes and was trying to get herself undressed when he came in.

"Let me help ye," he said, laughing as came to her aid.

"This is the only thing I do not like about these clothes. You can never get in or out of them by yourself," she grumbled.

"I have no problem helping ye do so," he replied.

"Of course you do not."

"Ye cannae blame me can ye? I know what ye look like beneath them."

Grace made a face at him. "What did you need from Madame?"

"Dinnae ask, love. I will tell ye as little as possible because that is the safest way. Just know it is all leading to something.

Something that will, hopefully, get us out of here. I will tell ye all when it is done."

"You do not trust me?"

"It has naught to do with trust, and ye know that perfectly well, so dinnae start. It is all to do with yer safety should they get their hands on ye. The less ye know the better. Do ye feel as though ye have lost anything else?"

"It would be hard to tell, I think."

"What is the last thing ye remember?"

"Going shopping for clothing."

Euan let go of a relieved sigh. "You have nae gotten worse. Maybe things have finally settled out."

"I hope so."

"In the meantime, I will be tasting yer food as I said earlier. It will nae harm me, but I will feel enough of it to know if it is safe for ye."

"You really believe they would go so far?"

"I know they would. They have."

"What!"

'I did nae participate in that; I had naught to do with it, but I know it has been done."

"Then I suppose I should tell you it is a good thing you gave me the sgian dubh."

"Why is that?"

"When I was standing waiting for the page to take me back, one of them tried to threaten me. He put a knife to my back and told me to tell you to stop interfering or he would show you what true grief was when he cut my throat."

His hands tightened on her dress as his anger rose to the surface for just a moment. "Lochiel did nae waste time getting started."

"You knew he would not, which is why you gave me the blade. His man was rather shocked to find the tip of it pressing against his groin, I must say."

Euan blinked. "Ye did what now?"

"I was able to get the knife out of my pocket without him noticing. When he told me he did not fear you, I told him you were not the one he needed to fear. By then I had the knife precisely where he would not want it, and I asked him how long he thought he would live if I shoved it in. I reminded him that not only am I Cameron, but I am your wife, and I *would* do it and enjoy watching him bleed out on the king's pretty floors."

Euan stopped what he was doing and started to laugh hard. "Christ, I wish I could have seen his face!"

A small smile played across Grace's lips. "Me too."

"Ye are perfection. It is truly a shame ye were born when ye were. Ye would have made a fine laird's wife."

"That is not what you are."

"No."

"Then why would I want to be the wife of one?"

"If I know ye, ye would have made me one somehow or another."

"This is not Macbeth."

"I did nae mean that way."

"Yes, you did."

"Fine. Maybe a little."

"How strange that I remember that."

"Aye, but I seem to recall ye reading it to me and Mam sometime before we left to go back to Scotland." Those were memories he knew she would still have.

"That must be it. What shall we do with the time we have?" Grace asked as he slid the dress away from her and untied the skirts.

"I have work to do and ye need to rest. I will be here with ye, but I want ye to rest as much as ye can."

"Sounds exciting," Grace replied, the words dripping with sarcasm and disdain.

Euan laughed. "Stop it, ye. Ye dinnae have to like it, but ye know it is what ye should do."

"Is there nothing I can do to help with your side of the plan?"

"Nae yet," he whispered as he kissed her shoulder. "Soon. I will nae leave ye out of this."

Grace shivered and leaned back against him but smiled as he pressed his cheek against hers. "No matter what happens, I hope you know how much I love you. I want to tell you in case I . . ." she trailed off, unable and unwilling to finish the thought.

"I know," he said. "I know ye do and I will always know that no matter what. If ye forget me I will just have to make ye fall in love with me again."

"You make it sound so simple."

"It is. For us, it is. We are part of each other, more, remember? Yer mind may forget but yer heart and soul never will."

Grace turned around and hugged him tightly.

"Everything will be all right, love, I promise ye. Ye will be mine always, regardless of what happens. We have fought too hard for this to let anything stand in our way."

"I believe you."

"As ye should, for I have never given ye reason to doubt me and I never will. Now, let us get ye the rest of the way out of this so ye can get some rest, even if that is reading a book from the study."

"I really do not want to. I want to do something, be useful," she complained.

"And ye shall be, but ye cannae do anything if ye are exhausted. I know ye feel well now, but ye should nae push it."

"I know," she admitted before huffing indignantly. "I hate feeling this way. I hate feeling so weak and powerless."

"I know ye do, and I would too, but this is what we have right now," he replied, stroking her cheek gently. "Please, *leannan*, I am begging ye: get some rest."

"You win," she said, smiling. "I will go, but only if you come and stay with me awhile."

Once Grace had allowed him to check her bandages and then gone to bed, she'd almost immediately fallen asleep despite her best efforts to remain awake, and Euan had time alone to think. He'd long understood why Grace always appreciated this time and he, too, had always made good use of it to think of his next step or to move forward with whatever he must. There was much to do and not much time to do it. All of it depended on whether Jeanne could accomplish what he'd asked of her.

He knew he should contact The Council and brief them, but he wasn't going to. They might try to get him to stop and he had no intention of doing so. They wouldn't understand this, it was beyond them, and for Euan it was critical. All of it was to save his country, of course, but there was more than that now. Now it was personal. He needed to prove to himself that he was more than what Lochiel believed him to be, wanted him to be. He needed to prove to himself that he was the man Grace believed him to be even though the truth was that he was both. It must be done without bloodshed, if possible, because that was the only way for him to show that he was beyond the simple ideas of a soldier at war on a battlefield. It was war, but war of a different sort, one where your wits mattered more than your strength. Euan knew that Lochiel and his men would resort to the tried and true methods of handling a threat like him, but they'd need to be smarter than that to win. The question was whether they knew it, too, and whether that knowledge would be enough to thwart him.

It was strange to confront a life he'd once lived, a life he'd accepted without question, only to discover how little of it had been what he'd believed it to be. Strange to have seen so much of the world, to have seen the future and what could be, and see how narrow his views had once been. Of course, he wasn't the only one whose views were narrow and unaware of the larger picture, but they had no scope to do otherwise. He wished he could tell them. Would it stop their present course? Would they change? Or would it make no difference because they didn't have the ability to see what it all truly meant, as he once hadn't.

Euan's mind strayed to the other battle he was fighting: the battle for his wife. Something was happening, and while he wanted to believe that it had stopped, it seemed unlikely. Though they seemed to have a reprieve; it might well come back. Whatever this was, it was stealing her from him piece by piece, and he was powerless to stop it. He could do as he had been doing and try to fill in the pieces she lost, but he wasn't sure it helped because she didn't have the emotional tie to go with those memories. She might remember what he'd said, but the words wouldn't truly mean anything.

There was, of course, the possibility that they'd both die here. If it started again and he couldn't close the mission before it claimed her entirely, she'd die and so would he. He'd asked her once if knowing she couldn't die made her feel powerful, and she'd told him he would be surprised at how quickly someone could get used to it. She'd been right because it was never something he thought of now. It made it strange to confront the possibility of his own death again, the same way he once had every time he'd left Achnacarry to follow Lochiel. He didn't fear it, which he found curious, but perhaps it was because Euan knew full well that he'd not be alone in it. Grace would go too, and this brought him comfort.

What he did fear was watching her die. The thought of watching her continue to suffer frightened him, along with the helplessness of being relegated to such a position. How did anyone watch someone they loved die? How did they watch them suffer the pain and the fear? He knew people did it all the time, but it was something he had a difficult time imagining. What does a soldier do when the enemy suddenly becomes something he can't fight; something he can't defeat or kill or stop? Euan would do all he could, but his options were becoming ever more limited, and he knew it.

He sighed and rubbed his face with his hands. If the only thing he could control was his fight with Lochiel, then that was the sole task he must turn his mind to. It was the one thing that could stop the rest, the victory that could get them out of here before the worst could happen. Euan stood up and crossed the room to place a kiss on Grace's temple. It was time for him to get to work.

Chapter 15

Thirty-six hours until the ball. That was all the time he had to do everything he must, and that was a tall order. Euan left Grace in the morning in order to see to other parts of his plan, knowing she'd be safe there in the daylight hours. The city was too busy to chance a bold attack on them in broad daylight. He knew Lochiel was not that foolish and so Euan didn't fear it. A blood feud was strategic and exacting, the moves careful.

Euan made his way along familiar streets, thankful for the knowledge his previous time here at the palace had afforded him. He knew where to find the less desirable elements because he'd spent plenty of time amongst them, and they were the ones he sought now. Entering a bookseller's, the place looked ordinary enough. Books of all sorts stacked everywhere, the clerk nondescript. You had to know that it was more than what it seemed, to know what to ask for, and Euan most certainly did.

"May I assist you, monsieur?" the clerk asked, surveying Euan over the tops of his glasses, taking in the fine clothing and bearing of the young man who clearly seemed to be of the aristocracy.

"Oui," Euan replied, falling easily into French. "Bonjour Cyrille. Ye dinnae recognize me?"

Cyrille blinked, his eyes going wide. "My, God. Euan Cameron. Look at you!"

Euan laughed and embraced Cyrille as he stepped around the desk. "Hello, my friend. Is Pierre here?

"He is, and he will be thrilled to see that *le Métamorphose Écossais* has returned."

The Scottish shapeshifter. A name Pierre and many of the others had given him what felt like another lifetime ago. Cyrille turned, disappearing into a back room, and moments later another man hurried out, his movements quick, but he stopped when he saw Euan.

"Well, here is a face I never thought I would see again."

"Hello again, Pierre," Euan said, grinning.

"Where in the hell have you been, boy? You just disappeared and we could get nothing out of the others as to where you had gone."

"I was sent home, but I am back for a very important reason and I need yer help."

Pierre gestured toward the back and Euan walked through the door, past Cyrille, who went back to minding the store. Pierre followed him and went to a table, pouring two cups of wine. Spread over tables in the center of the room were the tools of Pierre Faussaire's special craft: forgery. Faussaire wasn't, of course, his real name, as it was the French word for "forger," but the descriptor that those in the know would use to signal that they knew him and could be trusted. When he returned to the table, he put the cups down and took a seat.

"So, are you going to tell me why you are suddenly all tarted up, or will you make me guess."

"On assignment," Euan said, taking a drink from the cup set before him.

"Ah. Why am I not surprised?"

"Ye should nae be. It was why I was sent here the first time, to learn how to do exactly this."

"I remember, though you are far from the young man you were then. You are different."

"Much has happened since then."

"A war has happened since then."

Euan said nothing.

"I was wondering about you when we heard about it, if you had been sent to fight in it, if you survived, or if you were even there at all."

"Oh, I was there."

"Jesus, Euan, and you are still alive."

"By a miracle, aye."

"Did your chief send you again? Is it for him you act?"

"No. No, this time it is against him."

Pierre's eyebrows shot up. "Is that so? Why?"

"They wish to start a third war and I intend to stop them."

"What do you need from me to accomplish such a thing?"

"I need for ye to do what ye do best," he replied, pulling out a purse of coins and tossing it onto the table between them. "I believe ye will find this more than sufficient."

Pierre took the purse and opened it, then smiled. "Quite generous of you."

"This is a matter of extreme importance and I am willing to pay for the best: ye."

"You could do this yourself, Euan, you have the skill. I should know, I taught you."

"I will be doing some of my own, but there is nae enough time for me to do it all myself."

"Very well. Tell me what you need."

"I need ye to forge a letter and a list of signatures. Here is the list of names ye will need and the text of the letter itself," Euan said as he handed Pierre a folded piece of paper. "I will need this by tonight, midnight at the latest."

Pierre looked it over and then nodded. "Easy enough. You will have it by tonight, as requested."

"Thank ye. I wish I could stay longer and catch up with ye, but I cannae. I am being followed and dinnae wish to tarry here too long lest they get suspicious about this place."

"Always thinking. Go, and I will get to work."

Euan nodded and stood, making his way back out onto the street after purchasing a book to make it look as though he'd gone in there for legitimate reasons. He was aware he'd be followed and had planned for that. It was easy to get lost in the smaller streets and quarters near the palace, the places where market stalls were set up and the passageways teemed with people. Places where he could disappear into shadowed doorways and darkened alleys to let his pursuers pass him by without their even knowing. Euan walked down the street before stepping out into a more open road where he knew they would easily see him. He wanted them to think he was being careless.

It amused him to lead them on a merry dance through the more mundane tasks he'd added to his list just to throw them off. Buying some flowers for Grace along with some fruit that looked appealing, picking up gloves for the ball. All those things that would bore the life out of someone tasked to follow him, and that was entirely the point. When boredom arrived, it made you less observant, made it easier for the person to escape your notice and disappear. It was a mistake that Euan had only made once when he'd been assigned to such a duty.

As he arrived back at the house, he was conscious that it, too, was being watched. He could see them, though they thought they were inconspicuous. Euan wanted to laugh at how very distinctly conspicuous they were, and he was aware they had no idea what his training had been. It was something no one outside of a few select people knew, and something never discussed, though he was rather surprised Lochiel hadn't made it clear to these men by now exactly who and what they were dealing with. Instead, they were watching and waiting for him to make a mistake, a mistake that would never come. He went inside and upstairs, removing his hat as he entered their rooms.

"Did you get what you needed?" Grace asked as he entered.

"I did," he replied as he presented her with the flowers. "I saw these while I was out and thought ye might like them."

Her eyes lit up as she took them from him. "Oh, I do! They are beautiful! Thank you for the thought," she said, her smile bright.

"Tell me, how much do ye love me?"

Grace raised an eyebrow. "That is a question you should not even have to ask, but a lot. Why?"

Euan grinned as he produced two sacks from behind his back and handed them to her. Grace set aside the flowers and took them, peering inside before gasping and looking up at him.

"Aye, peaches and cherries. It is spring after all. If ye are locked away here, I thought I should make it enjoyable for ye. I also brought ye a book."

"Ooo, a book!"

Her immediate reaction made him laugh. "Aye, a book," he said as he handed it over from the bag he'd carried.

Taking it in her hands, she grinned. "Voltaire's 'History of Charles XII,' an excellent choice." Grace laughed and stood up to hug him. "Thank you. That was kind of you."

It was an embrace he was happy to accept, and he held onto it for as long as he could. "An original edition, too. I thought ye might like it. Ye seem to be still feeling well today."

"I am absolutely going to ask to take this home," she said in excitement. "And yes, I do. I am glad of it," she continued before she popped a cherry into her mouth and sighed happily.

Euan chuckled at her reaction. Maybe there was hope yet. Maybe it really had stopped. "As am I."

"Did you see anyone?"

"Nae exactly. I know they are following me, however."

Grace frowned. "I am surprised they did not try to do you harm while you were out."

"They would nae. Nae in daylight in front of so many others. That would be beyond stupidity and Lochiel is nae stupid. He will be far more subtle than that even if his men are nae."

"Then we should be safe at the ball, too."

"No," Euan said as he sat down. "There are many opportunities there. Many openings to slip poison into a cup, to pull someone into the darkness without anyone to see ye."

All of these were things Grace had never had to think about, and he knew it. Whenever she was in any place where it would have mattered, she couldn't be harmed. It was certainly nothing they would need to consider in their daily lives in the present. It was, however, something Euan had always been very conscious of due to his position. Any feud like this could mean he'd be taken down as part of it.

"It must be exhausting to have to live this way."

"Ye get used to it, I think. Ye grow used to always being alert and to seeing danger where others would nae. It is nae something ye have ever needed to concern yerself with."

"Except that now I do."

"Aye, now ye do. Stay to what I told ye: dinnae eat or drink anything and stay by my side as much as ye can."

Grace nodded her agreement. "Is there anything else I should know?"

"Aye. Yer piece in the game begins tomorrow night. Ye will need all of yer wit and yer charm for it."

"What would you have me do?"

"I need ye to occupy the king. Keep him away from Lochiel and the others. Work with Madame to keep him so entertained with the ladies that he will have no intrusion upon his festivities with talk of war."

"You want me to flirt with the king."

"Aye. Well, more than. I need ye to be tempting to him, just as ye do so well to me. I know what I am asking ye to do, but I also know ye can do it."

Grace sighed. "If that is what needs to be done."

"It is. Please, ye must trust me. If this comes together then all will be finished by the following day and we can go home."

"You will have to not get jealous about anything I do."

"I cannae promise that."

"You will have to promise you will not show it. If I must play my part, then so must you."

"All is off if he tries to take ye to bed."

"I agree to that. Are you sure we just cannot kill Lochiel and get it over with?"

Euan grinned and took her hand to kiss it. "Now ye sound like me, and I am nae sure how I feel about that."

"You would not want victory that easily, not for this."

"Ye are more than right. I need to beat Lochiel at his own game."

Grace laughed. "If anyone can, it is you."

"Aye, and he is about to be reminded of it. Let us talk of other things."

"Such as?"

"Anything that is nae missions or intrigues or illness."

"Hm," Grace said, trying to think but then frowning. "There is nothing I can tell you."

"Then I shall tell ye," he replied. "Let me tell ye of home."

"Home."

"Aye, our home. We live in the most beautiful place, *leannan*, and ye have made it a wonderful home. It is an old hunting lodge, but we restored it and updated it for our use. It sits at the top of the hill, and from our garden ye can see down to Inverlochy. Our bedroom has two windows, one that looks out upon that vista, and the other into the woods behind. It is nae, however, our favorite place in the house."

"What is?" Grace asked.

"The study is our favorite. There are shelves built into the walls and ye brought all yer books from home, as well as some that belonged to yer grandparents, to fill them. Ye have a favorite chair by the fire and mine is right beside it. We love to sit there of an evening and read together or just talk, always with a dram, of course."

"Of course."

Euan chuckled. "We have put some lovely and comfortable furnishings in it, and a great desk where ye sometimes set things out to study. Ye bought a cabinet to hold the whisky and crystal glasses and decanters."

"What do I like to read?"

These were the sorts of questions that broke Euan's heart.

Things she should remember about herself that she now couldn't recall. "All sorts of things. Fiction and non, poetry, histories. Ye have a fondness for Regency and Victorian literature and poetry. Ye love Shakespeare and love it when I read ye the sonnets. I acted out bits of Macbeth for ye once just to amuse ye, and ye laughed until ye cried."

"Why did I laugh? Macbeth is not funny."

"It is when I try to play all the parts and do it in a silly way."

Grace laughed. "You are right, that would be funny. I cannot imagine your portrayal of Lady Macbeth."

Euan smiled. "Love's not Time's fool, though rosy lips and cheeks within his bending sickle's compass come; Love alters not with his brief hours and weeks, but bears it out even to the edge of doom."

"That sounds so familiar."

"Sonnet 116, one of yer favorites and mine as well. That part is our favorite."

"And here you are, doing just that."

"Doing what?"

"Bearing it out to the edge of doom because you love me."

"Aye, and like it says, my love for ye will nae alter. It never could, except to grow. How could it nae? How could I nae bear anything for ye? I would walk through hell for ye, Grace, and if that is what I must do to bring ye back to me then I shall. It is nae even a question, just as it was nae one for ye."

"Tell me more."

"Ye love to walk in the woods with me, sometimes in silence, sometimes nae. Ye adored the autumn colors and I took ye all over Lochaber to see them. Ye were entranced, for they were naught like what ye had at home before."

"I hope to see them again."

"Ye will, beloved, ye will."

Grace rose from her seat and slid into his lap, letting him put his arms around her and snuggling into him once he did so. Euan knew her well enough to know that such displays of affection were an unconscious show of anxiety, a desire to be near him, the one stable thing she could hold onto above all else. He couldn't blame her and knew that he'd feel the same way were their positions reversed. She was always his comfort when his mind got the best of him and he woke up in terror from a nightmare. She'd hold him and stroke his hair, whispering words of comfort or singing to him as his heartbeat slowed to normal again. It was hard to remember a time now when she hadn't been there in such a way, and he wasn't sure how he had managed without her.

When she kissed him it took him by surprise, but the way she did it, slow, soft, and loving, told him all he needed to know about where her mind was and what she desired from him. He was happy to meet her in it, drawing her closer to him before he stood with her in his arms and carried her to the bed. As he set her down upon it and joined her there, he placed leisurely kisses on her neck, along her collarbone, her cheeks, her eyelids, arms, hands. There was plenty of time for this and he intended to take all he could, to pour everything he felt for her into it in the hope that she would feel how much he loved her in every kiss and every caress. At the same time, it was his own desire to have this memory in case the worst should happen, though he wouldn't let himself think about that. He couldn't, or it would drive him mad with preemptive grief.

As they lay beside each other afterward, Euan propped himself up on an elbow and smiled down at her. Grace reached up and brushed some of his hair away from his face and behind his ear, and he turned his head to kiss her hand once she'd done so, placing it against his cheek and holding it there with his own.

"I love ye, Grace. Dinnae forget that. Dinnae ever forget. No matter what happens, ye are my wife, and I love ye with all that I am. I will nae let ye go, and if the worst comes, I promise ye I will do all I can to repair it, even if I have to court ye all over again."

"I believe you would," she said. "But I hope you do not have to."

"So do I, trust me."

"I am so afraid of it, of forgetting you. I want so desperately to believe that I cannot, that there is no way I could forget a man who lives inside of my soul the way you do. But I have forgotten so much already, and the fear of forgetting the rest darkens and eats away at the edges of the things I still hold onto."

"I know, and I would be too if I were ye, but ye cannae dwell on that fear. Ye will drive yerself to distraction with it. Trust yerself and my love for ye and know I am doing all I can."

"You are, I know you are, I just hate this. My mind is such a large part of who I am — and what I do — that not being able to trust it, to know that there are huge holes, is frustrating."

"Aye, I can imagine. We are the same there, ye and I. As of right now though, it seems to have stopped, so let us focus on that."

Grace nodded and then smiled again. "You look so handsome this way."

"What way?"

"Hair down, undressed in bed with me."

Euan laughed softly. "Ye said something similar to me once before."

"Did I?"

"Aye, when we were first setting up the move to Scotland. I appreciated it then, too."

"Mmm well, you are, and I am a lucky woman that I get you all to myself."

"Do ye? Are ye sure about that?" he asked with a wicked smile.

"I had better!"

He laughed again, unable to help himself. "Of course ye do, ye daft lass." Grace scoffed and gave a lock of his hair a gentle, teasing tug. "Ach, be careful, ye know how I like that."

"Euan!"

Euan laughed harder and lay back down beside her, pulling her close to him and nuzzling her cheek. "I am teasing. Maybe."

Grace chuckled and nudged him with an elbow. "You are a ridiculous man."

"Aye, and I am *yer* ridiculous man. Now, get some rest. Ye look exhausted."

"Are you trying to tell me I look terrible?"

"Nae at all. Ye are beautiful, but I can read ye like no one else. Rest," he whispered before he kissed the tip of her nose. "Ye must be fresh for the ball on the morrow."

"Will you stay with me?"

"Aye, until ye are asleep. I have work of my own I must do."

Grace turned on her side, snuggling into him and closing her eyes. She was asleep in moments, and Euan rose to dress himself again. When the royal courier arrived a short time later, loudly announcing he had a gift for Madame Cameron from the king, Euan crept down the stairs to make sure it was not an ambush. It seemed odd until the box the man had brought was handed to him. Inside was a beautiful sapphire necklace with a note thanking Grace for her counsel and asking her to please accept the loan of this necklace from Madame's own collection for the ball. Hidden beneath the velvet the necklace sat upon was what he'd asked Jeanne for, and the courier had made it seem otherwise as a cover. If it was from the king, there'd be nothing amiss inside.

"Ye clever girl," Euan said in a whisper, smiling and retreating to the study.

Not long afterward there came another knock, and Euan left the study as the maid opened the door, careful to remain out of view. "Here are the stockings and gloves Monsieur Cameron requested for Madame Cameron earlier today," came the familiar voice.

Euan stepped into view and nodded to Pierre. "I thank ye for yer prompt service, monsieur," he said as Pierre handed him a small basket.

"Always a pleasure doing business with you, Monsieur Cameron," Pierre replied with a wink and a smile before he turned and departed.

Euan shut the door and smiled at the young maid. "Thank ye. Cannae have Madame looking ill put together, can we?"

"No, Monsieur, of course not!"

"Ye are dismissed for the evening. Madame is asleep and I will be retiring shortly."

The maid curtsied to him and Euan took the basket into the study. Everything was going precisely to plan. Now the real work began.

Chapter 16

Euan was kicked out of their room by Grace when it came time for her to be dressed for the ball the following evening. It was at her request, as she didn't want him to see her until she was entirely ready, and when she came downstairs, he seemed only able to stare at her. The gown she wore was a blue damask in the mantua style, the skirt covered in intricate silver embroidery to create a design almost like a brocade. The sides of the over-gown where they met the stomacher followed the same embroidery, as did the stomacher itself. Behind her was a train of the same embroidered blue damask attached to the back of the over-gown, where the sides of the gown had been drawn up into triangles and buttoned to show the embroidery on the back of the skirt. The heeled shoes matched the damask and, as a crowning touch, the sapphire necklace sparkled at her throat. All of it intensified Grace's already deep blue eyes and made it difficult to look away from her.

"My love, ye look stunning but I dinnae think that is even enough of a word to describe ye," he finally said as he crossed the room to take her hand and kiss it.

Grace couldn't help the blush as she smiled. "Thank you. You look handsome, as always."

"Shall we?" he said before Grace nodded and they walked out, Euan helping her into the carriage and making sure the dress was tucked inside.

Grace laughed at him as he got inside and shut the door. "I know, it is a lot of dress."

"It is," he responded as he joined her in laughing. "But ye look beautiful in it all the same."

The palace was crowded with people, invited guests as well as onlookers who wanted to see the glamorous fashions modeled on the courtiers. There were gasps as Grace stepped out of the carriage with the help of a footman; her dress was spectacular even by the French court's standards, and she somehow managed to wear it without seeming haughty; the same otherworldly air about her that Euan had noticed that night with the buck in the woods. A delicate beauty with a genuine smile was always disarming. There were more gasps and whispers as Euan stepped out behind her. They were striking together, and it didn't go unnoticed. Euan smiled, raised her hand to his lips, and kissed it before he tucked her arm in his as he led her inside.

When the herald announced them, they walked inside the ballroom and paid courtesy to all the guests there, a display which was returned. Jeanne was already there, and they made their way toward her as she smiled brightly.

"Monsieur and Madame Cameron! How glad I am to see you. Monsieur always livens up a party, and we have missed him at our table these last days."

"I am sorry to have deprived you of his company, Marquise. He has been so diligent about tending to me."

"It is the best reason of all for him not to be present. I must say you both look beautiful and that necklace was the perfect choice."

"Yes, thank you ever so much for sending it. It was exceedingly kind of you."

"Well, when your husband sent me a note asking if I would be so kind as to direct him to where he might find something special for you to wear this evening, I decided to send one of my own. As ill as you have been, you should have a chance to sparkle like a queen, madame. Or the mistress of a king," she said, winking.

Both Grace and Euan laughed, but the entire party came to a halt as the king arrived with the queen, and everyone paid them due courtesy, including Jeanne. Her relationship with the queen was cordial, as Jeanne didn't seek to replace the queen, nor act as though she had done so. She served a function, one for which the queen was grateful.

As the music started again, Euan pulled Grace close to him. "Ye know what to do."

She gave a small nod and he stepped back and smiled at her before he moved aside to speak to some of the other ladies.

When the king approached them, they paid him courtesy again. "Madame Cameron, you *do* look exquisite. You look as though you have come from amongst the stars with the way you shimmer in that gown."

"Thank you, Your Majesty. I wanted to be sure to impress you, as I have been so absent from your company of late."

"You have succeeded, and yes, you have been. Why?"

"I wanted to be sure I was truly mended from my illness so that I might be here. I certainly could not entertain you as I was."

"Then we are all fortunate you are well again," he said as he took Grace's hand and kissed it but did not release it. "I do thank you for your counsel of the other day, madame. It has given me much to consider."

"It is as I had hoped then, Your Majesty."

"Perhaps you may be as useful in that regard as the Marquise."

"If I can be then I would be more than happy to be of assistance."

"I think you could be. The both of you ladies," he said, looking at Jeanne before taking her hand in his free one and kissing it. "What a lucky man I should be to have two such angels in my confidence."

"Fortunate indeed," Jeanne said. "Madame Cameron would be quite the victory, Your Majesty."

"Would she?"

Jeanne smiled. "See how in love she is with the Captain? I

have tried to tell her how silly such affections are, how his head will eventually be turned, but she does not believe me. What a conquest for you if you are able to turn hers first."

Grace didn't let the shock of Jeanne's words register in her expression, smiling at the king instead. She knew that Jeanne was part of whatever Euan's plan was, and she was clearly trying to help Grace play hers.

"I think you are right, my dearest Marquise. It is possible that by the end of the evening she may know that such love does not always last for long. It burns brightly and then fades. In the end, we men are as we are."

Grace suddenly very much wanted to yank her hand back and leave, but she knew she couldn't. "I think I will not, but I look forward to you trying to convince me otherwise, Your Majesty."

He gave her a half smile and kissed her hand again, lingering a bit this time. "You shall dance with me."

Not a request but an order and it irritated her. "As you wish it, of course," Grace replied as she curtsied.

He released the hands of both women and went back to sit with the queen as Jeanne stepped up beside her.

"He will sit with her for a while, and then she will retire," she whispered to Grace. "I am sorry for what I said, but I saw what you were trying to do. I knew that for you to do such it was because your husband had asked you to. I know full well that you would never stray from each other."

"I know, and I thank you for your assistance," Grace whispered in reply.

"Flattery always works," Jeanne said. "He is a king, after all."

"He is a man."

"Too true, and all of them love to have their egos stroked, do they not? I would wager even Euan is the same."

"At times I think we all are. However, Euan has not lived a life of being constantly flattered. He has seldom heard anything other than brutal honesty."

"It is unfortunate," Jeanne said. "Louis is a good man at heart, but he does not understand what the world outside is really like. Every time he makes a decision, he is told it is the finest decision ever made by a king, even if it is the wrong one, and then his ministers quietly change things or try to find a way to get him to change his stance. He wants to be a good king to France, he wants to be loved, but do you know what he wants most of all?"

"No, what?" Grace asked as she looked over at Jeanne.

"Love, a true love where he is loved for himself. Not for a crown or the favor he can bestow, but for a woman to discover who he truly is and love that man that he hides."

"And you do not provide that?"

"In my own way but not, I think, in the way he truly desires. I wonder if he will ever find it."

"Surely you do not love him just because he is the king."

"At first, yes, I did. I will not insult you by lying about it for you are far more astute than that. No, at the start I was just like everyone else. Then I got to know him, and he pulled me into his confidence. He showed me his vulnerability and that, under it all, he was just as the rest of us: a frightened being yearning to be loved. I do love him, but I am not in love with him in the way you are with Euan."

"Do you think she does?" Grace asked, looking at the queen.

"No, but how could she? They were strangers. They have grown to be fond of each other, to love each other in their own way, but there is still not the kind of love he seeks."

"And you?"

"Me?"

"Have you ever felt such a love?"

"No," she said in a quiet voice, "but then I never expected to. I am not sad for it, nor do I wish you to be so for me. Your love is rare, madame, and you should hold onto it as tightly as you can. You are everything to him, and it is plain to see any time he or anyone else in his presence speaks of you."

Grace smiled for a moment. "He is the same to me."

"Clearly," Jeanne said with a small laugh. "Though I cannot

blame you. Look at him! You would think God himself had a hand in the making of him. There has been a great deal of speculation amongst my ladies."

"Speculation on what?"

"On whether the rest of him lives up to what we can see."

Grace's laugh was loud before she pressed the backs of her fingers to her lips and Jeanne grinned.

"Oh, do tell me, I so want to know."

Grace cleared her throat to try and stop laughing. "It does."

"Which part?"

"All of it."

"Indeed! So, one of those rare specimens who is not only gifted but talented in the use of said gifts."

"Yes, *quite* talented," Grace said through laughter she could no longer suppress.

Jeanne, too, was laughing now. "What a shame we shall not get to find out and try him ourselves."

"A *very* great shame," Grace said, grinning.

"Oh, you do taunt me, madame," Jeanne said. "You are terrible, and I adore you for it."

"I will not deny it."

"Of course you will not! You revel in it."

"I most certainly do."

"No wonder you are together, you are the same person!"

The two of them laughed together, Grace nearly crying from laughing so much. It felt good to laugh, something it felt as though she hadn't done in weeks, though it hadn't been that long here. Across the room, Grace caught sight of Euan with one of the ladies, and her laughter died.

"Now, you know full well he means none of it," Jeanne said.

"I know, but that does not make it easier to watch."

"You dearly wish to slap her back to Paris for her audacity, do you not?"

"More than," Grace said, a dark edge to her voice.

The change in her tone brought a surprised look to

Jeanne's face. "You do not strike me as the sort of woman prone to violence."

"I survived a war, Marquise, I am prone to a great many things."

"Touché, Madame Cameron. I suppose you would be."

"He does not suffer weak women, or silly ones, however."

"Clearly. Have you, like him, taken a life?"

"Besides my own?" Grace thought to herself, but she shook her head. She couldn't answer that with certain truth because she couldn't remember. She could only hope she hadn't had a reason to do so. "Not yet. It does not, however, mean I could not or would not if I felt justified in doing so."

"I am not sure I could."

"You could if the situation was right. Anyone can, I think."

"What situation would that be?"

"If someone came to you intent on ending your life, would you just sit and allow it, or would you fight back and seek to end their life instead, for daring to do such a thing to you?"

"Hm, I suppose you are right there."

"You would do it to defend the king."

"Yes, I would," she admitted.

"So, you see?"

"I truly had not thought of it, but I suppose you are correct. Everyone has a point, a line, and if you cross it your life is potentially forfeit."

"Everyone," Grace repeated, her tone firm.

The queen rose and all movement, music, and conversation ceased, all of them bowing or curtseying to her before she departed. Once she had, the music and the party resumed once more.

"Madame Cameron," the king said as he approached. "Come, we shall dance."

That he'd wasted no time after the queen had departed seemed to amuse Jeanne greatly. "Well, it seems I have been supplanted already."

"Nonsense," he replied. "No one shall be put above you, Marquise, only beside you."

"More like on either side of you tonight if you have your way."

"Something like," he said, smiling. "Now, come."

Grace placed her hand in his when he offered it and let him lead her out onto the dance floor. She knew full well that no one else would join them here unless he gave them leave, and she had a feeling he had no intention of doing so. He wanted to be the center of attention, wanted to be seen with her, wanted the other men to envy him. As she took her place in front of him, she saw Euan, and she couldn't tell if the look on his face was true displeasure or what he was putting on. Either way, it was obvious he was less than pleased.

When the music began, Grace moved through the set of the dance, thankful that at least the skills inserted with her remained for her use. It was intimate, as it was meant to be, and it was why he'd called it. It kept her close to him and, whenever he could, he used it to his advantage to touch her. A fingertip along her shoulder or the inside of her arm, a brush of lips across her cheek. He would never fully make a move in front of the court, but they all knew his intentions. When the dance ended, the king drew Grace's hand up between them and placed a lingering kiss on it. Grace, for her part, pulled off a stunningly convincing expression of a young woman smitten with a king.

"You dance divinely, Madame Cameron. I hope your other talents are just as divine, as I suspect they are," he whispered to her as he drew a fingertip along the line of her jaw.

Grace smiled, but there was nothing shy in it. "Perhaps you will find out," she whispered in return, "if you are lucky."

"Is that a promise?"

"Not at all. I am not so easy as that, Your Majesty."

"I see. You are presenting me with a challenge then?"

Grace let a wicked smile appear on her lips before she plucked her hand from his, curtsying to him. There was a small sound of shock that rippled through the room at her daring to step back when he hadn't released her. The smile that spread across Louis' face matched hers, just as she'd known it would. A king he may be, but he was a man all the same, and if you gave in too easily, he would grow bored. If she was to hold his attention all night, she needed to play the seduction game, give him something to chase.

"Play on!" Louis called out before he looked at Grace. "Fetch Madame and come to my side," he said before he returned to his seat.

Grace forced herself to smile and made her way back to Jeanne.

"Oh, well done, very well done indeed. I am suitably impressed," Jeanne said. "He will be thinking about that all night."

"He wishes us to come to him."

"Of course he does," she said before she took Grace's hand and squeezed it. "I know," she whispered, "but you can do this."

Grace took a deep breath and released it, then nodded, following Jeanne as the other woman led her by the hand to the king. In a way, it made Grace feel like a lamb being brought to slaughter by another lamb who wished to help the wolf sate his appetite for the bodies of young women who intrigued him. The two of them stepped onto the dais and another chair was brought and set between the queen's seat and the king's. Jeanne and Grace took a seat on either side of him and there was another shocked whisper at such a display before he lifted each of their hands in one of his and turned his head from one side to the other to place kisses upon them. Both women smiled sweetly and then turned slightly toward him to engage him in conversation.

* * *

Euan watched as Grace did precisely as he'd asked. Now that the queen had retired, Jeanne and Grace were the center of the king's attention and, as much as it grated on him to see in the man's expression exactly what the king wished from Grace, he shoved it down. Euan reminded himself that all of it was necessary, and he had to admit that his wife was playing it masterfully. He'd asked for this, and she was doing her job. Though he wanted to storm forward and pull her bodily away from the king and his roving hands and lips, he refrained. The soft whispers that perhaps Euan had lost his wife after all, the glances in his direction, irritated him, but what irritated him more were the smug looks upon the faces of the chiefs at what they were sure was Euan's comeuppance. He knew he was going to revel in seeing those tables turned in short order.

Euan continued to play the game as Grace did, flattering and flirting with the ladies close to Jeanne. He had to make it seem as though they were both focused on nothing but enjoyment, and enjoyment with people other than their spouse. It would make them seem easy to catch in a mistake when all it would really do was draw the trap ever closer. He heard Jeanne and Grace share a genuine laugh, and he smiled to watch them together. This was his wife doing one of the things she did best: finding common ground with someone and bonding with them over it. It was unconscious most of the time, but it was why she was flawless at it. It was who she was, the type of person she was, and what Caia had meant when she spoke of Grace being one of those beautiful souls who drew you to them and made you always want to be in their company.

"Monsieur Cameron."

The female voice drew his attention back to his current game, and he smiled. "Apologies, madame, I was simply wondering what the marquise and my wife were so amused by."

"Does it matter?"

"If they are talking about me, then yes."

"Let them talk," she said, stepping closer to him and placing a hand on his chest.

Euan looked down at it, then raised his eyes back to hers with a smile he knew she'd find tempting. It said what she wanted, though he didn't truly feel it. Indeed, he rather wished he could remove her hand from his body, but he had to play along. "Let them talk and then . . .?"

"You will be busy amusing yourself elsewhere and not notice."

"Perhaps," he replied, drawing a fingertip across the top of her hand where it still rested on his chest, and up along the inside of her ring finger. He felt her shiver, which brought a true smile to his face.

"You are the talk of court, monsieur, and we all wish to get to know you better. It is my hope I am the lucky one."

"Do ye, indeed? I make no promises."

"The night is young."

"Aye, it is."

"Let us go outside where it is less crowded."

"No," Euan replied, gently but emphatically, though he smiled. He wasn't about to leave Grace alone here, though he satisfied himself with the looks of irritation on the faces of Lochiel and the others as they realized they couldn't get close to the king. "Ye will need to be more creative than that if ye wish to seduce me away from my wife."

As the hours wore on, Euan could tell that the irritation of the chiefs was becoming anger. Louis was well into his cups by now, and it was clear there would be no discussion of anything tonight. Grace had more than succeeded in her task, and it was now time to free her from it and bring her back to him before anyone got any ideas about either bedding her or killing her. He excused himself from the women he was speaking with and turned to make his way toward where Jeanne and Grace sat, when he saw Lochiel approach them. He began to try to hurry toward her, but there were so many people it was difficult to move quickly, and Euan tried not to panic. He'd waited too long, and he could only hope to reach her before Lochiel made a move to end their feud.

Chapter 17

"Madame Cameron," Lochiel said with a bow as she stood and curtsied to him.

"Lochiel."

"Ye look to have made yerself invaluable tonight."

"No more than anyone."

When the king turned his eyes elsewhere, Lochiel reached out and grabbed Grace's elbow hard, bringing a shocked gasp from her, and pulling her close to him. The contact made her immediately dizzy, just as it had that first day, and though she tried to pull away from him, he held fast with an iron grip.

"Listen to me, lass," he hissed in a whisper. "If ye think ye are going to whore yer way into stopping us, ye are wasting yer time."

"I have no intention of doing any such thing. Release me."

"Then what are ye playing at?"

"Nothing, I just . . ." Grace found it difficult to focus, the world seeming unsteady in her vision, and she closed her eyes for a moment. "If he wishes to give me attention, I cannot say no. I am serving the king, as we all are."

"If ye keep it up ye may save me the trouble of yer murder, because Euan will do it for me."

"You assume he does not know that such a thing would be expected of me, and that I have no power to refuse it."

Lochiel chuckled, but it was a dark sound. "And ye assume he will care. He will kill ye before he surrenders ye, I promise ye that. Euan does nae like to share those things that belong to him."

"I am not a 'thing,' I am his wife. Please cease and desist in speaking of me as though I am property."

"Ye are," he spat, tightening his grip and making Grace wince. "Ye are *his* property, and he is mine. That makes ye mine as well, and if I thought I could get away with it, trust that I would kill ye here and now. Ye see, lass, yer death would break him, and he would be mine again to wield as I please. He may think he is free, but he is nae, nae as long as he lives. Even if I am gone, I have sons to whom he would be passed for their security. He is *mine*. Nae yers. *Mine*. Remember that."

Grace angrily yanked her arm free and moved past him. She needed to get away from here, and it was all she could think of as she hurried out of the ballroom. Her head felt so fuzzy, her vision expanding and contracting. The Hall of Mirrors sparkled in front of her, lit by what seemed to be a thousand candles. She walked toward them, watching the flames dancing in the crystal of the chandeliers and glass. Sliding onto a bench, she closed her eyes as the room began to spin. The sound of laughter rippled around her, and someone helped her stand. The arms were familiar, as was the feel of the hand that slid into hers. Another hand was placed on her waist. She wanted to open her eyes but found she couldn't, instead resting her head upon his shoulder. The one who held her began a slow waltz down the hallway, spinning her with him. Something tugged on Grace; this dance wasn't right. This wasn't the right time period for it. But the thought slipped away with another turn.

"I know you," she whispered.

"Nae for long," he whispered back to her, the voice as familiar as the arms that held her close. "Ye will forget soon enough. The time is almost here, and soon it will all be over."

"Forget? What will be over?"

"Aye, forget. Ye must. It is nae real. He is nae real. I am real to ye in yer dreams, but I am dead and so are ye. He has taken ye from me, love, from us. Ye must forget him so ye can return. Forget all that has come before and after that day when we died together, ye and me."

"No . . ." she whispered, attempting to resist.

Forget. Something in her mind called to her. *Remember me, soon ye will be the only one alive who will.* No, you cannot forget. He asked you not to forget. Grace forced her eyes open, lifting her head and looking up, but the Euan who held her was not hers. His eyes were pure black, his smile dark and cruel. Grace screamed and tried to pull away from him, but he suddenly locked her in a vice-like hold, her body pressed almost painfully tight against his. She struggled to free herself as he laughed at her and spun her faster, the mirrors becoming a blur until she couldn't think. In the mirrors were laughing faces, their eyes as black as those of the one who held her, calling her name. Her head ached as it made a desperate attempt to hold onto something, something she could no longer remember.

Around and around, music and laughter, until it all suddenly ceased. Grace fell onto her hands and knees, feeling as though she might be sick. She took deep breaths, and when the feeling passed, she opened her eyes again. Where was she? Shaking, she pushed herself up and looked around, feeling panicked. There was supposed to be something she must remember. She looked back to the ballroom, why had she been there? Grace shook her head to try and clear it before she stumbled out through the open doors. Air. She needed air.

"Come home to us. To me."

The words seemed carried to her on the breeze, and she walked down the stairs to find the source of it. Grace tried to force herself to remember something, anything. What was her name? Grace, her name was Grace, but she found it was the only thing she could remember. Where was she? Why was she here? How had she come to be there? There was more, she knew there was more, but she couldn't think of any of it. There was only a void, a blackness where those things should be. Her head ached terribly, and she only wanted it to stop.

"Grace? Are ye all right? I saw ye sit down to rest, and then ye fell forward onto the floor nae long afterward. Are ye feeling ill again?"

She whirled around quickly to see a young man standing there. He looked concerned; he knew her name. He was so handsome.

Remember me.

Grace winced, those words made her head hurt even more and she clutched it between her hands. "Who are you? How do you know me?"

* * *

Euan approached Grace as she stood in the gardens, keeping his steps slow so as not to startle her, because it was clear to him that something wasn't right. "Grace? Are ye all right? I saw ye sit down to rest, and then ye fell forward onto the floor nae long afterward. Are ye feeling ill again?"

Grace turned around and Euan's chest tightened as his wife looked at him with no sign of recognition before she held her head in clear pain. "Who are you? How do you know me?"

"Grace, love, it is me. Euan," he replied.

"Euan. I do not know anyone named Euan. I should go home. Please, find someone to help me go home. I do not know where I am or how I got here, and I feel so unwell."

"Of course ye know me. I am yer husband. Grace, please, ye have to know me," he pleaded, his voice tight.

"Husband?" She looked at him in confusion and then shook her head. "No, no, I have no husband. Please leave me be and send someone to help me."

Fear and pain clutched at Euan's heart as her words sunk in like a knife. *I have no husband.* She didn't remember him. The very thing they'd both feared had happened.

"Grace, ye have to come with me. Ye need to rest. Let me take ye home," he said as he moved toward her.

Grace backed up in a quick defensive movement. "No! Leave me alone! I do not know you!"

Euan understood her reaction even if she no longer did. With no memory of him she'd reverted to her previous distrust of men. There was nothing he could do but what he was about to do, and he made a swift move to grab her around the waist. Grace screamed in terror and fought against him, shoving at him and clawing at his hands and arms as she tried to get away from him. In the next moment, she surprised him by throwing an elbow back into his gut and he released her in shock. Grace fell to the ground but scrambled up, lifting her skirts as she started to run back toward the palace.

"Grace!" Euan called out as he ran after her. Catching up to her, he reached out, grabbing her left wrist and pulling her back around to face him. "Stop!"

"No! Let me go! Let me—" Her words were cut off and she cried out in pain. She looked up, her expression a mixture of confusion and extreme pain. "Euan? What is happening? How did I get here? I—" the words died on her lips as the pain turned them into a cry of pain, and then all she could do was sob.

"Aye, love it is me. Euan. Yer Euan. Grace—" He had no chance to continue as Grace's legs gave out beneath her and she collapsed into his arms, forcing him to kneel and lower her to the ground. "Grace!"

Euan tried not to panic as Grace collapsed but he couldn't stop it. Something about this felt different, felt wrong. This wasn't like the other times and he knew it.

"GRACE!" he screamed as he tried to shake her awake. "SOMEONE HELP ME!"

One of the pages had seen what had happened between them and had gone inside to alert the king and the guard. Guests flooded outside to see what was happening, but Euan took no notice of them as men hurried toward him. One of them lifted her up so that Euan could stand, and once he had,

Euan picked her up, following the two men back toward the palace. As they passed Lochiel and the others, he saw a small, satisfied smile cross the man's face and it made him sick. Euan hurried after the two men leading the way, now recognizing them as the king's guard. He was ushered into the private areas and shown into a room, where he laid her down on a table.

"The surgeon has been sent for monsieur," one of them said.

Euan nodded but he knew there was nothing the man was going to be able to do. This was something far beyond any of his capabilities. Euan took her hand in his, but it felt lifeless and heavy. "Love . . . love, wake up . . . please. Please nae yet, nae yet. Stay with me just a little longer, we are almost there. Please, I beg ye."

The king hurried into the room, followed closely by Jeanne, well and truly sobered by the shock of the news that something had happened to Grace. "What has happened?"

"I dinnae know," Euan said, not bothering with titles or trying to hide how distraught he was. None of it mattered to him now. "She went outside, and when I went after her she was confused. She did nae remember me at first, but then she did and collapsed."

"Has she done this before?"

"No. She has been ill, but nae like this," Euan said as he cupped her cheek. "Grace, wake up," he whispered through tears. "*Mo ghràidh*, please, wake up and come back to me. Please."

Out of the corner of his eye, Euan saw Jeanne's hand go to her mouth, saw the tears in her eyes. He knew what this looked like. She knew what he'd feared, and it was happening.

"Euan, I do not think—" Jeanne began.

"No." he said firmly. "She is still breathing and that means there is still a chance. We dinnae need the surgeon. Please, just let me take her home."

The king nodded to the guard, who dispersed to call off the surgeon and bring a carriage around for Euan. "Captain, I hope with all of my heart that she comes away from this."

"Thank ye, Yer Majesty," Euan said, forcing the words past the lump in his throat. "I must request a meeting with ye in the morning. With ye and the others."

"Will you not be tending to madame?"

"She would want me to do this no matter what. Please."

"Very well, if it is her wish, then you shall have it. I will make sure the others are alerted."

"Again, thank ye."

Euan scooped Grace up from the table as one of the men returned to let him know the carriage was ready and hurried out with her. Once he got her home, the house erupted in upset at the sight of Grace. He told them not to disturb him, and they understood it to mean that the death watch had begun. The maid helped to undress her and get her into bed, and then left the room. Euan knelt beside the bed and took her hand, kissing it before he dissolved into tears.

"God, love, please dinnae go. Hang on for me. I meet with them in the morning, and if I succeed, we can go home, they can treat ye there. They can fix this. I need ye here. I need ye with me. I need ye . . ." he sobbed.

There was no response from her, not even a tremor, and he felt deep down that it was already too late. He hadn't moved fast enough, hadn't been able to save her. He'd failed her despite his promise not to.

I have no husband. I do not know anyone named Euan.

The words repeated in his head over and over with the memory of the fear in her face, the utter lack of anything resembling recognition, and everything in him hurt. He knew she'd tell him he still had a job to do and she'd want him to do it. She'd said as much before this and he could not and would not let her down now. Even if she didn't know it, he couldn't fail her in this. The only true question was how much longer he really had.

Chapter 18

The image of Euan flickered and then faded away as Forbes strode through the doors to the chambers of his own Command. "Commander," he said with a bow.

"Good evening, Forbes. I take it your latest venture was successful?"

"Oh yes. If I come to her as him, she doesn't fight me. She's close."

"Excellent. What did you get this time?"

Forbes' laugh was cold. "Almost everything. She forgot him entirely. We also tried to see if we could get any idea of what the plan is to stop Lochiel and the others, but unfortunately he doesn't seem to have told her."

"And she is still alive?" the Commander asked in surprise.

"The link between them is still strong enough to pull her back, but not for long. That's what saved her, and we must rid her of it. The Companion was able to bring her memory of him back when he grabbed hold of her, but that won't work next time. He's strong here, but there's only so much he can do, and he'll soon find himself weakened as she gets worse. The opening to forget him has been made, the suggestion is there, and tonight caused a significant break in that link. I wanted to see if we could do it and we did. She's ready."

"What makes you so sure?"

"They can't leave until their mission is complete. We've had the time to do damage and that's what we needed. As long as the others keep whispering to the chiefs of war, the longer their mission takes and the longer we have access. He senses it, he feels her slipping away from him, but doesn't know what to do. She won't wake now, and she's already lost to him in that sense. We'll do one last small incursion to take everything away that he succeeded in bringing back, leaving her with only the moment she died for him."

"You could take more."

"I could but, as you said before, it's sweeter to take our time. Let him suffer, let him watch her dying, let him be helpless. The final time we pull her in, we'll pull her in all the way. It will make it impossible for him to find her and thus impossible to stop us. We can take everything that's left then, everything but that final moment, and she'll come to us willingly, as she must. It's time to make The Council pay for their mistake in sending her and for us to take our rightful control back from them. His time to save her has run out, and it's time for the Camerons to die."

Chapter 19

Grace hurried along a palace corridor, looking for something, though she didn't know exactly what that was. It was devoid of others, unlike how it normally was, and that concerned her. Where was everyone? The sound of her heeled shoes on the floor echoed off the walls in the vast, empty space. She stopped walking and looked around her, turning a slow circle. The corridor seemed endless.

"Euan?"

Euan. She was looking for Euan! Of course! Yes, he had to be here somewhere. She started down the corridor once more before she finally came to a door and pushed it open.

"Love? Are you here?"

She was met only by silence as she stepped inside a room she'd never seen before. There were objects everywhere, things she didn't recognize. Small stones with lines carved into them, a large piece of black glass. Jars and bottles. Grace frowned and picked up a bottle, unable to read the markings upon it. She set it down and investigated the black glass, seeing her reflection but nothing more. She picked up one of the small stones, tracing a fingertip over the carvings. It looked like a small fish. Where was she and why would Euan be in such a strange place?

"He is not here."

Grace turned around to find an old woman standing there. She looked bent and haggard, her hair long and stringy, hanging over her heavily lined face. Her clothing was tattered, her dirty fingernails long like claws, and Grace found her presence deeply unsettling. How had she gotten here without her noticing?

"What do you mean? Of course he is here. He should be here."

"He is not. He cannot be. You are in a place he cannot follow, and he cannot help you now."

"Help me?"

"Save you. He cannot save you. No one can."

"Save me from what?"

The woman laughed but didn't answer, and Grace moved forward to go past her. If Euan wasn't here, she needed to look for him elsewhere.

"Watcher," the woman said, grabbing Grace's wrist to stop her movement. Grace looked at her in shock at the use of the title, and the woman laughed at her again.

"Yes, I know what you are. I know *who* you are. You cheated Death. You stole from Him, stole a soul from that field."

"Stop, let go of me!" Grace said, trying to wrest herself free while fighting a rising panic.

The woman held fast and tightened her grip, bringing a small, pained sound from Grace. "You have come back now, back within His reach, and Death wishes to collect what you owe Him. If Death cannot have *him* then He will have *you*. You made the trade and you will honor it. You are cut away from them and they cannot save you. You fear being killed, but you cannot die. You cannot kill what is already dead." She yanked Grace close to her, her breath hot and putrid. "The dead can never leave, and you are no exception. You will *never* leave."

She released Grace, who stumbled backward, her head pounding. The dead can never leave. Had she died? Yes, she had, she had died. Culloden.

"You understand it now. You died here not long ago and yet you are back. You cannot exist here and will not for much longer.

Grace shook her head, unable to speak.

"Othila," the crone said with a dark smile.

"What?"

"The rune you hold is Othila. The rune of radical separation. A fitting choice, for it will come to pass soon enough. In fact, it already has."

Grace looked down with horror at the stone in her hand, at the carving, before dropping it and fleeing the room. When she was gone, the image of the woman faded, and Forbes laughed. It was gone now, all gone. Oh, how he relished taking this all from her. She was in their world now, and there was no getting out.

"Death to the Camerons," he whispered with a sadistic grin.

Chapter 20

Euan stayed beside Grace all night, somehow hoping she'd come around and that this wasn't happening. Nothing had changed, no matter how much he hoped it would. All he could do was wait for the morning to come so he could finish this, and they could be together. Whatever this was had managed to do what Lochiel himself had wanted to do and he hadn't even needed to act. Euan felt weaker now, just a little, but it was noticeable, and he knew what it meant. No one needed to tell him. She was almost gone. Euan stroked her hair and leaned down to kiss her forehead.

Death to the Camerons.

Euan stood up like a shot, grabbing his dirk and looking around for the source of the sound. What in the hell was that? It hadn't sounded human; it was like a hint of conversation carried on the wind. He looked back at Grace and knew she hadn't said it. Euan sat back down, wondering if he was hearing things, and the words never came again.

As morning crept in, Euan rose from her bedside and dressed himself. This was the moment they'd been working toward, and he could only hope his plan would work. Normally he'd feel far more sure of himself, but he found it hard to be so now. He made his way to the bed and kissed Grace. "Duty calls, love. I will be with ye soon."

He stepped away from her with great reluctance before turning his back on her. It seemed so final that he hated to do it, but he forced himself out of the room and away, grabbing a small bag on his way out. His horse was waiting for him as he'd requested, and he turned it toward the gate before riding out toward the palace. When he arrived, he did his best to ignore the whispers, knowing that they were all talking about what had happened the previous night. He couldn't think about it, couldn't let his mind dwell on the knowledge that the love of his entire existence lay dying and he wasn't with her.

"Captain Cameron to see the king. He is expecting me," Euan said to the page as he arrived.

"Of course, come this way, monsieur."

Euan stepped through the doorway and followed the young man toward the chamber where they'd all met previously. He took a deep breath to steady himself and released it before he opened the door. The king and the others were already present, and Euan bowed. He could see from what was laid out that they had already been back to talking strategy.

"Ah, Captain Cameron, welcome. I hope Madame Cameron has recovered?" the king asked, his tone hopeful.

"She has nae, Yer Majesty. There is no improvement."

"I am so very sorry for it."

"As am I," Lochiel said, though it was clear to Euan he didn't mean a word of it, and Euan refused to even look at him lest it break the last vestiges of his control and made Euan kill him.

"You asked to meet with me, Captain. What do you need to say?"

"I have come about Scotland."

"Come to yer senses at last?" Lochiel asked.

"No," Euan replied testily, still refusing to look at Lochiel. "I am here to ask ye nae to go forward, Yer Majesty. It is a fool's quest these men lead ye on."

"A fool's quest!" Murray shouted at him. "How would ye know anything, ye are naught but a whelp."

Euan ignored him. "Ye have heard from my wife what it was like, what it is like there now. There are nae enough men left to fight a war, and those that are there will nae fight for the Stuarts."

"Yer wife," Lochiel spat. "I knew she had something to do with this."

Euan finally looked at him, his glare deadly and dark. "Dinnae ye *dare* speak ill of her as she is dying," Euan hissed through clenched teeth. "She is a Cameron and deserves yer respect."

"How do you know they will not fight?" the king asked, bringing the subject back around before anything else could be said about Grace that might cause someone to end up dead in this room.

"The ones that are left fought for the Hanovers. The rest are imprisoned, transported, or executed. There is no one left for them to lead."

"I already told ye how we will handle that," Lochiel said.

"And I have told ye they will nae follow ye. Even if ye find any clan still supporting yer cause, they will nae risk their lives for ye now. Ye were nae there to see the retribution, but I was."

"How dare ye!"

Euan ignored the outburst and pressed on. He would deal with Lochiel later. "I will nae lie to ye, Yer Majesty: they will nae fight. Scotland is in tatters, and there is no taste for rebellion now. Nae anymore. They would join with the English before they would fight for the Stuarts again."

"Slanderous lies!" Murray shouted.

"Nae lies." From the bag he carried, Euan pulled a stack of parchment. "I have letters from the remaining clans pledging to fight against any landing force sent to Scotland — by France or any other country — on behalf of the Stuarts."

Lochiel and Murray's faces paled. "How did ye—" Lochiel stammered.

Euan smiled at him. "How did I get them? Ye did nae honestly think I just arrived here by accident, did ye? We got wind of yer plan, and I was sent to ask ye to cease."

"We?"

"The other clan leaders and myself."

"They would never have seen ye. Ye are naught to them, and to have ye in their presence would earn them charges of harboring a traitor," Lochiel said.

"Ye would be right, which is why I used my best asset to make contact with them. My wife was nae a soldier, so seeing her was no crime. If she were stopped or questioned, well, she is English, is she nae? Or at least they would think she was. I sent messages with her, and she returned with these signatures. The signatures of the chiefs," Euan said as he looked over at Lochiel. "And their sons," he added pointedly.

"Ye treasonous bastard. Ye have turned spy for the English, and that is how ye survived!"

Euan laughed, but it was cold. "No. I had no need to do such a thing and ye know it. I survived because that was what I was trained to do. I told ye I would fight against ye for my country, and that is exactly what I have done," he said as he handed the letters to the king, who looked through them.

"There are even seals on some of these, Lochiel," the king said.

"They are authentic," Euan replied. "The ones without are those who had their titles stripped from them, along with their seal. As ye will see, even the Murrays have signed."

Murray looked apoplectic, but Lochiel had no intention of giving up. "I still have my own men, Yer Majesty, and we have the Prussians and the Spanish."

"But you have no support at home, Lochiel," the king countered.

"The Camerons will come out to fight for me. It is their duty."

"No," Euan replied. "They will nae."

"What?"

Euan pulled the last piece of paper from his bag and held it up. "A document signed or marked by every living Cameron man I could find, saying they will nae follow ye."

Lochiel's eyes widened, his face reddening with rage. "If

the Camerons dinnae follow me, then they are traitors to their clan!"

"They see ye as the traitor. The traitor who left them to suffer and die."

"Who will they follow if not their chief, Captain?" the king asked.

"Me."

"Impossible!" Lochiel shouted.

"Definite," Euan replied as he handed the document to the king.

The king took it and looked it over, then slowly looked up at Lochiel. "Their renunciation of you as their leader, and their nomination of Captain Cameron to lead them into battle if he must, is plainly written here, Lochiel."

"They did nae know what they were signing!"

"They did. It was read to them and they were asked before they signed. The clan is no longer loyal to ye, and what is left of the regiment is under my control. Ye knew this day could come, knew that one day I could and would take them from ye if I felt I had to. Now I have, and there is naught ye can do about it. It is over for ye."

"Ye," Lochiel seethed. "After all I have done for ye, this is the path ye choose instead of fighting for me!"

"Wrong!" Euan shouted at him; his fury no longer able to be contained. "I gave ye *every* chance to stop this, and ye persisted. Ye forced me to do this, to humiliate ye and show ye in front of a king that ye are naught! I told ye they would nae follow ye, and ye did nae heed my warning to ye! I will repeat what I said to ye before: I am no longer yers to control! I have fought for ye all my life, but that time is done. Now, I fight for something bigger."

"Yer father would be ashamed of ye, at yer lack of loyalty!"

"I will nae allow ye to manipulate me any longer with the ghost of a man I never knew. I will nae let ye tell me what he would believe or what he would think of me. For far too long I let ye control me. I let ye direct me and I never questioned ye, even when I should have. I am more than the sum of what ye gave to me, and I will no longer stand for ye telling me what I am and what I am nae. Before anything else, I am a Highlander and Scot, and it is for the Highlands and Scotland I will fight, nae for ye."

"Lochiel, I am inclined to agree with the Captain that such an expedition seems ill fated if you do not even have the support of your own people," the king said.

"Dinnae listen to him, Yer Majesty. We can still take it with the Prussians and the Spanish. We dinnae need those traitors! They will pay for it with their lives when the time comes." Lochiel looked at Euan now. "And ye? Ye are dead to me. Yer mutiny has signed yer death warrant, and I will more than enjoy killing ye. I want ye to suffer, and I will make sure ye do. I will take everything ye love from ye first, until ye beg me for death."

"Ye cannae take what is already gone," Euan replied in a flat voice. "Everything I loved has been stolen from me by unseen forces; by war, by treason, by the English. I will nae beg ye for death because death is coming for me already. His breath is on my neck and I welcome him, for he will give back to me all that I have lost."

"Enough," the king said. "I have made my decision. France will not commit more money, weapons, or troops to another attempt to restore the Stuarts. We will not engage our allies on another front. The support is not there, and even if the young prince somehow managed to win, he would find himself tossed off the throne soon enough."

"But Yer Majesty!"

"ENOUGH!" the king shouted. "I am done with this talk! Take yourself from my court and trouble me no more with this. If you want to continue, I suggest you find someone else sympathetic to your cause, for I no longer am. Captain Cameron, please remain a moment."

Lochiel and the others stormed out, and Euan closed his

eyes, saying a silent prayer of thanks. It was done. His plan had worked. "What may I do for ye, Yer Majesty?"

"You truly love your country, and I appreciate that in you. You went against your own chief even though it could have meant your death, and still may. More, you went against the man who raised you. I know what that is like. I had to do the same with my uncle."

Euan nodded. "It is never easy, but ye do what ye must when yer country requires it of ye."

"Yes, you do, and I think both you and I know and understand that better than most. You may go but be careful. I feel this will not be over yet." The king stood and handed the documents back to Euan. "You should keep these. You may need them."

"Thank ye, Yer Majesty. It *is* over, at least for me," Euan said with a bow before he turned and left the chamber. A sense of relief flooded him, but it was short-lived as something ripped through him with such force it sent him to his hands and knees. As he tried to catch his breath, dread swept through him.

"Grace," he whispered before he forced himself up and ran for the forecourt.

Chapter 21

"Grace."

The sound of her name being spoken seemed to bring her out of wherever she'd been. She couldn't remember where that was, but it didn't seem to matter. She felt a cold wind on her face, and it carried with it a scent that was familiar. Her eyes opened, the light blinding at first until her eyes adjusted. She found she stood in the middle of a frozen moment. All around her were men standing still in positions suggesting they had been in action just before she'd opened her eyes. In their hands were swords, muskets, pistols. Some were in the process of falling, others charging forward. She turned and looked behind her to see a line of soldiers in red coats, all of them shouting and firing at the men running toward them. Smoke hung in the air, musket balls stopped where they were, and Grace frowned, looking down at her white dress. She knew this place, these men, but how? Who were they and who was she to them?

"Grace, love."

Grace turned back around to find a young man standing there, the only one moving amongst the stillness. He seemed familiar too, though she couldn't say why. He knew her and perhaps he could answer all of her questions. "Hello," she said, her voice as wary as her countenance. "Who are you and where is this? Why am I here?"

He smiled and walked toward her, picking his way through the motionless figures. "Ye have returned at last," he replied, ignoring her questions.

"Returned?"

"Aye, to me, to us. This is where ye belong."

Grace shook her head. "I do not know where I am or who you are, you still have not told me, so I have no idea what you mean."

"Who I am is nae important. Ye are here where we died, on this battlefield together, ye and I. Ye tried to save me but you could nae."

"Died? No, I cannot die."

"It will come to ye in a moment."

"If we died together, why do I not remember you?"

"Memories dinnae matter here. All that matters is that I have been waiting on ye. We can finally rest now that ye have come home."

Before she could reply, the memory hit her all at once and the stillness shifted, the men moving into action with a clash of steel and screams and guns for just a moment before it all froze once more. She knew where she was now. "No . . . no I do not want to be here! You have to let me out!" she said in a panic.

"Ye have no choice, lass. It is all that is left for ye now."

"You have to let me leave! You cannot force me to stay here!"

"I am nae the one who is forcing ye. Death is forcing ye. Ye cannae escape it, Grace. Ye are dead, and ye must go where yer spirit is to remain."

"Why will you not tell me your name?"

"I am Euan. Yer Euan, the one ye died for."

"Euan," she whispered to herself though the name dredged up no memory. She'd died for this man, but she couldn't remember anything about him.

"Aye."

Grace put her hands to her head. It hurt terribly, as though someone were squeezing it. "What if I refuse?"

"Ye cannae. There is no way out now that ye are here. Come to me. Come and the pain will all be over."

Pain. There had been so much here. The figures shifted

again, bringing sound, and then stillness. Grace closed her eyes to try to block all of it out, but it was no use. It was there to taunt her in the darkness behind closed lids. The sound of shots rang out and she could feel the balls strike her, her body jerking forward as she screamed and fell, the pain in her body now as excruciating as the pain in her head. Grace lay on the moor, sobbing and screaming.

"Ye dinnae have to remember more. All ye must do is come with me. Take my hand."

"No!" Grace said through her tears. Something didn't feel right about any of this.

The Council will be ours.

Grace looked up at the sound of the strange whisper, unsure of where it was coming from. The Council. What was that?

"Grace, it will do ye no good to fight this. Ye will suffer more than ye need to," he said, his hand extended. "I loved ye and still do. Come to me now and let me take the pain away. I have longed for ye."

Love. I loved you. Had she loved him? Grace pushed herself up shakily, backing away from him, her expression puzzled even as tears of pain continued to run down her cheeks. "Why were you stuck here, and I was not?"

"Something parted us, but it is gone now."

"I do not understand this."

"Ye dinnae have to. It does nae matter. None of it matters now. Please, come."

Something seemed to flicker, the men moving again but stopping just as quickly. A look of panic briefly crossed his face.

"Ye have to come, love. There is nae much time left."

Another flicker sent the men around her into a burst of action and this time the movement brought more pain for Grace. Something seemed to hit her in the chest, and she screamed in agony at the pain it brought her, falling to her knees, but when she looked down there was nothing there. She clutched her chest and there was a flash of something.

Laughter. His laughter. He was looking down at her as he lay beside her, long hair loose around his face, smiling.

I love ye, Grace. Dinnae forget that. Dinnae ever forget.

Forget. The voices had wanted her to forget. Grace looked at the man before her, at his outstretched hand. Something in her heart remembered him and she reached out her hand.

"Aye, that is it, come love. Ye must come to me. I cannae do it for ye."

ENOUGH!

The shouted word broke through in a way that seemed to surprise him, his expression becoming one of frustration, before he walked towards her. "Damn ye, woman! Hurry! There is nae much time! Dinnae let us be parted again!"

Go and you will be with him again. It is what you want.

Grace stood and stepped forward.

I will never leave ye.

His voice seemed to surround her even though he wasn't speaking. Where was it coming from?

Remember me as ye said ye would.

"Hurry!" he shouted at her impatiently.

As she got closer to him, she saw something in his palm, something golden. A ring. It drew her, she wanted to take it.

It is yours. Take it.

Her fingers reached out for it.

Kill her. The Watcher must die. Death to the Camerons.

Cameron. She knew that name. Somehow, she knew that name. Grace gasped and pulled her hand away, taking a step back.

Ye are a Cameron and ye earned those colors.

"NO! Take my hand damn ye!"

Grace shook her head in denial, the scene around her suddenly coming fully to life in a loud and cacophonous roar of men, steel, cannons, and gunshots. She saw him shout at her, but she couldn't hear him, his face a mask of rage. Without thinking, she grabbed a musket from the ground and swung it like a club, the butt connecting with his chest and sending him to the ground. The ring that had been in his hand rolled out onto the turf and she scrambled forward to pick it up, sliding it back onto her finger. As she got up to run, he seized her ankle and pulled her back down.

"You will not leave!" he shouted in fury; his accent gone. "You belong to us and we will never stop until you are dead!"

"NO!" Grace screamed, bringing the musket she still held down on his outstretched arm.

He screamed as the force broke his arm and he released his hold on her. Grace jumped up before he could grab her again and turned away, running into the crowd of charging men. They screamed and fell and pushed her, dying all around her as she ran back in the direction they were coming from, but she couldn't stop. Safety waited for her this way if she could only get to the other side. In the next moment, an explosion shook everything, the scene shattering like glass and becoming nothing but blackness.

Chapter 22

Euan raced out of the palace, not bothering to wait for his horse. Something had happened to Grace, he felt it, and he needed to get back to her. She couldn't leave without him, he had to be there. He couldn't and wouldn't let her die alone. He burst through the door of the house and took the stairs two at a time, throwing open the door to the room.

"Grace!"

He slid to a stop as he saw her sprawled out in the middle of the floor, face down and motionless. How had she gotten there? He hurried to her side, picking her up and turning her over.

"Grace, love. Grace," Euan pleaded as shook her and patted her face.

There was no response from her, and he realized she wasn't breathing, her lips starting to gain a hint of blue. He was too late.

"NO!" he screamed in desperation. "Grace! Please!"

Euan clutched her to him and wept, rocking her back and forth. She was gone, gone away from him, and he didn't know what waited for her or for him. He didn't know if they'd see each other in the hereafter, or if they'd be sent back in some other form, exiled from each other across centuries once more. The sound of a deep gasp for air startled him, and he pulled back from her in shock.

"Aye, breathe lass! Come back to me! Breathe!"

Grace's eyes fluttered open. "Euan?"

When she said his name, he couldn't help but to sob in relief.

"Aye, I am here. I have ye. Thank God above, I have ye now!"

"I know you," she whispered as she wrapped her arms around him, which only seemed to make Euan cry harder.

He couldn't explain what he felt; there was such a jumble of emotions. Relief. Happiness. Sadness. Pain. All of it mixed together in an overwhelming wave that swept through him. It was as though his entire world had been teetering on the edge of a precipice, only to be suddenly grounded and stable again. She remembered him, but how much?

"Please do not cry," she said in a weak voice as she smoothed some tears from his face.

"I cannae help it. I thought ye were—" he stopped short of saying the word. It felt as though to say it might make it happen. "Ye forgot me." There was so much hurt in those words and in his eyes when he said them, no matter how he tried to hide it.

Grace shook her head. "I could not forget you."

"But ye did, love. Ye did nae even know my name. Ye told me ye did nae have a husband before ye lost consciousness."

Grace frowned, and he watched her try to remember it but fail. "Why would I say that?"

"I dinnae know, but ye did. I tried to help ye, but I could nae get ye to come to me because ye did nae know me."

"Come to me," Grace whispered before she gasped and pulled back from him, holding her head as she had been doing whenever it hurt her.

Euan looked at her quizzically.

"Culloden. I was at Culloden. They wanted me to forget. Forget everything and come back so they could rest. I—" Grace whimpered as the pain seemed to increase. "You were shouting at me to take your hand, but it was not you. Not really you. I knew that. Somehow, I knew that, even though they did not want me to." She stopped and looked up, a frightened expression on her face. "Death to the Camerons."

Euan felt his blood turn to ice. "What did ye say?"

"Death to the Camerons. I heard them say it. They were whispering, but I heard them."

Death to the Camerons. The same words he'd heard as he kept vigil at her bedside the night before. They'd heard the same thing. "Who?"

"I do not know; I could not see them. You told me memories did not matter, nothing mattered. You told me I had to touch your hand, that you could not do it for me. You were so angry because I would not."

Euan shook his head, as confused as she was. "I dinnae know what ye are saying. That never happened."

"No, it did. It did, but it was not here. I was not here. I was somewhere else, and I was in danger, so much danger. I had to forget everything, but I did not forget you. You were still there in a place they could not reach," Grace said through her own tears. "Something in me remembered. He had his hand out, I needed to take his hand, but I would not. I ran from him, into the battle. There was an explosion, everything shattered, and then I woke up here with you."

He had his hand out. She needed to take his hand. Euan felt his stomach twist into a knot. "What did I look like?"

"You were wearing what you wore the day of the battle. Everyone was, even me. We were suspended in time somehow."

Time. "We need to see The Council. Right now."

"Why?"

Euan didn't answer her, instead pulling her up with him as he stood. Grace was unsteady and held onto him.

"Euan, we cannot. Not yet. We have to finish the mission."

"We have. It is done."

"You stopped them?"

"Aye, I did. The king has decided against another landing."

Grace smiled in relief and hugged him tightly, something Euan was more than happy to return.

"I could nae have done it without ye."

"I remember not being of much help."

"No, yer testimony to the king sat heavy with him. Ye did exactly what ye were meant to do. You befriended the Marquise and ye got an audience with the king."

"But it was you who truly stopped them."

Euan smoothed some of her hair back from her face. "We did it together, as we always do, and I will nae hear otherwise." He smiled and pressed his forehead to hers, closing his eyes. "Tell me what ye remember," he whispered.

"Everything," she whispered in reply. "I remember my mother, my grandmother, my training. I remember you. I remember home. I want to go home."

Euan sighed in relief. Whatever had happened, by some miracle she'd come back from it whole, and he was thankful for it. "I cannae tell ye how much I needed to hear that."

Grace reached up and stroked his cheek, just letting him hold her. After a few moments, he lifted his hand to cover hers, pressing it against his cheek. It was then that he felt it and pulled back, pulling her hand away from him. "Euan?"

"Yer ring. Ye have it again."

Grace looked at her hand. "Yes, they took it from me, but I took it back," she said before she cried out and pulled away from him. "Your marriage is a lie. It will make excellent balls for a rifle, perhaps one he will use to rid himself of you for good."

"What?" Euan asked, as confused as he was horrified by her words.

"No!" she cried out, stumbling away from him, and clutching her head in what was clearly intense pain.

"Grace, what is happening?"

"It hurts to remember. I am not supposed to remember what they did!"

"What who did?"

Grace shook her head. "I do not know!"

"If ye are nae supposed to remember, then how are ye doing so? Talk to me. Tell me before ye forget it."

"I was supposed to forget the nightmares." Grace

squeezed her eyes shut. "I remember because I heard it. The whispers. They said so. Make her forget."

"Do ye remember the nightmares now?"

"Only bits and pieces. Only the parts where the whispering interrupted my thoughts."

"Just enough to break yer focus. That is how ye remember."

Grace nodded in silence, still holding her head. "They wanted to take you away from me. They saved you for last."

The words made Euan feel sick. Whoever this was, they clearly wanted Grace dead, but they'd taken their time. They'd tortured her.

"But they did nae," he said in a gentle voice, pulling her back to him. "They could nae, nae truly. Ye were stronger than they were. I will contact The Council to update them on the mission and ask for one more day here before we go. Ye and I have loose ends to tie up before we can leave."

Later that night, he sat with her as she slept, close and protected with her head resting on his lap and her body snuggled against one of his legs. She'd been afraid to sleep, and he didn't blame her. He'd feared it, too. What if it was just another reprieve? But she was exhausted, and sleep found her whether she wanted it to or not. The thoughts in his head made him seethe with rage and made him feel sick, even though he had only hints of what had happened to her.

They'd done something to her mind, made her weaker and weaker, unable to mount any sort of effective resistance, then made her forget it had even happened. All of it taking place where he couldn't help her, in her dreams, the one place he couldn't follow her. Forgetting it ensured that she couldn't tell him what was happening, so he couldn't stop it or even try. He honestly had no idea what he would've done or how he would've helped her even if he'd known. What could he have done? Kept her awake for days somehow? They wouldn't have allowed Grace to return to The Council with those things in her head, it would've been too dangerous. What he couldn't figure out was how. How had this happened? What was this, and could it happen again? The only ones who could answer that would be The Council themselves.

Chapter 23

When she woke in the morning, Grace felt truly rested, and they were both relieved to find that she still remembered everything. He changed the bandages on her arm, and then sat with her as she ate. The conversation was relaxed, as it had always been before they'd come on this mission. Euan did his best to make her laugh, enjoying the sound of it. He realized he'd only heard her truly laugh twice in all the time they'd been here.

"I do wish ye could take that mantua gown with ye. Ye looked gorgeous in it."

"What would I do with such a thing at home? Wear it to cook dinner?"

Euan chuckled. "No, but it would be lovely for ye to have. Ye have nae worn anything quite as fine in all the time we have worked together."

"If you really want me to, you should ask them."

"The Council?"

"Yes, see what they say. If you were able to keep what you were wearing when they brought you forward, maybe it might work for me, too."

Euan pondered the idea, then gave a small nod. "I shall."

"I think you just want to be able to take me out of it."

"That is something I would consider a bonus and nae the main reason. At least someone who has seen ye in it can have that privilege, and it is nae the king."

Grace smiled and shook her head. "Madame was right."

"I told ye she was."

Grace kicked his leg under the table, and he raised an eyebrow.

"I cannae even feel any hurt from that, ye know."

"Shut up."

Euan laughed. "Ye are truly back now."

Grace rolled her eyes. "Let us get dressed. The sooner we finish this, the sooner we can leave."

As they walked into the palace together later that morning, Euan could hear the whispers again, but this time he knew they were because she was actually here and looking better than she had in the entire time she'd been present, and it made him smile. They could see her now as she truly was when she was healthy, no trace of strain upon her countenance. There was a gentle smile on her face as she entered on his arm, and he knew it was because she was happy in the knowledge they'd soon be home. For his part, he was still on guard for Lochiel's men, but he knew they wouldn't try anything in the middle of the palace with everyone to see them. They would end up dead, and it wouldn't be Euan's doing.

"Captain and Madame Cameron to see the king, if he would have us," Euan said to the guard in front of the door. "I also have Madame's necklace to return," Euan said, showing him the box he carried. The man nodded and the page standing near him hurried back with the request.

"I did nae expect to see ye here."

Euan stiffened and then turned around to face Lochiel.

"And clearly ye did nae expect to see me."

"No, I did nae. I would have thought ye might be gone by now."

"Murray is, and I will follow soon. No need to have apartments here if the king refuses to see us, and he does."

Euan nodded. "It is perhaps time to retire from war."

Lochiel smiled, though it was tired. "Ye cannae ever truly retire, can ye? I think ye know that better than most." He looked to Grace, his expression softening. "I would like to apologize to ye, for I cannae account for my behavior. I have never in my life treated a lass in such a way, and I am horrified by it."

Euan looked at him curiously, as Grace spoke up from beside him. "Thank you."

Lochiel didn't miss Euan's gaze. "I wish I could explain it but I cannae, just that I feel more at ease now than I have in some time. It was as if there was something in me, pushing me toward a fight I did nae really want, until I did nae remember that I did nae want it. I felt such a release from it yesterday after we left ye."

Euan felt Grace's hand tighten on his arm. "Something in yer dreams?"

"Aye," Lochiel said with a nod. "Dreams, a sense of something whispering in yer ear." He shook his head. "It is odd, but it does nae matter now."

"I am sorry it turned out this way," Euan said.

"As am I, lad, as am I. Ye did what was right, and the more I thought on it, the more I realized it. Someone had to stop us, and I feel as though it had to be ye. Ye were the only one who could, the only one who knew enough. As ye said, above anything else ye are a Highlander and a Scot, and it is for the Highlands and Scotland ye fight, even if that means going against yer own."

"I never should have had to."

"Ye are right. Those Cameron men who said they would follow ye made the right choice. The things I said to ye, I never should have said."

"They were the truth," Euan replied, his voice strained.

"Nae as true as ye may think, and it certainly does nae make them right, Euan. It does nae make what I did right. I thought I was doing what was best for ye, but ye were correct when ye said I used yer need for a father to make ye into what I wanted. Ye became all of that and more. What I did nae realize was that what I was creating would become stronger than I could have imagined and would someday be my downfall."

The conflict Euan felt was something he couldn't reconcile. This wasn't the same man he'd dealt with over the last several days, but the man he'd always known. Gone was the single-minded focus on war, and in its place was a man who looked worn by what he'd done and seen, by the suffering he knew he'd brought upon his clan. This was the man Euan knew wouldn't have dreamed of saying the things he had either to him or to Grace, and with his admission of hearing things in his dreams, Euan now wondered if he'd truly meant them. Had the words even been his own?

"Aye," Euan said.

The page reappeared. "The king will see you, Captain."

"Farewell to ye, Euan, I wish ye the best. Never forget who ye are and where ye came from. Never forget who and what ye are fighting for. I lost sight of that, and it will always be my greatest regret. Ye will always be a warrior, no matter what ye choose to do in yer life. Ye cannae take that out of ye. Use it well. Thank ye for what ye did here."

"Goodbye to ye, Lochiel," Euan said, bowing to the man.

Lochiel's smile was sad at the final gesture of respect from the young man who now owed him no allegiance and felt none. He nodded and turned, disappearing into the crowd of courtiers. Euan closed his eyes and lowered his head, trying to remain composed. Grace put a gentle hand on his chest, and he covered it with one of his own before he looked up at smiled at her.

"Come, the king waits for us."

The visit to the king was more of a formality than a personal visit. He was astonished to see Grace looking so well, but the conversation consisted of merely pleasantries and small talk. He thanked Euan for his intercession and the information he'd given, and then he dismissed them. It was not, however, truly the king they had come here to see. Euan had someone else to thank, and he very much wanted to do that in person.

Once announced, they were allowed entry to Jeanne's inner sanctum, and she was there before they'd even walked into the room. "Mon Dieu! Grace!" Jeanne cried out before forgetting all protocol and hugging her. "I feared the worst but prayed for you every day!"

Grace returned the embrace with a smile. "Thank you for it. It was close, but I seem to be past the worst of it now."

"And thank God for it! I do not know what Euan would have done otherwise."

"I came here to thank ye in person for all ye did, and to say goodbye," Euan said.

"Goodbye? You are not staying at court?"

"No. There are still battles of a different kind to fight in Scotland, and that is where we are needed now."

Jeanne's expression saddened. "I understand, but I cannot say I will not miss your company a great deal."

Euan smiled and held out the wooden box with the necklace she'd sent to him. "Ye will need this back, of course."

She took it and returned the smile. "I am glad it was of use to you."

"Without it, I would have had a much more difficult time."

"I can imagine. The king told me all about what happened yesterday. I wish I could have seen it. He said you gave quite the passionate speech."

"I simply spoke the truth."

"But it was the most powerful truth of all: it was your own."

"It is the only truth I can give."

"It the only truth anyone can give, Captain. Would you be so kind as to allow me a few words alone with Madame Cameron?"

"Of course," Euan said with a smile. "Farewell to ye, Madame. It was a great pleasure to have met ye," he said as he held out his hand, placing a kiss on hers when she gave it to him.

"And to you. Safe journey home."

***

Both women watched Euan depart before Grace turned to look at her curiously. "Is everything all right?"

"Indeed, I simply wished a moment of free conversation, as you and I have shared in your time here. One cannot speak so freely in front of a husband. Grace, my darling one, I will miss your presence and your humor. Thank you for sharing your magnificent husband with all of us. The ladies will be bereft when they learn of his departure."

Grace laughed. "I think he rather liked it."

"I do not know a man who would not."

"I hope things are different for you. I hope you find something more."

Jeanne smiled. "If I ever long for it, I shall think of you and Euan, and knowing it exists will be enough for me. I told you there is no need for sadness."

"Everyone should be loved."

"I am," she said. "Perhaps not in the way he loves you, but there is not one woman in a thousand who could claim such a love for her own. You are lucky in that you are the one in the thousand, and the rest of us take the next best thing."

"I wish it were not so."

"Wishing it was not so will not make it so, I am afraid. If that were the case, there would be a great many dead husbands and young women running off with their lovers."

Grace chuckled and shook her head. "I suppose that is true."

Jeanne studied her. "You are different."

"Oh?"

"I do not mean just now that you are well, but you are different than anyone else I have ever met and, I believe, will ever meet."

"What makes you say so?"

"I wish I could say. There is just something about you. You can be both strong and delicate, in such a way that no one can ever truly know the adversary you might be. I do believe Lochiel learned that the hard way."

"If he did, it was not from me. Not this time."

"This time. But before? Before you took something from him that he prized highly, and he hated you for it. You cheated Death, you pulled Euan from their clutches, and in doing so you set Euan free from a life that controlled his destiny."

"How do you know all of this?"

"Louis tells me much. I know what was said in that room, Grace. I know what Euan did."

"Tell me?"

Jeanne proceeded to tell Grace what she knew of Euan's meeting with the king and the chiefs. That there were harsh words spoken on all sides was not a surprise to Grace, nor was Euan's reaction to Lochiel's insulting her. It was when Jeanne mentioned Euan admitting to committing mutiny that Grace had to smother her look of confusion. Mutiny? What mutiny? She would ask him later. She did, however, frown at the mention of Euan's father.

"What a horrible thing to say."

"Indeed! What stood out to Louis was when he said 'I am more than the sum of what you gave to me, and I will no longer stand for you telling me what I am and am not.' It struck him enough to remember it word for word."

The smile that appeared on Grace's face was one of proud satisfaction. "They were words that very much needed to be said."

"Quite, but it gets better."

"Does it?"

"Yes! Lochiel told Euan that he was dead to him, and his mutiny had sealed his death warrant. He would enjoy killing him, wanted him to suffer, would take all he loved and make him beg for death."

"Good luck with that," Grace muttered.

"What Euan said in response was astonishing, and Louis told me it was branded into his very soul."

When Grace raised an eyebrow, Jeanne went on.

"He responded that he could not take what was already gone, that all he loved had already been stolen from him by forces unseen, that he would not beg for Death because Death was already coming for him, he could feel his icy breath and he welcomed it, for Death would restore all he had lost."

Grace closed her eyes and tried not to cry. "He was not wrong."

"What do you mean?"

"Everything he loves *is* gone," Grace said, opening her eyes again. "The life he knew, the people in it, the country he grew up in."

"I do not think that is all he meant. You were dying, after all, and he had no reason to believe you would survive. I saw him when you collapsed. He was disconsolate, weeping and begging you to wake and return to him."

Grace placed a hand against her chest, her heart aching. She could see it so clearly, as though she'd been there, but she knew it was because she would've been the same. "Euan," she whispered, trying to hold in tears. "I did not want to leave him; I would never want to leave him. I would do anything to come back to him."

"You have. Twice now. Once in battle and now this. But, Grace, even in all that misery, he insisted to Louis that they must meet in the morning. When Louis pointed out that Euan would want to be tending you, your husband told him you would want him to do this no matter what."

"I would have."

"I say all of this because I wish for you to know the things he cannot tell you. In all things, *you* are his focus. All he does, he does with you in his mind and his heart. The constant in his mind is always what *you* would think, what *you* would want or expect of him. Above all, your opinion is the only one that matters to him, and your opinion of him guides him in all choices. If he thought you would think less of him for something, he would refuse it, or at least hesitate. Men do not have words for such love, do not have a way to say it, but we do. I have never known a man so honorable, nor a man capable of such deep and unlimited love as Euan is."

"Thank you for telling me," Grace said. She knew Jeanne was right, in a way. Euan couldn't say any of that, or at least not that way. It was something only someone on the outside could see and put words to.

"I should let you return to him before he starts to wonder if I kept you here for a tryst with Louis," Jeanne said with a small smile.

Grace scoffed. "I mean no offense, but it would never happen. He is not for me."

"Oh, I know, though it would wound his pride to hear you say so. How could a woman not want a king?"

"Because so many women have had him, and I would be just another?"

"Yes, very true. Though I do like you a great deal, I would never let you share him with me on such a level."

Grace laughed. "Believe me, he is all yours, and you have nothing to fear from me on that score."

"Of course I do not! You have the beautiful and talented Captain!"

"I do indeed. Thank you for your company and your friendship," Grace said as she curtsied.

"None of that," Jeanne said as she stepped forward and embraced Grace in genuine affection. "Farewell to you, dear one, and if you are in France again, know that I expect you here."

Grace returned the embrace. "If we are in France again, I will come at once. You have my word."

Jeanne stepped away and turned to leave before pausing at the door and glancing back at her. "God help Scotland when the two of you return, for it does not know what is coming." She laughed and opened the door, closing it behind her.

Grace chuckled and shook her head. "You have no idea

how right you are," Grace whispered before she turned and left the room.

As she stepped outside, there was momentary alarm when she felt hands on her waist drawing her backwards.

"Hello to ye, love," Euan said, his voice immediately shutting down the panic before it could set in.

Grace smiled as her back came into contact with Euan's chest, and he slid his arms fully around her. Grace closed her eyes as he nuzzled her cheek then brushed his lips across it.

"What was that all about?"

"Just talk between women."

"That sounds a bit dangerous."

Grace laughed. "It was not, at least not this time."

"This time," Euan repeated with an amused expression.

"There are things men need not be privy to, and this was one of those."

"Ah, I see. One last walk in the gardens?"

"Oh, yes, please."

As they stepped outside, Grace took a deep breath and let the smell of flowers relax her. It was a beautiful spring day, and the courtiers were out taking in the sunshine, glittering and laughing, gossiping and plotting. Euan raised a parasol in his free hand, shielding Grace's fair skin from the sun's rays as they made their way down the stairs to the gardens.

"How very gallant of you," she said.

"Whatever else may be said of me, ye cannae say I am nae a gentleman."

"I most certainly could!"

"Ye dinnae count."

"Why not?"

"Because sometimes ye dinnae want me to be a gentleman, even going so far as to specifically request it, both in work and play," he replied, winking.

Grace rolled her eyes. "I have seen you not be one before I could ask you to do anything."

"Ach, now, those were different circumstances and ye cannae hold those against me."

"Can I not?"

"No, ye cannae."

"If you say so."

"Stop ye," he said, chuckling.

Grace smiled and squeezed his arm. "I suppose we do not have to worry about the feud any longer."

"I dinnae think so. Based on his reaction this morning, I am sure he has called it off, though it is nae as though he would go after ye here in front of everyone. I have an eye out all the same."

"Thank you for taking such good care of me."

"Ye say that as though I could have done anything else, or even would have."

"There is so much I want to say, but I will wait until we get home."

"Probably a wise thing. Come, let us nae think on anything but the beauty of the day and the gardens we are in."

When they finished their walk, they returned to the house and Euan helped Grace change into the dress from the ball. He hadn't asked about it, but he figured that it was worth trying to see if it worked. If it didn't, she'd be in her whites, and he could ask if they would send it on.

"Are ye ready?" he asked.

"Yes, more than. I very much want to be back where things make some sort of sense."

Euan nodded and Grace watched as he reached out to The Council with the message that they were ready for extraction and their mission was complete. Within moments, a Guardian was there, though it wasn't Caia, who was still with their bodies at the lodge. With Grace still severed from them, there was no way to pull her out in the traditional sense. Euan was gone in the next moment, and Grace took the woman's hands, closing her eyes for the transport.

The moment she arrived, Grace's link to The Council was restored and it brought with it a rush of energy that took her breath away. She stumbled, but the Guardian was there to catch her, holding her hand until it passed. She felt so disoriented as it all reconnected, just as she had when she'd arrived in France. She was home.

Chapter 24

When Grace arrived just after Euan did, the bond he shared with her, the one he'd lost, was immediately restored. He could feel her with him again. It had worked, and she was safe. He made his way to her and pulled her into his arms, holding her in silence for a long while, reveling in the renewal of the connection. He'd missed it far more than he'd realized.

"Ah, it worked!" Euan said as he released her and pointed to her dress.

Grace laughed and buried her face in his chest. He could feel her relief, the sense of knowing that everything she'd lost had been returned. The sense of safety.

"Ye look a bit out of place now, though."

Euan was dressed in his Watcher whites, just as they always were when Watchers and Companions returned to debrief with The Council. The clothing from wherever they'd been in the mission would remain there as if they'd just stepped out for the day. Museums would end up with "amazingly preserved" garments, as the pieces they left behind would eventually be packed away and forgotten in the timeline where they'd once been, only to be rediscovered later.

"I don't care. I'm just glad to be home."

"As am I."

"The Council is waiting for you," the Guardian said.

Euan nodded, not surprised they'd be meeting with the full Council after what happened. He took Grace's hand, walking with her to the Council Chambers. When the doors opened and they entered, they saw the Councilwoman's eyes widen as she caught sight of Grace's attire.

"Councilwoman," Euan said with a bow, as Grace did the same.

"I . . . well, that's very fancy."

Grace laughed, but Euan explained. "I liked it and asked her to see if it would work for her to bring it here, since she was nae coming back as a Watcher. Turns out it does."

Rochford chuckled. "Somehow, coming from you, that doesn't surprise me."

"It shouldn't," Grace replied.

"Ye traitor."

"Grace, we're all extraordinarily relieved and grateful to have you back with us," the Councilwoman said, trying not to laugh.

"I'm glad to be back."

"What happened?" Euan asked.

"We put Grace too close to when and where she'd died in the same timeline. It caused a sort of rift where her energy returning fought with what was already there. She should've gotten past it, but Lochiel saw her too soon. Had it even been an hour it would've been fine. The moment he touched her, there was a sort of convergence and it grounded her, severing our connection. It will be something we'll be more aware of in the future."

"And the rest?"

"We still don't know."

"I have an idea of what it might be."

"Go on."

"Grace said something that struck me when she was trying to explain what happened. She said she was at Culloden again, but everything was suspended in time. The only things that were nae were her and whatever was using my image. We were in the same clothing as we were then. It was when she told me he held out his hand and told her she needed to touch it that I knew: it was the same thing we saw when we first went back to Scotland."

"The timeline ghost?" Rochford said as both she and Grace looked at him in shock.

"Aye. Ye call it that, but I dinnae think that is what it is. It is something more sinister than that."

"What do you mean?"

"How many Watchers have fallen to such a thing?"

"Not many."

"And it happened just by touch did it nae? If they touched it, they died, just as Grace would have."

"Yes."

"At the time, ye said it was her energy that drew it out. What if that is what it is looking for? What if it means to do harm to Watchers and searches for that energy?"

"But we'd know if something like that was out there. We'd see it."

"Ye believe that because ye are overconfident."

"Euan," Grace said.

"Please, listen to me. There is something out there and it is after Watchers. This was a well-planned out strategy. Every move planned for maximum damage without detection. I know it when I see it because I used to do it. Something wanted her dead, and it wanted her to suffer before she died," he explained before he looked to Grace. "What did ye hear? Tell them."

Grace swallowed hard. "Kill her. The Watcher must die. The Council will be ours," she said before she closed her eyes. "Death to the Camerons."

Euan looked at Rochford. "It knew who and what she was. It targeted her deliberately and used her own memories against her at the end to try and lure her to touch it. Do ye nae see it?"

Rochford looked aghast, as did the other members of The Council. "How is it getting past us? Where is it hiding?"

"I dinnae know, and perhaps that is something to ask The Council of yer future. All I know is that ye had better warn all the current Watchers and start trying to figure out how to keep them out of danger. At the same time, ye need to start developing a strategy to fight back. Ye are at war, and it already has the upper hand."

War. The word seemed to reverberate in the silence.

"We ended it . . . this can't . . ."

"Ye ended the traditional notion of it here, but this is something else. This is what ye now call guerilla or psychological warfare." Euan had learned those terms in his modern studies, words for the things he and the others had done as a matter of course. "Ye dinnae have time for denial, Councilwoman. Tell the other Watchers and request a meeting with the future Council. It is the best place to start. I will do all I can to help ye with what skills I have, though I dinnae know how effective it will be against such an enemy."

"It will be welcomed, Euan, as your help always is."

"Companion Cameron," said one of the other Council members, "without your Watcher's assistance, how did you manage to complete the mission?"

Euan couldn't help the smile that spread across his lips. He was proud of his work and had no intention of hiding it. "She did help me. Perhaps nae as much as she might have had she been well, but she did what she could. She told the king the truth and so did I. When that did nae seem to be working fast enough it was time for . . . other measures."

"Such as?"

"The Marquise wanted to stop this as much as we did. I enlisted her help in getting someone loyal to her to go into the rooms of Murray and Lochiel while they were at supper with the king, when it was certain they would be gone for a long period. From there, they were to find any letters they could with seals from any of the clans, remove the seal intact, and give it to the Marquise."

Grace's eyes widened as she stared at him in shock, as did the other members.

"The Marquise sent them to me hidden in a box with a

necklace for Grace to wear to the ball. I spent that night attaching the seals to the letters I had forged, purporting to be from the other clan chiefs. The letters stated that they would fight with the English against any force sent by France into Scotland. Some of the seals I made myself from memory, because I knew I would need them: Campbell, Grant, Munro. The last piece in the game was the list of Cameron men who had renounced their allegiance to Lochiel and given it to me instead. That was forged, too, written from a list I had given to a forger of all the names I could remember. I then sealed it with the Cameron seal," Euan explained, holding up his left hand. The hand that contained the Cameron crest on his wedding ring.

"Euan, that was brilliant!" Grace said, grinning as widely as he was.

"I told ye I had skills ye had never seen, love. War quickly makes ye learn to do what is required to survive and to win. The fate of Scotland and the future hung in the balance, and I was nae going to lose."

Chapter 25

The Council sent Grace to Medical and to Andy who, as the Head of Medical, was in charge of the Cameron Watcher's medical team. She was to be checked over to make sure there were no ill effects from what had happened, as well as to see if he could access any of the nightmares and the information in them. If this could be done, the nightmares could be stored to be viewed by The Council, so that they might be able to better understand what they now faced. Euan stayed behind to confer with the Council members and answer what questions he could. He'd made sure to tell them that he was certain Lochiel had been under the effects of the same thing that had gone after Grace, but in a different way. Whispers and dreams, pushing for war.

"Grace," Andy said with an expression of sheer relief as she entered Medical. "I cannae tell ye how good it is to see ye."

"As good as it is to see you, I imagine."

Forgoing formality, Andy hugged her tightly. They were close in age, with Andy being a few years older, but he'd known Grace as part of The Council for years. His father had been her doctor here when she was a child, and though he hadn't been introduced to her then, Andy had seen her when he was helping his father around the ward, preparing, just as Grace had done with her grandparents, for his future role. When his father retired, Andy had taken over, and formally met Grace in her final year of university. The genuine friendship that had blossomed between them once Grace became the Evans Watcher was unexpected, but one both of them needed: someone else who understood the life they led, and there had been a number of occasions where he'd joined her for a drink at her flat and they'd spent hours simply talking.

Caia had been surprised when she'd found out about the relationship, as had Rochford. When Grace had come in after Culloden, there had been a moment when he'd thought he was alone with her, in the silence after he'd done what he could. He'd wept then, truly wept, holding her hand and stroking her hair, apologizing to her for what had happened. He hadn't seen the two women come in, and he hadn't seen them leave, and it was that moment which had revealed the depth of the friendship to the both of them. When Euan became part of her life, her friendship with Andy hadn't ceased. Rather, it had deepened. She became far more open, and there were parts of her life that only Andy knew about because he'd been the one to care for her in their aftermath. He was thankful that Euan was accepting of him and their friendship, but Andy made sure he was very respectful of Euan's time alone with Grace in order to keep it that way.

Right now, however, none of that mattered. Andy didn't care who saw them or what they said about it. His friend had very nearly died in a way he couldn't have saved her from, and that was far too much for even *his* reserved sensibilities to bear quietly. Grace returned the affection just as earnestly as it was given, and his arms tightened just slightly when she started crying into his shoulder. He struggled with his own tears, but he could let those go later when he was alone. It wasn't what she needed right now. She needed strength and comfort. She needed him to be Andy as well as Dr. Fraser.

"Dr. Fraser, we're standing by for Watcher Cameron," said one of his staff.

"Thank ye, Joan, but I'll see to Watcher Cameron on my own."

"Yes, Dr. Fraser," the young woman said before she went to disperse the others.

"Come on," he said. "Let's get ye someplace with a bit of privacy."

Grace nodded and wiped her eyes, allowing him to lead her back to the ward.

"Well, dinnae ye look all dressed for a party," he said, smiling.

The remark made her chuckle. "Euan wanted me to bring it back."

"I can see why. Ye look beautiful in it."

"Thanks," she replied as he guided her into a room and shut the door, where she collected linens from a drawer so she could change. "I'm going to need your help."

"Ach, well, I get to undress a beautiful woman. My lucky day," he said.

"Stop it," Grace said, unable to help laughing.

It made him laugh as well, and he unlaced and untied where directed. "Christ, it is a wonder anyone ever got into bed with all of this work."

"The work is the fun part. Anticipation."

"Is it now? I'll have to keep that in mind."

"Euan can tell you all about how to play that game with these clothes."

"As long as the anecdotes are nae about ye, that's fine."

"Ew, no."

Her reaction made him laugh harder. "I mean, I love ye, and ye are gorgeous, but that would be far more information than I need."

"Yeah, it would be," Grace said as she stepped out and made her way to the table, lying down and closing her eyes.

"Caia has been alerted and yer real body has been brought here. Ye are going to go to sleep for just a couple of minutes so we can make the transfer and then check ye out, all right?"

"Got it."

In the next moment, Grace's eyes closed, and Andy made

the transfer. For her, it would be a bit like nodding off, and when she opened her eyes again, she'd be back in her own body. The exhaustion would, unfortunately, be there, as it always was, but she'd be herself again. Her eyes opened, but within seconds Grace started to panic. She sat up quickly and held her head, her breathing becoming fast and ragged.

Andy was there in an instant. "Hey, hey, it's fine, ye are fine. Calm down and breathe."

"No! Andy how long was I asleep! This is how . . . I always had a headache and . . . I can't breathe!"

"Just a minute, as I said ye would be. Take a deep breath Grace, come on. No one can get to ye here," he said, grabbing an oxygen mask and placing it over her mouth and nose. "Breathe for me. Shhh."

Grace struggled to calm herself and regulate her breathing, and Andy placed a hydration patch on her arm, something they used when Watchers went on long missions.

"Ye are a bit dehydrated, and that's causing the headache, that's all it is."

She nodded and closed her eyes.

"Christ, what did they do to ye?"

Grace burst into tears, great heaving sobs that shocked Andy. He'd never seen her this way, at least not since her grandparents had died. Sitting down beside her, he put an arm around her shoulders, and she turned her face into his shoulder. It was raw emotion, powerful and heartbreaking, and he found himself in tears with her. It was impossible not to be in the face of this. He could feel the fear and the pain radiating from her in waves.

"Grace," he said, "I'm so sorry."

"It was . . . I can't even remember everything. I just know that these people want me dead and they came so close! They attacked me in my dreams, made me forget everything, made me forget Euan — but they saved him for last so it would hurt more."

"What!"

"I forgot him. Everything about him. They took my ring and—" Grace shook her head.

The instructions he was sent before she arrived pained him to think of. The Council wanted him to attempt to access those memories. He didn't want to do it now, didn't want to even try; the thought of putting her through it was abhorrent, but he had no choice. He looked at her before he reached out and took her hand. "Sorry is nae enough, but I assure ye that ye are safe now. I promise. Ye are safe with us and ye are home."

"But what if they can still get in?"

"They cannae. Ye have yer connection back, ye are yerself again, while ye were nae when ye were there. The opening is gone. I would *never* let anyone hurt ye, just as Euan would nae, and I would nae lie to ye."

"Okay," she whispered, her voice trembling.

"Before ye fell asleep and left yer mission body, I saw the work Euan had done on yer arm. Glad it was in the notes because I was wondering about that. He did a fine job tending to it."

Grace looked down at her arm to find the injury gone. "It didn't feel great when he sewed it up."

Andy winced. "I suspect nae."

"It's going to take a long time, isn't it?"

"What is?"

"To mentally and emotionally heal from this, to not feel frightened every time I forget a word or have a headache."

"Probably," he admitted. He'd promised not to lie, and he wouldn't. "But ye should see a Specialist to help ye."

"Not sure I'll have a choice."

"Probably nae."

"What is it you need to do?"

"Make sure this body is nae harmed in any way, but it should nae be."

"And what else?"

"What do ye mean?"

Grace gave him a look and he sighed.

"Right. They want me to see if I can pull those memories so they can study them for things ye cannae remember, as well as for how it was done."

She shook her head vigorously, her lower lip trembling as she fought back tears. "No!"

"I know, trust me I do, but I'll get ye to sleep so ye dinnae have to go through it again. Ye will never know, I promise ye. We may nae even be able to get to them, but we have to try."

Andy watched Grace swallow hard and force back her own fear, becoming Watcher Cameron and not the terrified Grace.

"Then let's get it over with."

* * *

Once Euan finished with The Council, he was sent home. Waking up in his own body and not finding Grace beside him induced a momentary panic before his mind caught up and he remembered her body had been moved to Council Medical. He rose from the bed, stretched, showered, and changed his clothes, then had Caia return him to The Council. Now he made his way toward Medical to wait for Grace.

Sitting down on a bench across from the doors, he sighed and rested his head against the wall, closing his eyes. He was looking forward to truly going home and taking Grace with him. He'd run her a bath, bring her some tea, pamper her in whatever way he could think of. She'd be exhausted, perhaps more than usual, but he'd see to her comfort so she could rest. Euan was relieved that it was all over, that he'd managed to pull it all off, and that she was alive because of it. More than anything, he was far more tired than he could ever remember being. His return to his own body had taken from him all the abilities that made a mission body invulnerable, and with that the stress and exhaustion had kicked in. He felt the weight of all of it; of all he'd done and said, all that had been said to him, the pain of all of the allegiances and bonds that had been broken.

"I must admit, that was a masterpiece of work with the seals and the letters. I'll have to remember that."

Euan looked up quickly. "Grace?"

A young woman stepped out from a doorway and smiled at him. "No."

She looked familiar, but in a way he couldn't place. "Who are ye?"

"Me? I'm the reason they tried to kill her. They wanted to kill her in order to prevent my ever being born," she replied as she sat down beside him.

"What?"

"I'm the Cameron Watcher who stopped them."

Euan blinked and sat up. He could see it now, the resemblance. "Wait . . ."

She laughed. "Relax. It's fine. My Council knows I'm here and, yes, I'm one of your descendants eventually."

Euan shook his head in disbelief. "This is . . ."

"Strange? I.m sure, but I had to meet you. I begged them to let me."

"Why?"

"Because it starts with you. Don't you see? You change everything, you and Grace. Fundamentally change it all. Any new Watchers will now be trained differently because of you. Mostly though, you start the Cameron line. Every Cameron Watcher from now on will be just as much a soldier as anything else. Trained in strategy and tactics, in personal combat. The Council won't do it, but the Camerons do it for themselves."

Cameron Watchers. Soldiers. "I dinnae want that for any of ye."

"Not soldiers like you were. And the abilities serve all of us well. No one forces us, we choose it. It's in our blood. It's from you."

"Do any of ye ever decline?"

She looked at him as though he'd asked either the most foolish question in the world, or an insulting one. "No. It's an honor to do it, to follow you. Why would we say no?"

"I dinnae understand how my adding any of that changes anything? Grace is still who she is."

"She is and isn't. They'll figure this out eventually, but when you two collided, when she chose you? Something happened that has never happened before. It created a different sort of bond, the one you can feel. It severed her ties to the former line. When she died, she really did die. The Watcher that she was died at Culloden. The tie that binds you together is the start of the new. That day she became the first Cameron Watcher."

"They dinnae know this?"

"Not exactly, no. We're not even sure we do now. This is their best guess, but whatever you have has never been duplicated. When the next Cameron Watcher is born and comes to her duty, they'll start to realize that whatever it was between you imparts something to the future Watcher, which has never happened before. There are traits all of us have that don't match anyone else in the Watcher's immediate family because they're yours."

"That sounds impossible."

"It should be, but it isn't. Then again, everything we do should be impossible and yet . . ."

"Why would it need to kill Grace to get to ye?"

"Easy, and it's not an 'it' it's a 'they.' We call them Divergents. If they kill her, the Cameron line dies, and I'm never born. None of us are. If I'm never born, they could successfully attack The Council, and everything would be lost."

"But why would that even be necessary?"

"I told you. I stopped them. I found a way to lock them where they are, to make it so they can only operate in certain ways. We can't stop them entirely, but we *can* limit the damage they can do. They can only operate in the divergent spaces, the spaces where history can go one way or another. You were right with what you said: it's a war. Long and ongoing, a war of attrition. They tried to attack us outright once. That's when The Council sent me."

"How did ye stop them?"

"Just the same way you would've; I outplayed them." A wicked smile crossed her face, a smile Euan recognized very well, and it made him laugh.

"Can ye tell us who and what they are?"

"No, sorry. That time will come, but not yet. In the meantime, they'll show up where they can, in the places we can't control, and they'll try to take as many of us as they can. Their idea is that if they take enough, the future Watchers will be too young to take on the work, and then there will be no defense. We aren't, however, that easy to be rid of. We know what to watch for, so they don't get any of us often."

Euan frowned. "The best we can do is be wary here and now, since they seem to be starting earlier, trying to find a weakness in the past where we dinnae know about them."

"Yes. You know what they are now, though, how they appear."

"If ye know this already, why did the future Council allow this Council to send Grace?"

"Ah, well, that's a bit more complicated. It was necessary for her to go. What happened there had to happen because it will inform new protocol. The severance was expected. The rest? Not so much."

Euan echoed her phrase: "What happened there?"

"The simple answer is that they were the ones pushing Lochiel and the others to war, which you already know. They were aware a Watcher would show up, but they didn't expect it to be *her*. They were attached to Lochiel when he touched her, and it gave them an opening to get to her while she was weak. That was all it took. From there, they could pull her into their space while she slept and have free access to her. That's why she always felt so sick when she woke up. It's like how we travel, and when we get there, we're sometimes dizzy. It's that, but worse. The headache was from their pulling things out of her mind. It was a good thing The Council didn't bring her back here in that state, or there's a good chance they would've let the enemy right in the front door."

"But ye knew she would go on that mission."

"We did, but we had no idea that such a convergence could even happen, much less that it would."

"What was their intent in doing her so much harm? Why nae just get it over with?"

"The harm was just a bonus, a way of getting back at a Cameron Watcher to make her pay for what one of us did to them. Maybe she might break and kill herself, save them the trouble. If not, the point was to make her forget everything on either side of her death that day and make sure she suffered as much as possible before she did. If it was the only thing she had left, the only thing she remembered, they could lure her with what was left of your bond. They would convince her to go with you, and as soon as she touched them? Dead. She had to do it herself, had to do it willingly. They can't just reach out and kill someone. Thing is? They have no idea how your bond works. They had no idea that it's more than just The Council joining you, or your memories together. You're part of each other, and they couldn't take that. It's the memories living there that kept her from touching the Divergent using your image."

"She would nae have survived if they had nae sent me."

"No, she wouldn't have. Your finishing the mission closed the divergence, and that's what pulled her out and away from them. They couldn't keep her in the space they were using because there was no longer a divergence for them to hide in. My Council will tell yours all of this." She studied him. "You know, you look just how I imagined you would."

"Do I?"

"Yep. It's kind of cool, really. All of the Watchers keep the name, you know. We're all Camerons no matter what our parents' names are."

"Councilwoman Rochford did nae."

"Yes, she did. Rochford is her Council name. When she goes out, she's Alice Cameron."

"She is still a Watcher?"

"Yep. A damned good one, too. You're not keeping any Cameron Watcher off the field, and trust me, The Council wouldn't want to."

"Do ye still live at Achnacarry? I know Councilwoman Rochford says she does."

"Oh yeah. I love it there. Scotland is still awesome, and the Highlands are still gorgeous."

Euan laughed. "Good to know. I suppose I will nae be seeing ye again."

"Probably not, but it was an absolute honor to meet you, Euan. I got to meet the man who is responsible for so much of what I know. It's not every day you get to do that: tell your ancestors how awesome they are and thank them."

"Thank me for what?"

"For being you. For not losing. For fighting for something bigger than yourself. If you only knew how much you're responsible for. Well, you and Grace."

Euan nodded. "I will always do what I can."

"I know. We all do."

"Were ye waiting around to meet her, too?"

"No, just you. I was only allowed one. I'll try to convince them to let me see her another time. They kind of owe me."

Euan held out his hand. "I am glad to have met ye . . ."

"Elizabeth," she replied, shaking his hand.

"Elizabeth. Thank ye for the information."

"Of course. Like I said, my Council will tell yours everything I just told you, but just in case they decide not to tell *you* I thought I'd beat them to it. Councils are weird like that sometimes," Elizabeth said before she stood up and began to walk away from him.

"Elizabeth," he called out.

She stopped and looked at him over her shoulder. "Yeah?"

"Ye be careful out there."

Elizabeth smiled and gave him a look that was pure Grace. "You too."

Euan watched as she disappeared around a corner and shook his head. At least he knew now. He'd been right, and he wasn't sure if that was good or bad. They'd all need to be careful from now on. This ran far deeper than any of them could've imagined, and if they were trying to kill Grace in order to entirely prevent the Cameron line from continuing, the attacks would never stop. They'd always be trying to find new and inventive ways to get to them. Not only was she a target, but he now knew that he was, too. If they could get to him, kill him, it was as good as killing her. The door across from him opened and Grace walked out, dressed in the linens they'd normally wear on a mission. The court dress would be cleaned, preserved, and packaged for Caia to bring to them later.

"Well, there ye are at last. Did they say anything?"

"Everything looks fine, which is a relief. They were able to get some of the stuff I remembered as well."

She was trying to act as though she were fine, but he knew better. He could read her like a book, see it in every bit of her. He could feel it. Her eyes were red and swollen from crying, and he had a feeling much of it was due to finally being able to relax in a place where she knew those beings couldn't get to her. Euan stood up and walked over to her, caressing her cheek before pulling her into his arms. "Good. Let us go home. Ye will nae believe the story I have for ye."

Grace smiled. "Ooo, intriguing."

"Ye have no idea."

"Andy commends you on your fine surgical skills, by the way."

"Does he now? I am glad it met with his approval, but I am more glad that it is gone as though it were never there."

"You and I both."

"Cannae imagine ye would want to explain that scar."

"Definitely not. What would I even say? 'Yeah, I got it when I went to Versailles to try and stop a third landing for the Jacobite rebellion in the 18th century. Turns out that clan chiefs are a superstitious bunch who don't like someone trying to get in their way, so they drag women out into the middle of nowhere, tie them to a tree and threaten to kill them. All I got was this scar; what a crappy souvenir.'"

Euan laughed. "I think I would rather like to see someone's face when ye say something like that."

"They would think I was mad."

"Well, ye did marry me."

"Is that madness? Not sure. I suppose it's debatable."

"Ach, come, I am nae that bad." Grace raised an eyebrow with an amused half smile. "At least nae all the time."

"Mmhm."

"Let me take ye home, away from all of this. Ye need some time alone."

"No," she said quickly, almost too quickly, her body tensing.

"Why? What is the matter?"

"I don't want to be alone."

"I did nae mean it that way. I will be with ye, of course I will be. I just meant away from everyone else here who may want to speak with ye or want something from ye. Ye need rest."

"Oh," she said, relaxing. "Right. I don't know why I thought that."

"Because that is how they left ye: alone. But ye are nae alone, and ye never will be."

Euan kissed her forehead, and she closed her eyes before resting her head on his shoulder. He heard the doors of Medical open and looked up to see Andy step out. When he met Euan's gaze, he looked sad and uncomfortable.

"Hello to ye, Andy."

Grace lifted her head and turned it to look at Andy curiously.

"Hi, Euan. I . . . uh . . . could I see ye alone for a moment, please?"

"Why?" Grace asked, wary.

"There's something I want to show him. Ye should go on home, I will nae keep him long."

"No, I don't want to go home without him."

There was something in Andy's expression that troubled Euan. He turned to Grace. "Why dinnae ye sit and wait for me inside, love, if it will nae be long. I know ye are anxious."

"Okay," she replied, turning and walking back inside with him. "I'll wait here."

As Grace sat down in a chair in the open area, Euan followed Andy, who didn't say a word until they'd reached what seemed to be his private office. Andy shut the door behind him.

"What is this about and why could Grace nae be here?"

"Because she has suffered enough," Andy said as he made his way to his chair and dropped into it, rubbing his face.

"Aye, she has, but that still does nae answer my question."

"Please sit. I want to show ye something. Two things, in particular."

Euan sat down in one of the chairs in front of Andy's desk as Andy typed something into the terminal at his desk and turned the screen toward Euan before turning off the lights.

"We were able to get some of those nightmares. The Council wants to study them, to see what was used, how it was done. I dinnae think they'll be ready for this, and I wanted ye to see it before they did. I have nae uploaded them yet. Ye need to know what happened to her, and I think to truly know, ye need to see it. She will nae be the same for a while, and this will tell ye why."

Euan swallowed hard but nodded, and Andy started up the file. What followed was far worse than Euan could have imagined. That first nightmare, he and his men pulling her into darkness, was like something straight out of a tale told to terrify people on a dark night around a fire. As the next nightmare began, he watched it unfold with creeping dread. They'd gone into her dreams as just him alone, and then they'd done her physical violence. The cruelty of the things they'd had him say sickened him. Worthless. Useless. I don't need you, don't love you, regret tying myself to you and coming here.

"I would tell ye whatever I needed to in order to get into yer bed. And oh, it was sweet. Sweet how much ye loved me, how much ye wanted me to love ye. Sweet to achieve such a victory over one who had made it her mission to never love anyone."

Euan closed his eyes, the words bringing tears to his own eyes even as he heard Grace's tears turn to great sobs. Of course they would. How could it be otherwise? He forced himself to open his eyes, to watch this.

"I no longer have a wife."

"No," Euan whispered. "After this, I did nae. Ye stole her from me."

The scene switched now to the next incursion on the same night, and when Euan saw the faces of the men assembled there, he gasped in shock. He knew those men, all of them; they were his friends. He watched as the one who'd gone in as Duncan pressed Grace, watched as Grace pushed back against what she knew in her heart was wrong. She'd known. Even then, those deeper memories had pulled at her, allowed her to resist. The charges of infidelity made him furious, and he was happy to see she ignored them until they got physical with her. More violence as Duncan struck her twice.

"Ye know, as I left, I heard him say 'mo leannan bòidheach' to the mistress before the door closed. That did get a moan from her."

"Ye son of a bitch," Euan growled.

They'd used something so personal, so intimate, to break her. They'd somehow gotten from her mind that he'd call her that, and he did. Often. Even when they weren't in bed together. When they cut her arms, Euan's hands flattened on the desk as he stared in horror, wanting to scream with her as her wedding ring was ripped from her finger using the blood dripping from the wounds to lubricate it. This was the moment they'd taken their marriage from her, the moment he'd ceased to be married to her in her mind.

"It belongs to me now. It will make excellent balls for a rifle, perhaps one he will use to rid himself of ye for good. Would nae that be poetic?"

Euan shook his head and buried his face in his hands. No wonder she'd been so ill and in such pain the following morning. What they'd done to her was beyond cruel, a form of pure, sadistic torture. It was Culloden he feared seeing, not sure he wanted to know what they'd done to her there, but Euan watched it play out, not surprised at how the cruelty had suddenly disappeared. There was no more need for it. She was there, broken and alone, no defense, no recollection. To treat her thus would frighten her, make her more likely to run than come to them. It was all done on purpose, all strategically planned, all part of a longer game. Euan could barely breathe as he watched her reach out her hand for her ring. Closer and closer. He could hear what she'd heard now.

Go to him. You want him. Take it, it is yours.

He felt a small sense of relief as her mind pushed back, sent her memories of him and his words to her, reminded her of his love so that she'd know this man before her wasn't him.

Kill her. The Watcher must die. Death to the Camerons.

Grace gasped and stepped back from the man, something triggering a memory. She'd been so very close to touching him, millimeters from death. Euan watched as she backed quickly away in spite of the man's fury, the battle returning to life, but what he didn't expect was what came next. Watching Grace fight back, hitting her enemy with the musket, breaking his arm and snatching her ring from the ground, pleased him a great deal.

"You will not leave! You belong to us and we will never stop until you are dead!"

Euan's heart was pounding as the battle swallowed her up

when she turned and ran from him, back toward the Jacobite lines, back to where her heart and her deeper memory told her the true Euan would be, toward the safety he'd always promised. Euan placed his hands on the desk and dropped his head, losing his composure entirely.

"Turn it off," he whispered. "No more. Please, turn it off."

"There's nothing else," Andy said, "but now ye know why I wanted ye to see this first."

"How could anyone do this to another person?"

"Ye know there are people like this out there. Surely ye ran across them in yer time."

"Aye, but nae like this, nae with a woman. This was—"

"Torture," Andy finished. "Pure and simple. They wanted her to suffer and made sure she did. I cannae tell ye how angry it makes me, and I know it's worse for ye. I hated to see them use that violence against her, as ye did, to use her past as fodder for the game. I treated those injuries, saw them firsthand. I know what that did to her. I was proud of her for breaking that bastard's arm."

Euan shook his head. "What do we do? How can I possibly fix this?"

"I dinnae know if ye can if I'm honest. She'll need to see a Specialist, but I'm nae even sure if *they'll* be able to repair this. All ye can do is be there for her while she sorts this out as best she can."

"I wish it had been me. I wish I could take this from her."

"Of course ye do, so do I, but we cannae. Try to take comfort in the knowledge that ye are so deeply embedded in her soul that they could nae take ye from her no matter how hard they tried. Ye are there, always there, giving her strength even if ye dinnae know it."

"I am so angry," he said, and though his voice was quiet, the rage was clear. "So angry that they used things so personal against her, that they broke her using a name I call her. I cannae call her that now."

"Give it time and ye likely will be able to do so again."

"I am nae sure I can do it, nae now that they have tainted it. I will find something else."

"This will be difficult for a while, but ye will get through it together."

"Aye, we will."

CHAPTER 26

EUAN WAITED UNTIL HE had control of himself before he returned to Grace so they could go home to the lodge. He didn't want her to see him upset, wasn't ready to talk to her about the things he'd seen. When they returned, there was a palpable sense of relief to be home where it was quiet and familiar. He guided Grace upstairs, drew a bath for her, let her soak in it as he sat with her talking about things they might do on their break, and washed her hair for her. By the time she emerged, he nearly had to pour her into bed. At least this time he knew the exhaustion was natural, and he was relieved to slide into bed beside her and hold her close. He had no idea what time it was when he stirred to the realization that Grace wasn't there. His heart jumped and he sat up, instantly awake, scrambling out of bed after switching on the bedside lamp.

"Grace?" he called out, listening for a response but hearing nothing.

Heart hammering, he headed for the bedroom door and opened it, hurrying out and down the stairs. There were no lights on that he could see, and it only deepened his concern.

"Grace?" he called out once more, slight panic now edging his voice.

Still no response. Euan stepped into the study, thinking perhaps she'd gone there to sit quietly in the darkness, but she wasn't there. He checked all the other rooms with the same result, and each empty space only pushed his panic closer and closer to the surface. Opening the back door, he stepped outside.

The early spring air was still icy cold, and it made him shiver, but he pressed on. Crossing the drive, he stepped into the woods, a few steps taking him out again to where the hillside ended, and Euan stopped short just at the tree line. Grace stood there at the edge of the hill, her arasaid wrapped around her over the white nightdress she wore, feet bare. Her hair was down, strands of it blowing in the cold wind coming up from the glen below.

"Grace," he said, his voice quiet, not wanting to startle her.

She turned just slightly to look at him over her shoulder.

"What are ye doing out here, *leannan*? It is freezing."

"Thinking," she replied just as quiet as he'd been. "Couldn't sleep."

"Ye scared me. I woke up and ye were gone."

"I'm sorry, I didn't mean to."

"I know," he said as he closed the distance between them. The cold made his bare feet ache, but he knew they'd go numb soon enough and he wasn't going to leave her out here. "Ye want to talk about it?"

"About what?"

"About what's troubling ye and keeping ye from rest."

"Where do I even begin."

"Wherever ye need to," he said, echoing her own words from the mission back at her.

Grace turned her gaze back over the vista. "I don't even know what I'd say. I don't know if there are words for it."

"Why dinnae ye come inside and I will make some tea."

"Do you think the earth remembers all of the things that have happened upon it?" Grace asked, ignoring his suggestion to go indoors. "Do the trees and the soil and the rocks remember, silent guardians all, watching the world move around them while they stay the same?"

"What?"

"So many things have happened. Do you think the hills here remember the fires that consumed the homes burned for retribution? Do they remember the screams and tears?"

"Grace—"

"Do you think they do?" she asked, turning her head to look at him.

"I dinnae know. Why would ye wonder about it?"

"Memory is a strange thing. I wonder if any memories are exactly as the reality was, as it truly happened, with no tricks of the mind to sharpen or soften. I would imagine that the only place such a thing would be true would be in the things that make up the world, those things that soak up the energy of our lives as we move through them. Culloden remembers. The moor remembers, the trees. If you go you can feel it. It's why certain things never change when a timeline repeats. It is etched into the earth, fixed."

Euan frowned. "Aye, it does, but ye know yer memory is fine now."

"Is it? How do we know? Truly know?"

"You can remember all of those things ye forgot."

"But are the memories tainted now? Details added that weren't there before? How do I know what's real and what isn't?"

Her last words hit hard, but he understood now, understood what troubled her. "I suppose ye cannae know, except for those things ye can ask others to confirm for ye. I would hope that if such a thing had been done to ye, the memory would seem off and ye would question it."

"There are things no one can confirm."

"Such as?"

"I remember everything, now. I remember what they did to me," she replied, her voice breaking for a moment. "But I don't know if those memories are real, and no one can tell me that."

"I can," he said, his heart aching to know that she remembered now. He'd been hoping she never would.

"How?" she asked, turning around to face him.

"Please, come inside *mo ghràidh*. I will tell ye all, but ye will catch yer death if ye stay out here this way, and we have had enough death to last us for eternity."

Euan held out his hand to her and she took it, allowing him to draw her away from the edge and to his side. She didn't resist his leading her back to the house, and they walked into the kitchen. Euan turned the light on over the stove so that there was at least a dim light, and then put the kettle on. Grace sat down at the table, watching him move about. As the warmth of the kitchen penetrated the cold that shrouded her, she began to shiver and wrapped her arasaid around herself.

Once the tea was ready, Euan brought the pot and cups to the table, followed by sugar and milk. "What do ye want to know?"

Grace shook her head, poured herself some tea, and wrapped her icy hands around the hot cup. "I'm not even sure, but how do you know anything about them?"

"Andy was able to get everything, I dinnae know if he told ye that."

"He did tell me."

"When he called me in, it was because he wanted to show me. He wanted me to know what they had done to ye, truly done, so that I would know what ye were facing. Why ye might react a certain way without even realizing why, things like that."

"He didn't show me."

"Why would ye want him to? Ye lived it."

"I don't know. None of it seems real now. Not the mission, not what happened."

"But it was, and it did happen. I know what ye are doing, as it is probably what I would do."

"What I'm doing?"

"If ye convince yerself it was nae real, then ye can shove it down and act as though none of it ever happened. Ye dinnae have to face it."

"Have you done that?"

"More than I probably should have, aye."

"I don't want it to be real. I don't understand how anyone could do such things to someone else."

"It is less frightening that way, is it nae?"

"Something like that."

Euan reached out and placed a hand on her forearm. It was warm from the cup he held, and Grace seemed comforted by that. "It was both real and nae real. What happened to ye was real, but the things you saw and heard were nae. I would never do any of that to ye, never say those things, and I hate them for having put it in yer head that I would. I hate that they used my likeness, nae to mention the likenesses of Duncan and the others. They would never do those things either."

"I know," she said. "It was why I was so confused, or at least one of the reasons. None of it squared with what I knew of you, what I still know. Those two nightmares were the same night, and in between them, you came to me and asked why I was crying. You comforted me after I'd just had a nightmare where you'd done and said the most horrendous things."

"I had no idea, but even if I had, I would have done the same. I would have told ye it was all false. It sickened me to watch it, and to watch myself do and say those things was beyond anything I could imagine."

"Mo leannan bòidheach." Grace whispered.

"I would never say that to anyone but ye. Never. I have never said those words to anyone before ye, either. They have always been yers, but I cannae say them to ye now. I will find something else."

Grace was silent for a long moment. "I was tempted to point out that a gold ring would make terrible musket balls. There's not enough material."

Euan blinked, then laughed. Even in the middle of this, she found a way to be humorous. "Aye, true enough, though ye could certainly buy some proper ones with it."

"But then it wouldn't be poetic enough. You wouldn't use my wedding ring to kill me."

"True, but that seems a bit much if I am honest. Then again, if I were to do that, use yer ring I mean, I would just paint some poison on the inside and let ye wear it."

Grace raised an eyebrow and looked at him.

He laughed. "What?"

She smiled. "Saying that from experience?"

"No. Never had occasion to poison someone. I preferred the more direct method anyway, where they knew it was me doing it. Someone taught me about it."

"Who?"

"Cannae remember now." It was a lie he hated himself for telling, but he wasn't ready to talk about it with her yet. He could see she didn't quite believe him but wasn't going to press it.

"I wonder what those things did with the memories they stole."

"Did?"

"What happened to them? Did they just disappear when they were removed?"

"Oh. I am nae sure we will ever know."

"But now there is an enemy out there who knows all about me. Every private moment, every word, every piece no one else knows. Any secrets I had belong to them now."

"Maybe, or maybe they were nae able to access those, just take them."

"I hope that's the case."

"I think ye cannae dwell on it because ye dinnae know. There is no way for ye to know. Ye just have to focus on what ye do know. Ye were so close, Grace, so close to dying, and I cannae tell ye how terrifying that was to watch."

"What do you mean?"

"I saw that final piece, Culloden, and what happened there. Ye were the barest hint from touching him before ye pulled away from it. Even though I knew ye lived through it, it was still horrible to watch. Ye got back at him though, at least a little."

Grace wiped some tears away from her cheeks gently. "I just . . . I don't know what I'd do if you weren't here. The thought of not knowing you terrifies me, because now that you're here I can't imagine life without you. You mean everything to me, and you are the only person in the whole world who truly understands me, every part of me. You've made my life better in every way, and they tried to take that away from me. They saved it for last because it would hurt more, and it did. It still does. To know I forgot you, forgot our life, our wedding, and then you entirely is just—"

"I know," he said, cutting her off. "But ye did nae. My love, ye got all of that back, and in the end, they could nae take me from ye entirely. They might have removed me from yer mind, but nae yer heart and yer soul, just as I said they could nae. I live in yers as ye do in mine."

"You're right. I'm borrowing trouble, as your mum would say."

"Aye, but I cannae blame ye as ye try to make sense of this. I know why they want ye gone, these people."

Grace lifted her eyes to meet his, her expression wary. "Why?"

"They are called Divergents, and they are trapped in a space somewhere, and in this place, they can only work in the places where history may go one way or another, the very same places we show up. They apparently tried to attack The Council and were banished there."

"What? When? I've never heard of this."

"Has nae happened yet for us, I think."

"Oh. So then how do you know?"

"I had a visitor named Elizabeth," he said, smiling. "A future Cameron Watcher beyond Alice."

"What? Really?"

"Aye, apparently she asked her Council to allow her to come see me. Ach, Grace, she reminded me so much of ye. She is the one who traps them, and if they kill ye, she is never born."

"None of the future Cameron Watchers are," Grace said in shock.

"Exactly. Kill the root and the flowers never come."

"They're trying to change the past to affect their future."

"Ye are nae safe from them, Grace. Ye never will be. I will nae be either."

Grace sighed and sat back in her chair. "Then we'll have to be vigilant."

"Always."

"What else did she tell you?"

"Essentially that the bond between us is unlike anything ever seen before or since, and they still dinnae know what it is or how. Whatever it is, it endows certain traits in the next Watcher, traits from us, that only they possess. We are, apparently, legends."

Grace snorted in amusement. "Alice told me that once, too, remember?"

"Aye, so it was interesting to have someone past her say the same."

"Do they still live here?"

"Aye. I asked. Did ye know Alice still goes out on missions?"

"Wait . . . what?"

"That is what Elizabeth says. She is still the Cameron Watcher."

"How, if I'm the Cameron Watcher? I'm really confused. Maybe she goes by something else because I'm there? Either way, that's a lot of work to be both Watcher and Councilwoman."

"I have a feeling she may nae work as a Watcher as much as ye do."

"Maybe," Grace said as she poured herself another cup of tea.

"Anyway, closing the mission is what got ye out. It closed the space and they could nae hold ye there."

"That was what the shattering was."

"Aye."

"I'm not sure if I'll ever be able to . . ." she began but stopped.

"Able to what?" Euan asked, prompting her to go on.

"Forget this. These attackers wanted me to, but they failed."

"If ye really wanted to, you could always ask Andy if there is something he can do for ye in that vein, to make ye forget it."

"There is, but I don't want him to. I need to remember that this can happen, what it felt like, so that if it happens again, I can see it coming."

"A fair point," Euan said, going silent and tapping his fingers on his cup for a moment. "May I ask ye something?"

"Of course."

"At the ball, do ye remember what Lochiel said to ye?"

Grace's expression darkened. "Yes."

"Will ye tell me?"

"I don't know if I should."

"Why nae?"

"It was . . . well, it wasn't him anyway."

"Please. What did he say to ye?"

Grace swallowed hard. "He said that if I was trying to whore my way into stopping them, I was wasting my time, that I would save him the trouble of my murder because you would do it for him if I let the king bed me."

"What! No, I—"

"He insisted that I'm your property, as you are his, and because I'm yours, I'm also his. In the end, he said that if he thought he could get away with it he would kill me there and then because my death would break you and you would be his again to wield as he pleased."

There was a dark undercurrent of rage in Euan's features, just as there had been the day of the duel. "I would *never* harm ye," he said through clenched teeth. "Would I allow the king to have ye? No, but I would nae have harmed ye to ensure it. There are plenty of other things I could do. He is right that I would nae want to share ye, but that is because I love ye far too much to inflict such an indignity upon ye. Ye are part of me, ye dinnae belong to me."

"I knew that even as he said it."

"I believe ye. He was right about one thing: yer death would have broken me. It would have destroyed me utterly. But he would nae have me to wield because I would be right behind ye, even without the bond taking me. I would crawl into the grave beside ye and hold ye while they buried us, for I would nae leave my love to face the dark and cold alone lest ye be afraid. I could nae be without ye, Grace, and the world without ye in it is nae a place I would want to remain."

"Euan, I—" Grace whispered before she dissolved into tears.

Euan stood and moved his chair closer to hers before sitting down and drawing her into his arms as she wept. "Tell me ye would nae be the same," he whispered.

"I can't, because I would be."

"Aye, I know. I thank God every day for the miracle that allowed me into yer life. The miracle that brought ye across two centuries to my very door, come to claim what was yers. There is nae a woman in the world I could have loved the way I love ye, no woman who could have called to me the way ye did, or who could have drawn me to her the way ye so effortlessly did. There would never be another who could, just as I know full well there is nae a man alive or dead who can reach ye and understand ye as I can."

Euan's own words, about his welcoming death because it would restore to him what he loved, echoed in his mind as she cried against his shoulder. He knew that it was as much for her own pain as it was for his honest admission of just how vulnerable he was when it came to her. To do him the worst harm, one needed only to hurt Grace. Lochiel had known it and had tried to exploit it, and it was why he'd been so incredibly vigilant. He knew his weakness, knew his enemy, and he would be damned if anyone would get past him to drive the knife into his heart. Nothing and no one would take her from him, and if they tried, they'd find themselves dead.

"I will say, however, that Lochiel and the others should have been thanking the Lord they did nae have to deal with ye unencumbered. They would have been in for a hell of a surprise otherwise."

"Probably. Can you imagine the both of us there if I was myself?"

Euan smiled in dark amusement. "Oh aye, I most certainly can, and I am a bit put out we did nae have that chance. Oh, what I would nae give to see ye tear them apart when they insisted they controlled me still."

"You proved more than amply how wrong they are."

"Still would have liked to hear ye as ye lit into them."

Grace laughed. "Would have been fun."

"And then ye could go with Madame and put all those court ladies to shame as ye used yer mind as well as yer looks to seduce every man in the place."

"Why would I want to?" Grace asked, wrinkling her nose. "I already had the best one."

"That is very kind of ye to say, *leannan*. I disagree, though."

"You can disagree, but you're still entirely wrong."

"What makes me better than any of them? They did nae spend their lives doing the things I did, like killing people."

"No, they spent them doing something else, but there is no shame in what you did. You had a reason; you were at war. You didn't try to hide it; it was clear what you meant to do in those situations."

"Nae all of them."

"The ones that involved you actually killing people, not plotting to kill people."

"Aye, that is true."

"That's the difference, you see. At court, people must be duplicitous. They must hide what their true motives are and play games. They can trust no one. At least in war, we know exactly what we're doing and who our enemy is as they stand across from us."

"There are things nae so pure leading up to it."

"Yes, but when it comes down to it, you're not hiding. It isn't politics."

"Nae sure how this makes me better?"

"Because you're honest, Euan. You don't hide who you are, and when you were there, you charmed everyone by being yourself. You didn't pretend to be what you weren't, and someone being real can be the most intoxicating thing when you're wading in a sea of artifice and deceit."

"A sea of artifice and deceit. I like that, very apt."

"Well, it is."

"I dinnae disagree in the slightest." He wasn't sure if she knew just how right she was, or how deeply that deceit went. The parts of him that were not a simple soldier had been developed at Versailles and in Paris by those who were among the best at what they did.

"I think I will request to return to see a Specialist."

Grace lifted her head and looked at him curiously. "Why?"

"So much of my past was pushed to my present with this mission, so many things I had tried to bury that now will nae remain there anymore. With all I was forced to confront, I dinnae think it will do well for my mind to try to act as though all of this did nae happen."

"I think that's very smart and self-aware."

"Ye should as well."

"No," Grace replied. "I've had enough with people being in my head."

"Grace, I am nae sure they will give ye a choice in the matter."

"No," she said adamantly, and he knew it would do no good to press her. "They can't force me to go."

"All right. Do ye think ye are easy enough to return to bed?"

"Worth a shot."

"If ye are nae . . . well . . ."

Grace laughed and shook her head. "You'll try to help me?"

"Or at least give ye something to do with that energy."

"You're terrible, you know that right?"

"Dinnae ever hear ye complain in the moment."

"And you won't, either. Come on, let's at least attempt to

sleep," Grace said as she stood and then took his hand, trying to pull him out of the chair.

"Ooo, look at ye, so eager! Ye want me now, dinnae ye?"

"Stop it," she said, though she was laughing.

Euan rose from the chair quickly and wrapped her up in bear hug before he kissed the top of her head. "Come on, I know ye need the rest."

* * *

The following morning found Euan in the Cognitive Specialist area of Council Headquarters. He was nervous, but he knew he had to do this. There was so much he wanted to say but couldn't, so much he wanted to make sense of on his own before bringing Grace into it and confiding in her. He had to learn to let go of the lies, the secrecy, the need to remain silent that had been drilled into him and didn't allow him to speak even when he wanted to. The first visit had helped so much, and it was his hope that returning would do the same. He wanted to be free of it all, free of his past, of the things he'd done. He could see now that, while he thought he'd done them willingly, he'd actually been forced — at least as far as the war was concerned. He'd been given no other choice, didn't know how to demand one, or how he could possibly say no to his chief.

"Companion Cameron?"

Euan looked up and stood, surveying the man in front of him. He looked kind and friendly, though his hair was more gray than the brown it had once been, and the eyes behind his spectacles were understanding and comforting.

"Aye."

"A pleasure to meet you. I'm Specialist George, and I'll be seeing you today. Come with me."

Euan followed him into an office, and George shut the door behind them. The room was dim, but they always were. It helped people to relax, and Euan had appreciated it the first time. There was a scent here that reminded him of home, something they'd probably done on purpose to further encourage his relaxation.

"Would you like any background noise? Rain? A stream, perhaps? May I get you a drink?"

"No but thank ye."

"Very well," George said with a smile. "Have a seat, would you? I understand you're here hoping to work through a great deal of your life, from your youth through the time you encountered Watcher Cameron. If you find I'm to your liking, you'll be seeing me for the duration."

"Aye, I do, and that sounds fine with me."

"Well then, let us begin."

ABOUT THE AUTHOR

Eilidh Miller, FSAScot, has a BA in English and studied history as an undeclared minor to better inform her literature studies. A recent winner of the Robert Burns Literary Award and a Fellow with the Society of Antiquaries of Scotland, Eilidh was very active within Southern California's Scottish community, spending a great deal of time volunteering with the charitable organization St. Andrew's Society of Los Angeles.

A long-time historical reenactor, Eilidh loves research and educating the general public about historical events, as well as entertaining them with tidbits no one would believe if they weren't documented. She extends this same energy to her work, extensively researching the historical periods she includes in her writing to ensure that the information she presents is correct, even going so far as to travel internationally to access archives and scout locations.

She resides in the Pacific Northwest with her husband, daughter, and feisty Shiba Inu sidekick while working on her master's degree in the history and politics of the Highlands and Islands.

You can keep up with Eilidh on TikTok – @authoreilidh – or her Facebook page to keep up to date on the next release, special content, and information on appearances.

Facebook: eilidhmillerauthor

Excerpt from "Echoes of the Rising" the 3rd book in the series, coming in April 2021!

When next he woke, he realized he was no longer moving and no longer in the carriage. Beneath him was a bed, though he could feel that his eyes were covered. Moving his hands to try and touch his face, he found them strapped down, and it brought immediate panic. What torture was he in for now?

"Easy boy, easy," someone near him said in English, his voice different from any of the others he'd heard over the last four days. "You are fine."

"Where am I?" Euan asked, almost afraid to hear the answer.

"At the palace. Well, more specifically at the barracks, but close enough."

"When did I get here?"

"About a day ago."

"Untie me!" Euan demanded, his panic beginning to give way to anger.

"Cannot do that, I am afraid, for it is for your own safety. You need to stay where you are, as you are in rather rough shape."

"Aye, because those men tried to kill me!"

"They did go a bit overboard, I think."

"That is an understatement!" Euan snarled.

A soft laugh emanated from the unseen person beside the bed. "It is the only statement I can give. You will recover, but you did well. They tried to break you, but you would not give in."

"I did nae realize giving in was an option. What was it they wanted me to do?"

"Beg them to stop, plead with them, bargain, things of that nature. You did not, however."

"I will nae give anyone such satisfaction." Euan replied with far more determination than he felt.

"Ah, and that is why you are here. You are strong and strong willed, a soldier. Now you will learn how to harness that to your advantage."

"Who are ye?"

"My name is Jacques, and I am the captain of the king's guard. You need not tell me who you are, I already know."

"I dinnae want to be here!"

"You have no choice, I am afraid."

"This was nae—"

"Was not what you thought?" Jacques said, interrupting Euan. "I am sure it was not. However, you cannot leave. You are here now, and you will learn what you were sent to learn, though we will all speak to you in English for the time being. You have a few days to rest, to let some of that swelling go down, and then we begin again. Take advantage of the time while you can, you will most certainly need it."

"Please, uncover my eyes," Euan asked, his voice now absent of the determined edge it had held only moments ago and betraying a child's fear.

"It is for your own good. You could not see out of them anyway, as swollen as they are. You must begin to heighten your other senses, Euan. Without your sight you must instead learn to hear, to smell, to feel."

Euan heard Jacques' footsteps walking away from him, and the panic rose once more. "No! Wait! Please!"

Silence was the only response to his plea, and Euan struggled against the ties that bound him before he fell back to the bed, letting loose a scream of anger that made his breathing ragged. The moment he was free he was leaving this place. This was not what he'd been sent here to do, and he was sure Lochiel wouldn't have allowed such treatment of him.

"Let me out of here!" Euan screamed in fury.

"And if we do not?"

Euan went still, barely breathing, the fear of that voice creeping into his heart and clenching it with an icy grip. "That is what I thought. Nothing," he said with a chuckle. "Jacques, we should send this petulant baby back home. He will not make it."

"Now, now, Alain. He is just a boy, and though you will never admit it now, you were this way, too. We all were. Answer the question, Euan. What will you do?"

The calm of Jacques voice was maddening, making it impossible to tell what was going through the man's mind or giving any hint as to what answer he was expecting. Euan was silent for a long moment before he spoke. "Ye will let me go sometime; ye have to, for ye have a job to do. But I promise ye this: when all of this is over, I am going to make ye pay for what ye have done to me."

"Are you? Fascinating," Jacques said.

"I would like to see you try, boy," Alain sneered.

"Especially ye," Euan hissed.

"If I do not kill you first."

"Do it," Euan said, his tone cold. "Go on. Either way I win. If ye kill me I am free and ye hang for murder. Dinnae think for a moment I would nae be missed."

OTHER BOOKS BY THE AUTHOR

The Watchers — The Watchers Series: Book 1

Echoes of the Rising - The Watchers Series: Book 3

The Gathering - The Watchers Series: Book 4

Queens & Spies - The Watchers Series: Book 5

Her Father's Daughter

Captain Merrick

www.ingramcontent.com/pod-product-compliance
Lightning Source LLC
LaVergne TN
LVHW041554060526
838200LV00037B/1285